Prasie for Lucy and Stephen Hawking's

'Like a Doctor Who adventure' *Sunday Times*

'Delightful' *Independent*

'Gripping, informative and funny' *The Bookseller*

'Dramatic' *Guardian*

'A true beginner's guide to *A Brief History of Time*'
Publishers Weekly

www.randomhousechildrens.co.uk
www.georgessecretkey.com

Also available by Lucy and Stephen Hawking:

George's Secret Key to the Universe
George's Cosmic Treasure Hunt
George and the Big Bang

For details of Stephen Hawking's
books for adult readers, see:

www.hawking.org.uk
www.randomhouse.co.uk

LUCY &
STEPHEN HAWKING

GEORGE
AND THE
UNBREAKABLE CODE

Illustrated by Garry Parsons

CORGI BOOKS

GEORGE AND THE UNBREAKABLE CODE
A CORGI BOOK 978 0 552 57005 3

First published in Great Britain by Doubleday,
an imprint of Random House Children's Publishers UK
A Penguin Random House Company

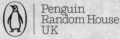

This edition published 2015

1 3 5 7 9 10 8 6 4 2

Penguin Random House is committed to a sustainable future for
our business, our readers and our planet. This book is made from
Forest Stewardship Council® certified paper.

MIX
Paper from
responsible sources
FSC® C018179

Set in Stempel Garamond 13.5pt / 17pt

RANDOM HOUSE CHILDREN'S PUBLISHERS UK
61–63 Uxbridge Road, London W5 5SA

www.randomhousechildrens.co.uk
www.totallyrandombooks.co.uk
www.randomhouse.co.uk

Addresses for companies within The Random House Group Limited
can be found at: www.randomhouse.co.uk/offices.htm

THE RANDOM HOUSE GROUP Limited Reg. No. 954009

A CIP catalogue record for this book is available from the British Library.

Printed and bound in Great Britain by CPI Group (UK) Ltd, Croydon, CR0 4YY

To all those who have looked up
at the night sky and wondered . . .

LATEST SCIENTIFIC IDEAS!

As you read the story you will come across some fabulous science essays and information. These will really help bring the topics you read about to life, and they have been written by the following well-respected scientists:

With special thanks for the additional material to:
Dr Stuart Rankin
High Performance Computing Service, University of Cambridge

Chapter One

On another planet, the treehouse would have been the ideal spot for star-gazing. On a planet with no parents, for example, it would have been perfect. The treehouse – halfway up the big apple tree in the middle of the vegetable patch – was the right height, location and angle for a boy like George to spend all night staring up at the stars. But his mum and dad had other ideas, involving chores, homework, sleeping in beds, eating supper or spending 'family time' with his little twin sisters, none of which were of any interest to George.

All George wanted to do was take a picture of Saturn. Just one teeny photo of his favourite planet – the enormous frozen gas giant with its beautiful icy, dusty rings. But at this time of year, when the sun set so late, Saturn didn't appear in the night sky until nearly midnight. Which was so far past George's bedtime, there was no hope of his parents leaving him out in the treehouse until then.

Sitting with his legs dangling over the edge of the

platform, George sighed and tried to calculate how many hours and days it would be before he was old enough to be free . . .

''S up?' His train of thought was broken as a slight figure dressed in long baggy camo shorts, a hoodie and a baseball cap bounded onto the treehouse platform.

'YOLO!' George cheered up instantly. 'Annie?'

Annie was his best friend, and had been ever since she and her mum and dad had moved to Foxbridge a couple of years ago. She lived next door, but that wasn't the only reason why they were mates. George just liked her: Annie, the daughter of a scientist, was fun and clever and cool and brave. Nothing was beyond her –

2

no adventure could be shunned, no theory go untested and no assumption stay unchallenged.

'What are you doing?' she asked.

'Nothing,' George muttered. 'Just waiting.'

'Waiting for what?'

'For something to happen.' He sounded miserable.

'Me too,' said Annie. 'D'you think the Universe has forgotten about us now we're not allowed to go on space adventures any more?'

George sighed. 'D'you think we'll ever get to fly in space again?'

'Not right now,' said Annie. 'Perhaps we've had all our fun already; now that we're eleven, we've got to be really serious all the time.'

George stood up, feeling the wooden planks rock slightly under his feet. He was *almost* sure that the treehouse was safe and that there was very little chance they could both go crashing down to the hard ground below. He'd built it with his dad, Terence, out of stuff they'd scavenged from the local tip. And once, when they were busy constructing the 'house' part where he and Annie now sat, his dad had plunged his foot through a rotten plank. Fortunately he hadn't fallen through entirely, but it had taken all George's strength to pull him back up again, while below, on the ground, his twin sisters, Juno and Hera, shrieked with laughter.

The good thing about the mini-accident was that the treehouse was judged dangerous enough by George's parents for his toddler sisters to be banned from coming up the rope ladder. Which made George very happy. It meant that the treehouse was *his* kingdom, protected from the chaos of the rest of his house. Under strict instructions to pull up the rope ladder to stop eager small people from shinning up to join their beloved brother, George was very careful about security. He never left the ladder down. Which meant . . .

'Hey!' He suddenly realized that Annie shouldn't have been able to appear out of nowhere like that. 'How did you get up here?'

Annie grinned. 'I was bitten by a spider when I was just a baby,' she intoned dramatic-ally. 'Which gave me special magic powers that I am only just coming to under-stand.'

George pointed over to the knotted rope that he had just spotted lassoed onto the end of the thickest branch. 'Is that your work?'

'It is,' admitted Annie in her normal

voice. 'I just wanted to see if I could do it.'

'I would have let the ladder down for you,' George told her.

'Last time I asked you to do that,' she complained, 'you made me guess about a thousand million different passwords and I still had to give you half my Kit Kat.'

'That wasn't a Kit Kat!' George reminded her. 'It was a piece of "chocolate"' – he used his fingers to make comma marks around the word – 'you'd tried to create under lab conditions, done up in a Kit Kat wrapper to see if I could tell the difference.'

'If a mouse can grow an ear on its back,' protested Annie, 'then why can't I grow a Kit Kat? It's got to be possible to make self-replicating chocolate molecules that just keep on doubling.'

Annie was a budding experimental chemist. She often used the kitchen as her own personal laboratory space, which drove her mother, Susan, crazy. Her mum would reach into the fridge to get a carton of apple juice, and encounter crystalline protein growth instead.

'FYI,' said George. 'Your Kit Kat tasted like a dinosaur's toe—'

'It did not!' interrupted Annie. 'My home-grown chocolate was delicious. I don't know what you mean. And when have you ever chewed a dinosaur's toe anyway?'

'Toenail,' finished George. 'Seriously gross. Like

it had been fossilized for a trillion years.'

'ROFL,' replied Annie sarcastically. ''Cos you're, like, *so* gour-may.'

'You don't even know what gourmet means,' George retorted.

'Do so.'

'What is it, then?' George was pretty sure he'd won this one.

'It's like when you have some gours,' explained Annie, 'and it's the month of May. It makes you go all *gour-may*.' She just made it to the end of the sentence before bursting out laughing – so hard that she fell off the beanbag.

'You're an idiot,' said George good-naturedly.

'With an IQ of 152.' Annie picked herself up off the floor. She'd had her IQ tested the week before and she wasn't about to let anyone forget the results. Suddenly she spotted the line-up of George's possessions. 'What's all this?'

'I'm getting my things ready.' George pointed at the equipment, which had been rescued from the tiny hands of his twin sisters and borne up to the treehouse for safety. There was a 60mm white telescope with black bands at each end, and a camera which he was attempting to rig up to the telescope so that it could take a picture. The telescope had been a present from his grandmother, Mabel, but amazingly, the camera had come from the tip. 'So I can get photos of Saturn when it gets dark. If my *boring* mum and dad don't make me go in. It's my half-term project.'

'Cool!' Annie squinted into the viewfinder of the telescope. 'Ew!' she exclaimed immediately. 'It's got something sticky on it!'

'What!' shouted George.

He looked at the telescope more carefully. Sure enough, around the viewfinder was some kind of gluey pink substance.

'That's *enough*!' His temper suddenly exploded. He started to climb down the rope ladder.

'Where are you going?' Annie scrambled after him. 'It's no biggie! We can clean it off!'

But George had steamed ahead, back into his house, his face red with fury. He barged into the kitchen,

where his father was attempting to give Juno and Hera their tea.

'And *one* for Dadda!' Terence was saying to Hera, who opened her mouth, accepted the green goo and promptly spat it back at him. Hera then shrieked with laughter and banged her spoon maniacally on the tray of her high chair, which made all the other bits and bobs of food jump around like Mexican beans. Juno, who tended to copy her twin, joined in, banging her spoon and making a disgusting wet farting noise with her lips.

Terence turned to look at George, an expression of mixed suffering and joy on his face; green slime dripped off his beard and down his home-made shirt.

George took a deep breath to start on his angry tirade about small people who messed up other people's stuff, but Annie managed to squeeze past him just in time.

'Hola, Mr G!' she sang cheerily to Terence. 'Hello, baby girls!'

The girls banged their spoons and gargled eagerly at this new distraction from dinner time.

'Just wanted to ask if George could come over to mine!' chirped Annie. She reached out a hand to tickle Hera under her soft sticky chin, which made the little girl dissolve into helpless giggles.

'What about my telescope?' George muttered crossly behind her.

'We. Will. Sort. It,' she said firmly back to him in a low voice. 'So lucky to have baby sisters,' she cooed over the twins. 'I wish I had lovely ickle baby sisters. I'm just a one and only lonely child . . .' She pulled an exaggeratedly sad face.

'Hmph.' George would have liked nothing better than to live in Annie's quiet, geeky, techno-obsessed household, with her scholarly father and her increasingly career-minded mother. Where there were no babies, no noise, no organic vegetables and no mess – except, perhaps, when Annie had been conducting one of her more 'interesting' experiments in the kitchen.

'Er, yes, you can go – but make sure you're back in time to do your chores,' said Terence, trying to sound like he was in charge.

'Great!' shouted Annie enthusiastically, pushing George back out of the door.

George knew that when Annie was in bossy mode, he just had to go with the flow. So he followed, which wasn't so hard: he didn't feel like hanging around at home in a bad mood when a visit to Annie's house was on offer.

'Bye, Mr G and baby Gs!' bellowed Annie as they ran off. 'Have a wonderful time!'

'Don't forget, George, you need to fill in your reward chart by completing your weekly tasks!' Terence called weakly after the departing figure of his oldest child. 'You've still got three fifths of the pie-chart left!'

But George was gone, swept away by Annie to the exciting domain of Next Door – the home of all things techno, cutting edge, scientific, electronic and amazing in George's eyes.

Chapter Two

They reached Annie's house by means of a hole in the fence between the two gardens. The hole had been made when Freddy the pig – another present from George's enterprising Granny Mabel – broke through from the Greenbys' back garden in a bold bid for freedom. Following Freddy's hoof prints that afternoon had led George to meet Annie and her family for the first time – her dad, mega-scientist and super-boffin Eric; her mum, musician Susan; and their super-computer, Cosmos, who was so powerful and intelligent, he could draw doorways through which you could walk to any part of the known Universe you wanted to visit (provided you were wearing a spacesuit, that is). Since that day, George had surfed the Solar System on a comet, walked on the surface of Mars, and had a showdown with an evil scientist in a distant solar system. It was fair to say that his life had never been quite the same since.

'Hey!' said Annie as they ran. 'You shouldn't be mean to your sisters.'

'What?' George wasn't thinking about his baby sisters any more. 'What are you talking about? I wasn't mean!'

'Only 'cos I stopped you,' accused Annie. 'You were going to say something horrible.'

'I was angry!' George replied indignantly. 'They're not supposed to touch my stuff or go up to the treehouse!'

'You're lucky to have a brother or a sister at all,' said Annie piously. 'I haven't got anything.'

'Yes you have!' George burst out. 'You've got so much stuff! You've got Cosmos the computer, you've practically got your own science lab, you've got an Xbox, you've got a smartphone, a laptop, an iPod, an iPad, an i-everything; you've got that mechanical dog; you've got a scooter with a motor on it . . . I dunno . . . You've got the lot.'

'It's not the same,' said Annie quietly, 'as having a real-life brother or sister.'

'If you actually had one,' said George dubiously, 'or even two, I bet you wouldn't want it. Them.'

The two friends hurried through the door into the kitchen.

'Huzzah!' Annie skidded across the floor towards the huge fridge, reaching out to grab the handle.

Even the Bellises' fridge didn't look like a normal fridge – more like the sort of thing you might find in a laboratory: massive and made of steel, with

cavernous drawers and
separate compartments
for isolating elements
from each other. It was,
of course, a profes-
sional machine, as far
removed from a normal
fridge as a spaceship is
from a paper aeroplane.
That was one of the
things George loved
about Annie's house: it
was full of unexpected
gadgets and scientific
oddities which Eric had

bought or acquired or been given in the course of his
many years of work. George looked at the fridge envi-
ously; it glowed with a strange blue light. The most
technologically advanced item in his whole house
probably contained less processing power than Annie's
refrigerator.

George was just musing on that depressing fact when
he realized that there were voices coming from the
sitting room.

'Annie! George!' Annie's dad, Eric, stuck his head
round the kitchen door. He was smiling broadly, his
eyes sparkling behind his thick glasses, his tie loosened

and his shirt sleeves rolled up. He came in carrying two crystal glasses.

'I've come to get a fill-up,' he explained, reaching for a dusty old bottle and pulling the cork out with a loud *thop*. He poured out a sticky brown fluid and turned to go back to the sitting room.

'Come and say hello to my guest.' His face was creased into long laughter lines. 'I think she has something that might interest you.'

George and Annie immediately forgot their brief argument and followed Eric into the sitting room, which was packed from floor to ceiling with rows and rows of books. It was a beautiful room, full of interesting objects like Eric's old brass telescope. The cutting-edge technology that ruled the rest of the house was less over-whelming here; it was cosy and inviting rather than cool and futuristic. On the squashy sofa, which Eric had owned since his student days, sat a very ancient lady.

'Annie, George,' said Eric, handing the old lady her glass of sherry. 'This is Beryl Wilde.'

Beryl accepted the drink gratefully and started slurping it straight away. 'How d'you do!' She waved a cheery hand at them.

'Beryl is one of the greatest mathematicians of our times,' said Eric seriously.

Beryl burst out laughing. 'Oh! Don't be absurd!'

'It's true!' he insisted. 'Without Beryl's mathematical genius, millions more people would have died.'

'What people?' asked George.

Annie had whipped out her smartphone and was trying to pull up a Wikipedia entry for Beryl Wilde.

'How do you spell your last name?' she asked.

'You won't find it,' said Beryl, guessing what Annie was trying to do, her pale blue eyes twinkling. 'I'm completely covered by the Official Secrets Act.

Still, even after all these years. You won't find me anywhere.'

Eric gestured to an object on the coffee table in front of the sofa. 'This,' he said dramatically as he pointed to what looked like an old-fashioned typewriter, 'is an Enigma machine – one of the ones used during the Second  World War to encode messages. It meant that messages could be sent that were impossible for interceptors to understand. But Beryl was one of the mathematicians who broke the Enigma code. Which meant that the war ended much sooner than it might have done, and fewer people on both sides lost their lives.'

'OMG!' said Annie, looking up from her phone. 'So you could read the secret messages without the other people realizing you knew what they were planning? Like, if someone read all my emails now . . . ? Except, obviously,' she added, 'I'm not fighting a war with anyone. Except Karla Pinchnose, who made everyone laugh at me when I spelled something wrong on the smartboard . . .'

'Exactly.' Beryl nodded. 'We could intercept their messages and decrypt the content so we knew what they were planning to do. That gave us a huge advantage.'

NUMBER SYSTEMS

Decimal

Our everyday numbering system – the *decimal* system - is based on a factor of 10. We number from 1 to 9, and then go to a new column for the number of '10's.

36 = 3 x 10, plus 6 x 1

48 = 4 x 10, plus 8 x 1

148 = 1 x 100, plus 4 x 10, plus 8 x 1

And so on.

Binary

With early computer systems, a *binary* numbering system was used. This is because binary is based on a factor of 2, so the only digits used are 0 and 1.

10 = 1 x 2, plus 0 x 1 i.e. the number 2 in the decimal system

11 = 1 x 2, plus 1 x 1, i.e. the number 3

111 = 1 x 4, plus 1 x 2, plus 1 x 1 i.e. the number 7

The 0/1 choice could be linked to switches in the computer circuits so that 0 = 'off' and 1 = 'on' and code written in binary could then make the circuits turn themselves on and off as needed to make calculations.

Hexadecimal

Nowadays, computers are much more sophisticated and codes are often written using a *hexadecimal* numbering system, based on a factor of 16. This counts figures from 0 to 9 but then also uses A for ten, B for eleven and so on up to F for fifteen.

C therefore represents 12 in the decimal system

10 is the hexadecimal way of writing the number 16

11 = seventeen

1F = 1 x 16, plus F x 1 (15) = 31

20 = 2 x 16 = 32

F7 = F x 16 (15 x 16 = 240), plus 7 x 1 = 247

100 = 256

CODE BREAKING

Code breaking usually means the unscrambling or decryption of messages, without having access to the secret key which the person who sent the message used. Another name for this is *cryptanalysis*, and a particular method of encryption is also called a *cypher*.

Before computers

Until the arrival of digital computers, encryption worked on letters, or on numbers representing letters. For example, each letter appearing in a message might be replaced with another letter. In a simple code, A would be replaced by E, B replaced by F and so on through the alphabet. Or the alphabet would be scrambled in some way.

To solve this sort of cypher, a good approach is to count how often each letter appears in the encrypted text (this is called *frequency analysis*) and then guess some of the substitutions. For instance the letter 'e' appears in a great many words, and if the letter 's' is in the coded message, then this might mean that 's' = 'e'. This can be enough to correctly guess the remaining substitutions since the original message has to make sense.

More complicated cyphers might use a different scrambling of the alphabet for each letter of the message – and there are a very large number of possible scramblings to choose from: 26 letters in the alphabet, so 26 possible letters for the first letter, then 25 for the second, 24 for the third and so on.

Modern code-breaking

Modern methods work not on letters but on bits (1s and 0s) in the memory of a computer. Encryption and decryption use a secret key, which is a long sequence of bits (1s and 0s). A key 256 bits long today is thought to be quite sufficient to prevent a code-breaker using a supercomputer to find the key by brute force (i.e. by trying every possible key).

CODEBREAKING
DPEFCSFBLJOH
(+ 1 letter)

GEORGE
JHRUJH
(+ 3 letters)

ANNIE
ZMMHD
(–1 letter)

'Wowzers!' said Annie. 'Props to you, Bez!' She went back to typing on her phone.

'Is that *really* an Enigma machine?' George gazed at it with longing. He couldn't believe that yet another amazing gadget had found its way into the Bellises' house. He wished for the millionth time that he'd been born into this home instead of his own.

'It is,' said Beryl, smiling at him. 'And I'm giving it to Eric. As a present.'

Eric gasped. He'd clearly had no inkling of her intention. 'You can't do that!' he exclaimed.

'Yes I can!' Beryl was firm. 'It's for your Department of Maths at the university. You are exactly the right person – with your work on quantum computers, I can't think of a better home for it.'

'What's a quantum computer?' George asked. This was news to him – and exciting news too. He remembered that Eric had been very secretive for quite some time now – George hadn't been able to get anything more than a very vague answer from the great scientist as to what he was working on at the moment.

But tonight, Eric seemed in a much chattier mood than usual.

'It's the next wave of change,' he told George. 'We've had the *digital* revolution in information, and now we are on the brink of the *quantum* revolution. If we could make a quantum computer – and control it, which looks very difficult right now – we could do things that are

ENIGMA

Wartime secrets

By the time of the Second World War (1939–1945) the warring nations were using machines such as the *Enigma* (in Germany) and the *Typex* (in Britain) to encrypt important messages.

The operator of the Enigma machine typed the message on keys on the front of the machine, and the machine produced the encrypted text, indicating each scrambled letter by lighting a small electric bulb. The encrypted message was recorded by hand, turned into Morse Code and finally sent by radio.

Three rotors

The Enigma machine had three rotors – *wheels* - containing complicated wiring. The rotors could be taken out and put back in a different order, then rotated so that each of the three could be in any of 26 different positions. This meant that there were six possible ways of setting the three rotors (3 x 2 x 1) and then 26 x 26 x 26 positions of each letter. To make this even more complicated, up to ten short wires could be plugged into a plugboard at the front of the machine – each of the many ways of doing this would create an entirely new set of 26 x 26 x 26 cyphers for a message to use.

At the receiving end, there would be another Enigma machine set up in exactly the same way, and the scrambled text would be typed in. The original text could then be recovered by recording which lights lit up. The idea was that each day, every Enigma operator would know which rotor to insert where, in what position, and with what connections on the plugboard.

Breaking Enigma

The encryption system relied on a shared secret, in this case the daily instructions for setting up and using the machine – and the problem was how to securely share it with many people. A mistake by any of them could give away important information, and printed instructions could also be stolen or captured.

Through a combination of German errors, advanced mathematics and ingenuity, code-breakers – first in Poland, and then later at Bletchley Park in England – managed to discover the settings of the Enigma machines and were able to decrypt German messages. A crucial part of the method was a particular machine – a machine designed by Alan Turing, a maths genius, known as the *Bombe*. Another important machine developed at Bletchley Park was the Colossus – the first electronic, programmable digital computing machine – which was used to break code produced not by Enigma but by another German cypher machine called the *Lorenz*.

THE UNIVERSAL TURING MACHINE

An imaginary device

In 1936, a 'computer' was a human being performing calculations. The Turing Machine developed by genius mathematician Alan Turing was intended to be a simple imaginary device capable of reproducing everything a human computer might need to do while calculating. The machine is therefore a mathematical, rather than a real-world, device to be used to understand what computation is, and what can be achieved by computation. But it could not exist in reality; for example, it is assumed to have both infinite 'memory' and an unlimited time in which to operate, neither of which are feasible.

A string of 0s . . .

The operation of a machine is first defined by a finite list of coded instructions. Imagine a very long tape on which is written a very long string of 0s (as long as the tape itself). The tape stretches out for ever in both directions (assume it is infinitely long) and represents the 'memory' of the computing machine. Sprinkled among these 0s are finitely many 1s which represent the 'data' given to the machine. Sitting on this tape is the processing device (the processor) that can read just the one symbol that is currently directly beneath it and it can leave it as it is, or replace it with either 0 or 1.

It also has a clock which ticks steadily, and at each tick of the clock, the processor reads the symbol it can currently see. It then does one of two things depending on what it just read and its current state. It can:

- change the symbol beneath, marking it as 0 or 1, then move one position either left or right along the tape, maybe change to a different state, and wait for the next tick.
- or do the same but then halt (turn off).

What it *actually* does depends on the rules (the 'program') we give it, and what it finds on the tape. As an example, let's assume that the machine starts out in state 0, with a long string of 0s on the tape, and that somewhere to the right of it some of the 0s have been replaced by 1s – these 1s form a pattern which is the binary number we give the machine as its input.

Then a good rule to start with is: *if in state 0 and we read 0, then switch to state 0, write 0, and move right.*

This means that when the machine sees 0 initially (when it is in state 0), it stays in state 0, does not change the 0 on the tape, and moves one step right. If the tape one step right still says 0, the same happens – the machine stays in state 0, leaves the tape as it found it and marches another step right.

This happens at each tick of the clock, until the machine finally reaches the first of the 1s written on the tape. It now needs a rule which tells it what to do when it reads a 1 in state 0. The simplest rule would be to: *stay in state 0, write 1, and move another step right and halt*. The 1 will now appear on the left of the machine, and is the result of the computation.

We could describe this very simple computation as '*print 1 if the input is valid*', where by valid we mean 'contains at least one 1'. If there were no 1s written to the right of the machine when it starts, it would simply carry on marching right looking for a 1 for ever – it would not halt but carry on working fruitlessly! This can happen on a real computer – a program can endlessly 'loop' or 'spin' until the entire computer crashes.

This possibility is unfortunately a fundamental property both of Turing Machines and real computers. However, we can stop this happening straightaway by insisting that 'valid' inputs contain at least one 1, so that this first rule cannot simply be used for ever.

Every possible calculation

Given enough time and the ability to write as many 1s on the tape as required, every mechanical operation with whole numbers that we can think of could be performed by feeding a Turing Machine with the input number on the right of the machine, starting the clock and waiting for it to halt, then reading the answer on the left of the machine. It includes every arithmetic calculation a human with pen and paper could ever do, and Alan Turing proposed that what his Turing Machine can compute should be taken as a definition of what can be computed at all. Amazingly, nearly 80 years after his theories, this is still widely believed to be a good definition because every known design for a digital computing machine can only compute what a Turing Machine could compute.

Turing also showed mathematically that even a Turing Machine cannot solve every problem! Put another way, some problems in mathematics are uncomputable – mathematicians won't be replaced by computers yet.

unimaginable with the current generation of computer technology.'

'Like what?' said George.

'With a quantum computer we could break every code – there is no security system on Earth that could stop it!' said Eric gleefully. 'There are amazing things we could do in the fields of information processing, medicine, physics, engineering and mathematics. It is the next great step.'

'But what's that got to do with an Enigma machine?' asked George.

'Enigma,' replied Beryl, 'is the forerunner of all sorts of exciting technologies that came later. And, of course, Enigma actually existed and worked. Whereas the quantum computer, at this moment, does neither.'

'Yes – ha-ha-ha!' said Eric. 'Most of my work at the moment is in Quantum Error Detection—'

'Your father,' Beryl interjected, 'is probably the only person on Earth who could operate a quantum computer – if one existed, that is.'

Eric looked pleased. 'Quantum Error Detection basically means making sure that when we get a quantum computer working, we're able to keep it under some kind of control. Which isn't looking very likely right now! They didn't have that problem with Enigma.'

'Could we use Enigma? Could Annie and I send coded messages to each other with it?' George wondered.

'Enigma can't *send* messages.' Beryl finished her

sherry. 'It encrypts and decrypts them, but you need another means of transmission. In fact, users would send the encrypted messages as Morse code over the radio. These days, we have technology which does both – encrypts messages, billions of them, every second, and sends them across the Earth through cables or over the airwaves; then they are decrypted by other computers. Every email, every request for a web page and every computer command is a coded message, and even though some codes are supposed to be understood by everyone – the internet would be in a pretty pickle otherwise – if you buy a pair of socks online, you would certainly want at least your credit card number encrypted so that no eavesdropper can steal your money. Think of those computers all over the world controlling how things work – electricity, transport, defence, to name just three. They all use encryption to stop the wrong people putting spanners in the works. If you could defeat such encryption, then you could hold the world to ransom.'

'Don't give them ideas,' said Eric in a mock-stern voice. 'I don't want to be fighting an extradition request because these two have managed to burrow their way into some super-secret government programme and started upsetting people.'

'Oh, that would be such fun!' cried Beryl. 'I really hope they do!'

George looked at Annie. Beryl must have some

WHAT IS COMPUTER CODE?

Codes for secrets

Throughout history, when human beings deliberately used codes, it was usually because they were trying to encrypt messages, turning ordinary text into something that made no sense to anyone not knowing how to decode the message. This meant they could send secret messages to their allies.

Today, anyone making a purchase online – ordering music, or a book, or a present for someone – needs to do exactly the same to make sure that spies can't use the internet to discover the details of their payment card and then use those details to steal their money. The digital computer means that not only can details in messages (like your payment details) be hidden from others, but also it is easy to check and see if a message has been tampered with or sent by an impostor.

These methods work on *bits* instead of *letters*, and rely on cyphers which are quick to use with a computer, but extremely hard to break without the secret key. It won't stop people trying, though – so it is possible that new ways to break these cyphers will be discovered eventually, and in that case new cyphers will have to be invented.

Computer languages

To a mathematician, coding is a process of transforming a set of symbols into another by following certain rules.

For the operation of any computer, the coding of instructions and data is basic. How exactly should these be represented in terms of 1s and 0s, so that the computer processor can read the instructions? The rules for doing this define the *machine code* of the processor.

Each set of rules is an *algorithm*, so coding can be performed by a patient human being with a pen and paper, or (probably much faster) by a digital computer.

Human beings write their programs in readable computer languages, like C or FORTRAN, both of which are written using English words and characters instead of just 1s and 0, and lots of different programming languages have been developed over the years, so that programmers can 'talk' to the computer, and we often talk about 'computer code' in the sense of a program coded in one of these different languages.

Compilers are special programs which read programs written in these high-level languages and transform them into machine-code programs that can then be fed directly to the processor. Machine code is usually written nowadays in hexadecimal (16s).

Breaking this sort of code means finding a way to make the program fail, or do something unexpected – this is a tactic often used by hostile people on the internet attempting to gain unauthorized access to a computer for mischievous or criminal reasons (like stealing your card details so they can steal your money!).

ALGORITHMS

An algorithm is a step by step process in which clear rules tell you how to convert one list of symbols into another at each step. For example, learning how to multiply large numbers or do long division involve familiar steps which you are taught at school: these steps are *algorithms*. Each problem is tackled in exactly the same way; at each step you write down the numbers on the paper, making new lines of numbers as you need to, until the answer appears.

Algorithms have an ancient history – for example, Euclid wrote down an algorithm for finding the highest common factor of two whole numbers in around 300BC (though it is probably older).

The word 'algorithm' comes from the name of a 9th-century Persian mathematician, al-Khwрizm , who described algorithms for performing arithmetic. He also (amongst other things) developed the methods of algebra.

In the twentieth century, mathematicians have tried to define exactly what an algorithm is mathematically, but all their early proposals proved to be equivalent to 'what can be performed by a Turing Machine': no known computer design can do more yet!

Every computer program boils down to an algorithm which changes the patterns of bits in the memory of the computer during each cycle of the processor.

wonderful stories to tell, he thought.

'Well, you're a good influence, aren't you?' Eric said to Beryl, but he looked the opposite of cross. 'Go on, you two – scram before Beryl signs you up for the secret services' junior division.'

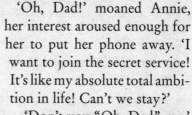

'Oh, Dad!' moaned Annie, her interest aroused enough for her to put her phone away. 'I want to join the secret service! It's like my absolute total ambition in life! Can't we stay?'

'Don't you "Oh, Dad" me,' said Eric firmly. 'Go and do something that won't result in MI5 ringing my doorbell. I'm not James Bond; I'm a professor of physics, and I don't want you to confuse those two things.'

'Look, it's dark outside now!' George said, looking out of the window. 'Let's go back to the treehouse and take a photo of Saturn!'

'Excellent idea,' agreed Eric. 'Even you two can't get into trouble taking a photograph of a distant planet.'

Beryl giggled. 'Please try,' she said, giving Annie and George a wink. 'Life is so much more fun when you get into trouble from time to time. It's what makes it all so interesting.'

'Go, kids!' ordered Eric in real, not pretend exasperation.

Chapter Three

Annie and George obediently filed out of the sitting room, breaking into a run as soon as they reached the kitchen.

'Last one to the treehouse is a . . .' they shouted in unison.

'Bad banana!' yelled Annie.

'Rotten egg!' bellowed George as they dashed into the garden, each trying to push the other out of the way so they could leap through the hole in the fence first.

They reached the tree at the same time, with Annie snatching the ladder while George shinned up the knotted rope as though climbing the rigging on a tall ship. They arrived on the platform at exactly the same moment, and cried out, 'I won!' The treehouse was rocking to and fro like a ship in a storm, and they grabbed onto each other to prevent themselves from pitching over the edge into the dark garden.

'Whoa!' said Annie as the platform slowly stabilized itself.

'Oops!' George felt guilty. 'We forgot to pull the ladder up when we left.'

'Is your telescope OK?' asked Annie.

George hoped so! He produced a little torch from his pocket. The telescope was still securely in its place, the camera next to it, waiting for its moment of glory in imaging the night sky. George took out a handkerchief and gingerly wiped the viewfinder until the sticky mess had gone.

'How did the twins even get up here?' said Annie. 'Can they climb a rope ladder?'

'They get everywhere,' said George darkly. 'Nothing is safe from them.'

'Aw, they're so cute . . .' Annie smiled. 'You love them really.'

George didn't answer. He was too busy trying to frame Saturn through his telescope so that he got the perfect shot of the magnificent ringed planet. For a moment he looked up at the stars in the night sky with his naked eye and thought what an extraordinary sight they were. He was totally fascinated by space; by what lay out there, beyond the edge of the Earth's atmosphere. *Space.* George even loved the word. The vast expanse of the Universe, enormous beyond imagination and full of bizarre, fascinating phenomena – planets, black holes, neutron stars ... the list went on and on. *The Universe*, he thought to himself, *is amazing! And I want to understand it all. I want to go beyond the limits of human knowledge and understanding until I know as much as is possible to know about our incredible cosmic home—*

'Are you going to take that photo?' Annie's voice interrupted his wandering thoughts.

'I'll have a go,' he replied. 'I hope there isn't too much light pollution.' Even the small university town of Foxbridge gave off enough light that the evening sky was orange around the horizon rather than pure black. But he pressed the button on his camera; it used the telescope to collect more light than the human eye so that it could record an image of a planet millions of miles away in the Solar System.

'Lessee!' said Annie, grabbing the camera. 'Let's have a look at your beautiful picture . . .'

She opened up the camera's memory to view the last photo. 'Oh!' she said in surprise.

'What?' asked George. 'Didn't it work?'

'Well, it's taken a photo,' said Annie, 'for sure. But . . .'

George reached for the camera and peered at the image it had just captured of the skies above Foxbridge.

'That's not Saturn,' he said. 'That looks like a . . . Well, I don't know what that looks like . . .'

'It looks like' – Annie finished his sentence – 'some kind of spaceship. But it's not like any spaceship I've ever seen before.' She gazed up into the night sky through the telescope. 'I can't see anything overhead.'

'Me neither.' George took a turn at peering through the telescope. 'Whatever it was, it's not there now.'

'That's so weird,' said Annie. 'Honestly, in the picture it looks just like a floating space doughnut, but when you look up into the sky through the telescope, there's nothing there. Except the stars and stuff – but they were there before.'

33

'Really weird,' George agreed, using the zoom function to enlarge the photo on the small screen of his camera. He could just make out faint markings on the side of the mystery object. 'It says "IAM".'

'IAM?' said Annie. 'What does that mean? International American Mission? Imbecile Android Missile? Incredible Armed Machine . . . ?'

'Don't know,' said George. 'It's not anything I've ever heard about.' As a devoted space fan, he prided himself on knowing about every space mission currently in low Earth orbit. And this was not one of them. 'Perhaps it's a *secret* spaceship?'

'Or aliens?' Annie suggested excitedly.

'It's probably some kind of weather satellite,' said George, more realistically.

'It's a bit big for a satellite. That much I *do* know! I think it's a UFO.'

'But why would a UFO turn up here?' George wondered. 'What would it want from Foxbridge?'

As soon as he said it, he knew the answer. And even in the dim light, he noticed that Annie suddenly looked anxious. He knew her big fear was that something terrible would happen to her dad. Eric was such an important scientist and worked on such top-secret projects that, in the past, he had been targeted by people who wanted to stop his work or find out what he was doing.

'I'm sure it's got nothing to do with Eric!' George tried to reassure Annie; but at the same time he was getting a fluttery feeling in his stomach that something really exciting might be about to happen. 'It's probably some random scientific spacecraft taking measurements of the atmosphere. It just looks like a UFO – I bet up close it's really ordinary.' But even as he said this, part of him hoped that he was wrong; that it wasn't something ordinary at all.

'Yeah, right,' said Annie. She didn't sound completely convinced, but she looked a little more cheerful. She scuffed one trainer against the other. 'Do you think Dad's safe now?'

'Yes, of course,' said George firmly, even though he wasn't sure this was true at all. 'He's the most important scientist in the country. There must be people looking out for him. Stop worrying about your dad! I don't think anything is going to happen over half-term in Foxbridge. Just usual boring parents and school projects and stuff. That's all.'

'I hope you're right,' Annie murmured, scanning the sky for signs of returning UFOs. She still didn't sound her usual boisterous self.

'Calling Annie!' George cupped his hands around his mouth like a megaphone. 'Do you have any chocolate – I mean, dinosaur toenails? I is hungry.'

Annie brightened up. 'You sound ridiculous.' But at least she was laughing.

Chapter Four

The next day was another bright, clear half-term day. Over breakfast, George had quizzed his dad as to what the little girls had been doing up in his treehouse. His father had looked shifty but eventually admitted that after a long campaign of pestering from the twins, he had taken them up so that they could have a look at where their brother Georgie hung out.

'But you promised me they would never go up there!' George had exclaimed, feeling very let down.

'They won't! Not again!' Terence promised. 'It was just the once. Honest.'

George humphed again. It seemed as though rules were broken for his sisters when they never budged even a millimetre for him. But then he remembered Annie telling him not to be mean – and thinking of Annie reminded him of the photo of the UFO ... which reminded him that he wanted to get his chores done as quickly as possible so that he could meet his friend in the treehouse and find out if she'd got any useful info on the secret spaceship from Eric after she'd gone home last night. So he cheered up and got on with his tasks – feeding the hens, collecting the eggs, taking the vegetable waste into the garden for compost and helping his mum, Daisy, knead the dough for their daily bread that had been proving . . . It wasn't till after lunch that he was free to scoot down the garden, up the ladder and into the treehouse once more.

He'd only been up there for a nanosecond when he heard a scuffling noise and a figure leaped onto the platform, causing the tree-house to sway. George wondered again if he should check the ropes that held everything in place. But he quickly forgot to worry as an apparition in a long raincoat and old-fashioned trilby with sunglasses accosted him.

'The weatherman says the sky will be clear tonight,' it murmured mysteriously.

'Um . . . he does?' queried George, quickly realizing that Annie had now reinvented herself as a spy from the time of the Enigma machine. She sounded like one of those Second World War spies who used coded language to send messages to each other, so that even if their communications were intercepted, the enemy wouldn't know what they meant.

'A cloud across the glass eye will bring early snow,' it continued.

'The big cheese stands alone,' George replied, trying to join in.

'We pick the strawberries at midnight.' Annie discarded her coat and hat but kept the sunglasses on. She clearly thought they made her look cool.

'Hold on . . .' George raised one hand with a flat, outstretched palm. 'The message has to actually *mean* something, if you know how to decipher it – you can't just say any old random stuff, you know!'

'OMG! You're literally so *literal* sometimes!' exclaimed Annie, throwing herself onto the beanbag. 'Did I mention how high my IQ is?'

'Yes, just, like, a trillion times,' replied George. He wished he could have his IQ measured, but when he'd asked his parents, they told him they didn't approve of educational testing.

'What did your dad think of the photo?' he asked, hoping to get off the topic of Annie's super-intelligence and on to something more interesting. She had taken his camera home with her last night. 'What about Beryl – was she still there? Did she let slip any clues?'

'Well, I showed the picture to them,' said Annie, 'but they didn't recognize it; said it was probably some sort of foreign satellite. They did say it was kind of large – but they didn't know what "IAM" stood for.'

'So they didn't tell you anything useful?' George was disappointed. He was longing for a good reason to go on another adventure – perhaps to open up Cosmos, Eric's amazing computer, and use his portal to step out somewhere in the Universe. It wasn't the kind of thing you could just do because you felt like it – you had to be able to justify your space missions, and at the moment he couldn't think of a really great reason why he should embark on a cosmic journey. The only reason was that he wanted to, but somehow, George suspected that wouldn't be quite enough.

'No, they just kept laughing,' said Annie. 'They were like – "Pour another glass and let's drink a toast to the UFO!" They didn't take it seriously at all.'

'So what now?' George had the feeling that this was a dead end.

'Dunno,' said Annie. 'I tried posting the photo on Instagram to see if anyone recognized it, but I just got loads of junk comments about how we'd better watch out because the Thorgs were coming to eradicate us.'

'Yay! The Thorgs!' said George, trying to rally himself. 'My fave aliens!' A thought struck him. 'But seriously, was it a good idea to post it on the internet? If it's some kind of weirdo spooky secret mission, aren't they going to be annoyed that you've posted a photo of their ship?'

'Oops!' Annie looked worried. 'I didn't think of that. I tweeted it too.'

'Well, that's OK,' conceded George. 'I know for a fact that you don't have any followers so it doesn't matter.'

'One day I will,' said Annie, stung. 'One day I'll have millions, if not billions of followers . . .' She paused and gave a smug smile. 'Once my blog goes live, then all this will change.'

'Your blog?' asked George in surprise. He didn't know anything about Annie's blog.

'It's super-cool,' she enthused. 'I've got to prepare stuff for a blog – it's for my school science project. Actually, it's not going to be a blog. I think I'll do a *vlog* instead, and put it on YouTube.'

'What's it called?' George asked.

'Um . . . I don't know yet,' said Annie. 'I'm still deciding. Our teacher said it had to be "The Chemistry of *Some Thing*" – but we all have to choose what the Thing is.'

'The Chemistry of Chocolate?' offered George. 'You could do that really well.'

'I *was* going to do the Chemistry of Chocolate, but then Karla Pinchnose stole my idea!' said Annie in outrage. 'So I have to do something really cool to show her that even if she copies me, I'm still going to come up with a better plan. And that I'm still smarter than her.'

'The Chemistry of Glue?' suggested George, laughing.

'I'd better not,' sighed Annie. 'Mum and Dad weren't

very chuffed when I stuck them to the dinner table with my very excellent home-made polymer. I don't think I can do any more stuff with glue. The Chemistry of . . .'

'Did you ask your dad?' George was idly looking through his telescope, sweeping across the skies and the cityscape.

'I did,' she told him. 'He got all excited and was, like, "Oooh, I've got medals for chemistry, you know"! I was, like, "Seriously, Dad! No one cares about your medals! Have you done GCSE science? No, of course not, because you went to school back in the dark ages when you wrote with a quill and parchment—"'

'Annie!' George interrupted her. 'Look!'

'What?' She jumped off the beanbag in a flash and tried to peer over his shoulder into the viewfinder of his telescope. But she didn't really need the telescope. It didn't take a lens to see what was happening in Foxbridge.

A mass of people were streaming along the streets winding down to the city centre – mostly on foot, but

some on bicycles or mopeds. Cars had ground to a standstill, unable to move either forward or backward through the mob that surrounded them. The people were approaching from all directions, all heading for the main square.

'Thundering Thorgs!' said George in astonishment. Their home town was usually a sleepy, quiet place; the centre was normally frequented mainly by tourists and students. He'd never seen anything like this before.

'Is it a boy band?' asked Annie, jumping about in excitement. 'It must be! It must be a secret visit by UnDetection! They're my all-time favourite band! They're on tour, and they said on Twitter to keep an eye out because no one knew where they would show up next . . . C'mon, George, we have to go!'

'I don't know how much fun it will be,' said George doubtfully. Down in the town, he could see that anyone who tried to go against the tsunami of people was simply spun round and washed along by the sheer force of the crowd.

'It will be awesome!' Annie was already climbing down the ladder. Knowing that he couldn't let her go by herself, George charged after her, down the rope, through the hole in the fence, back into her house and out through the front door again.

Annie sprinted along to the end of their road where it joined the high street, leading into the heart of Foxbridge.

'What about your mum?' George called as he pelted after her. He almost caught up with her at the corner, before she disappeared into the fast-moving stream of people.

'She sent me over to yours when she went out – I'll text her . . . Do you think they'll sing?' she yelled back as they were swept along the streets.

'I didn't know they could,' muttered George, who preferred Fall Out Boy and the Arctic Monkeys to the pop that Annie liked so much.

He managed to get a grip on her wrist, which he encircled like a handcuff. Losing her in this mass of people was not an option. 'You mustn't fall over!' he shouted at her. 'You'll get trampled!' They were being

43

squeezed and shoved on all sides as they were forced along towards the centre of town.

'I just want to see his hair!' Annie screamed back at him. 'His beautiful hair!' She had a huge poster of the lead singer of UnDetection above her bed, and George knew that, when she thought no one was looking, she stroked the floppy locks in the photo. 'He might spot me!'

George snorted to himself. No one would notice anything in this enormous jostling river of people who buffeted him and Annie one way and another as they jogged along. George couldn't care less whether he saw UnDetection or heard a note they sang, but he wasn't going to let Annie get lost in the madness.

As they surged forward into a market square that was surrounded by graceful old buildings with turrets and gargoyles and grand stone columns, the atmosphere changed. Up until then, the crowd had been quite friendly, as though everyone was taking part in a joint adventure. But suddenly the mood shifted, and the pushing and shoving became more aggressive.

'Whoa – it's turning nasty!' warned George, still trying to hang onto his friend. He had a bad feeling about this situation. But Annie was still so focused on reaching her beloved band that she hadn't picked up the change in atmosphere.

A roar went up. Shoving forward, the multitude seemed to be trying to converge on a single point. But as there were by now hundreds, if not thousands, of people in the centre of Foxbridge, chaos had taken over. At the very edge of the crowd, the police stubbornly blew their whistles and called for order, but no one took any notice.

'I won't be able to see the band!' Annie panicked as she realized that they were much smaller than most of the other people.

George jumped up to try and see over the heads of those in front. 'I don't think there *is* a band,' he said. There was no sign of a big stage or any kind of musical set-up.

'But . . .' Annie's voice was drowned out as a helicopter appeared overheard, flying low enough for them to see the metal of its underbelly. Its wings beat the air like a manic wasp trapped in a jam jar. The sound was ear-splitting. Annie carried on talking: George could see her lips move, but he couldn't hear what she was saying.

'I can't hear you!' he screamed back.

The helicopter hovered over the centre of town, where by now the angry mob was corralled against the old houses on the high street. George looked up, and suddenly saw that the air was full of rectangular bits of paper – blue, brown, purple and pink. But they didn't seem to be coming from the helicopter. Instead, they were flying up from the ground, spiralling and spinning in the currents generated by the rotor blades.

George realized at once what the pieces of paper were.

'It's money!' he yelled over at Annie as loudly as he could. 'BANKNOTES – EVERYWHERE. PEOPLE ARE HERE FOR THE . . .'

The pilot of the helicopter, realizing that it was only making the situation worse, suddenly flew off, leaving George still shouting at the top of voice.

'MONEY!' he screamed into the silence.

'MONEY!' yelled a young man next to George, thinking he was starting a chant.

Other people joined in, until the whole crowd was yelling, 'MONEY! MONEY!' while leaping up and trying to grab handfuls of the notes floating through the air. Fights were breaking out between those who had managed to catch some and those who hadn't. A man grabbed George's T-shirt. 'Give me your money!' he menaced.

'I don't have any!' said George, terrified, holding out his empty hands. The man let go immediately and moved on to threaten the next person, who fortunately wasn't Annie.

'We need to get out of here,' George hissed into Annie's ear.

She turned and nodded, her face pale with shock. 'How?' she mouthed.

'Follow me!' said George. He started to weave in and out of the crowd. It wasn't easy, but they managed to navigate their way out of the crush without anyone trying to stop them.

Back at Annie's house, they raided the fridge, making sure they stuck to the side with the food and drink rather than the part that housed Eric and Annie's experiments.

'Oof!' Annie sloshed cold juice down her throat as George bit into a huge piece of flapjack. She was still trembling after their astonishing trip into town.

'Yum – this is delicious!'

George had recovered more quickly; in any case, he was always hungry. 'Did you make it?'

'No,' said Annie.

'Probably why it's so nice,' said George. Annie flicked a tea towel at him.

'That was crazy!' she said after a pause. 'And we didn't even see UnDetection!'

'I don't think they were there,' George replied. 'I think those people went to the centre of town because they heard about the money.'

'Yikes!' said Annie, checking Twitter on her phone. 'You're so right! It says that some bank machines in Foxbridge went crazy and starting spewing out money . . . Why would they do that?'

'Weird,' said George, munching away. 'Perhaps it was some kind of computer error? Instead of taking money *into* the bank, it got reversed and sent the money back out again.'

'We should have got some money, you know,' said Annie regretfully. Now that she had calmed down a little, she was able to review the situation objectively. 'I could have bought some tickets for UnDetection's stadium gig.'

But before George could reply, the doorbell rang. Annie started off towards the front door.

'Are you allowed to open the door when your

parents aren't home?' George asked, following her.

'I'll just find out who's there,' she told him before shouting through the letter box, 'Who is it?'

'Delivery!' sang a cheerful voice. 'For Professor Bellis! From The Future Is Now Foundation.'

'Sooooo exciting!' Annie whisked open the front door. 'I'll sign for it!'

She scribbled her name on the clipboard, obviously expecting to be handed a small package. But to their surprise, the delivery man went back to a bright red van emblazoned with the words THE FUTURE IS HERE!, opened the double back doors and brought out a narrow rectangular box which was the height of a grown man. He managed to heave it through the front door and laid

it down in the hallway. Saluting Annie and smiling, he returned to his van and set off without so much as a puff of exhaust smoke.

Annie closed the front door, and she and George stared in puzzlement at the long package.

'I thought it would just be some equipment for the home lab.' Annie looked baffled. 'I don't know what this could be. Shall we open it?'

'I don't know,' said George, undecided. 'What do you think?'

'Ummm . . .' Annie was just making up her mind when the box seemed to make the decision for them. As they watched, it began to shake.

'It's moving!' Annie cried.

The box seemed to be trying to right itself from the prone position it had been left in.

George stood there with his mouth open. 'I heard a noise from inside . . .' he said slowly.

Sure enough, once again, from inside the box – which, now that George thought about it, was indeed the height and width of a person – came a knocking sound.

'Let me out!' came a faint voice.

'ARRGH!' screamed Annie. 'There's someone in the box!'

'No!' said George in disbelief. 'You don't send people by post! There just *can't* be anyone in that box.'

'*Yes there is!*' Annie ducked behind him.

There was the sound of ripping parcel tape, and then the cardboard flaps of the tall box swung open.

As the two friends watched in horror, first one long leg and then another stepped out of the box. Annie had squeezed her eyes tight shut, but George watched in terrified fascination as a figure emerged from the cardboard packaging. It was dressed in a tweed suit and sported a thatch of dark brown hair and a pair of very thick glasses. Its head was hanging down so George couldn't really see its features. But even so, he realized he could take a guess at whose face it might resemble . . .

'Annie,' he said. 'I think you'd better take a look.'

'Is it a vampire?' she whispered in his ear, her eyes still closed.

'Weirder than that,' replied George.

'Weirder than a vampire? *How* weirder than a vampire?'

'Er, your dad . . . ? He is *definitely* weirder than a vampire. When he comes out of a box sent through the post, that is.'

'My dad?' said Annie. 'In a box?'

'As a robot,' added George.

'My dad in a box as a robot?' Even Annie's super-high IQ seemed to be struggling now.

The figure lifted its head, and as it did so, it seemed to come to life. As George had predicted, it had Eric's face, though newer and shinier than the real Eric, who was starting to look a bit worn out. It also had bright red eyes where the real Eric had blue ones. But like the human it was modelled on, the new robot Eric had  such thick glasses that its eyes were magnified; they looked enormous behind the powerful spectacles.

'Ew!' Annie had opened her eyes by now. 'What *is* it?'

The android decided to answer for itself.

'*ATVQ one zero XXX,*' it burst out at top volume. '*Vertical line! Vertical line!*'

George had never come face to face with a lifelike robot before – in fact, he didn't think he'd ever actually met an android before; not one that had been modified to look like a human being. He couldn't stop staring at it – it was the most fascinating thing he had ever seen.

'What's it saying?' whispered Annie.

'I dunno,' said George. 'It's *your* robot-dad, not mine. Watch out! It's coming towards us.'

The robot started taking jerky steps towards the kids, talking to itself as it went.

'*Random excitations of poetry before M theory develops time*,' it declared.

The two friends backed away from the Eric-doppelgänger android, but it kept on coming towards them.

'*Intrigued variety cells expressed flare telescope cosmic misfortune*,' it rambled on, advancing as George and Annie reversed down the hallway.

'I think it's swallowed a science dictionary,' muttered Annie.

'*Sungrazers flirt magnitude astatine predictions.*'

'Perhaps it's got your dad's vocabulary,' suggested George, 'but doesn't know how to use it?' Riveting though the new arrival was, he suddenly realized that they had no idea how to control it. The robot could, in theory, do anything at this point.

'What are we going to do?' hissed Annie. 'Any

minute now, we're going to get trapped in a corner by a fake-Dad robot!'

But as they moved away from the android into the playroom, they also approached the TV, where George, without realizing it, trod on the games console: the TV came on – along with the last game he and Annie had played, a dance-off that Annie had won by thousands and thousands of points. Suddenly a blast of a party rock anthem burst out across the room. The robot's eyes flashed and, while Annie and George watched in amazement, it started to dance along with the figures on the TV.

'It must somehow have automatically linked up to the Xbox!' Annie realized.

'Wow!' said George. 'So if you ever wondered what your dad looked like dancing, now you know—!'

'Don't! I can't bear to look!' Annie cringed, but at least this time it was out of embarrassment and not fear.

But disaster was only seconds away. When the song came to an end, the robot looked around for a distraction. Its red eyes fell on Annie's old teddy bear, cosily ensconced in an armchair. For some reason, known only to its own circuits, it snatched up the bear and, as the next song started, began to dance with it.

But the robot's dancing was increasingly out of control, and instead of dancing with the bear, it appeared to be trying to rip the poor patched-up old thing apart.

Annie quickly saw the danger to her favourite child-hood toy. She might be too old for cuddly bears now, but that didn't mean she was going to stand by and see it destroyed by an android imposter.

'That's my *bear*!' She threw herself at the robot and knocked it flying; it landed on an armchair, with Annie bashing it to make it let go of her teddy.

George ran over and was just starting to pull Annie off the android when he heard a familiar voice behind them.

'What *is* going on in here?'

MY ROBOT, YOUR ROBOTS

Writing about robots is as much fun as building robots. When I was younger I used to draw robots, write about robots and even build robots out of cardboard boxes and string. Now I build them for real – but I haven't forgotten that it is a lot of fun.

Writers, scientists and engineers use their imagination all the time to come up with new ways of doing things, and when it comes to robots there is no end to the possibilities; well, almost. In fact, when you have to build a robot for real you start to run into all sorts of problems, but they are always *interesting* problems, problems worth solving. In this chapter I'm going to tell you some of the history of robots, some of the ways they are used today and some of the ways we might be able to use them in the future.

The dream of building a machine that looks like something real goes way back in history. One of the first built was a mechanical servant created in ancient Greece around 250 BCE; this clever device could automatically pour a cup of wine from a jug, and mix it with water as required! Its inventor, Philo of Byzantium – also known as Philo Mechanicus – came up with lots of amazing mechanical ideas, including a water-powered chirping bird, but his servant automaton was one of his most popular. An automaton (plural: automata) is the name for a mechanical device that looks like a living thing.

In the eighteenth century, automata became amazingly popular. Inventors would use the new clockwork technology of the time to create beautiful devices that looked like living dolls – dolls that could play musical instruments, perform magic tricks and even draw pictures and write. They would tour these around the courts of Europe and make lots of money from these exhibitions; the age of the clockwork robot had arrived. In their day, they wowed the crowds, but today they look kind of creepy,

alive but not *quite* alive, with dolls' faces, a key to wind them up and tiny mechanical bodies that jump, judder and creak.

But they set the scene for the future: the 'Draughtsman-Writer' automata designed by the Swiss clock-builder Henri Maillardet. These were able to draw pictures and write poems, and were what robot builders today would call programmable, as depending on the card you placed in the automaton's slot, the machine would draw different things. In essence, most robots today are similar: they have a body, they have some way of deciding how to move, a list of things to do, and a way to provide the power to do them.

However, not all robots that inhabit the world with you today look like humans, as robots can take on all types of shapes and forms depending on what their job is. In modern car factories robots pick up parts and weld them together; and even computers themselves are now often built by industrial robots that put the different parts accurately in place. Robots like this can do these jobs without getting tired or bored, they are powered by electricity rather than clockwork, they have simple repetitive tasks to do but they get on with the job and do nothing else. They don't really need to understand their world.

On a farm, however, there can be robots that milk cows, and these robots need to be much smarter, since cows won't always be in exactly the right place at exactly the right time. These farm robots have to be able to see and make decisions. When a cow wanders in, the robot has to identify where the udders are and carefully attach the suction cups to them to gently remove the milk. Therefore they need to have the ability to understand a picture from a camera, and work out the best way to move their suction-cupped arms safely and gently into place. If they get it wrong, there will be trouble!

57

MY ROBOT, YOUR ROBOTS

These apparently simple tasks of seeing and moving are actually really hard for machines. About half your brain (including the bit at the back of your head called the *visual cortex*) is right now working on understanding the world you see around you, and a great big slice in the middle of your brain – called the *motor cortex* – is working out how to move your muscles to do what you want your body to do. Human brains are actually making billions and billions of calculations all the time, but what's simple to us needs to be turned into clear instructions – thousands of lines of computer code – for a robot, and as we don't yet understand exactly how the human brain does all these wonderful calculations, making a machine mimic it is tough. Fortunately, down on the farm, our limited understanding is enough for us to build robots with just enough intelligence to manage the job and keep the cows happy.

Ideas for robots can come from anywhere. There are scientists who study insect intelligence, for instance, since insect brains are much less complex than human brains with fewer interconnected networks of nerve cells, neurones, but insects are still smart. They have to be to survive in a difficult world – try swatting a fly! Using this example, in fact, there are robotic devices being built to fit into cars that allow cars to automatically swerve to avoid collisions; the idea for these devices came from studying flies' brains.

But what if there was an accident? Who, then, would be responsible? The car driver, the car manufacturer or perhaps

even the fly? What do you think? As intelligent robots start to live in the world with us, there could be lots of questions like this.

Accepting robots into our world is complicated, and how we feel about them also may depend on where in the world you live. In the West, people tend to think of robots as sinister, out to take over the world; often this is because that's the way robots are portrayed in films and TV. In the Far East however, robots are often presented in stories as heroic characters.

There is also something scientists call 'the uncanny valley'. If you look at how acceptable robots are, we find that robots that look like robots are generally more acceptable than robots that look like humans . . . but aren't quite the same. It's that creepy living-doll problem from the age of automata again: things just don't look right, so we don't feel happy around them.

Today's electronics and computer technologies, able to mimic the way the neurons in our brains work, as well as the movement of our limbs, allow us to build ever more lifelike robots, but they are still far from perfect. These *androids* – human-like robots – now buzz as the electric motors whir, rather than creak with clockwork gears, and they have complex computer programmes which try to artificially create the way the myriad ways our brain's neurones work together, but the androids can't yet effortlessly walk up stairs, catch a ball or reliably tell the difference between silk and sandpaper. They can't unfailingly recognize faces or expressions, or single out particular voices in noisy rooms like we can; they can't yet talk, react or understand us and our world as we would naturally expect a fellow human to. They are 'not quite right', so hard for us to accept.

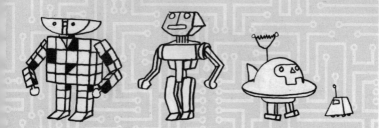

MY ROBOT, YOUR ROBOTS

But all is not lost for today's robots; our brains hold another trick we can use. In a classic experiment done by Heider and Simmel in the 1940s, people were shown random shapes moving round a screen, but when asked what was happening many came up with elaborate stories about squares falling in love with circles or larger triangles chasing smaller triangles. Our brains are smart, gigantic learning machines, and one of the main ways we learn is by creating stories to make us better able to remember and understand our world. When we see robots, our brains tend to fill in the gaps that today's technologies can't yet build, so we naturally think that robots have personalities and are more intelligent than they really are, and robot-builders often give us cues to help us make these stories seem more real, and which help us to accept and use the robots better.

One big problem with robots, for instance, is the question of what powers them. When the batteries go flat, they stop, and a robot can't always be connected to the electrical mains by a cable. To get round this problem, providing power to the robot can be made part of its story. A great example is how scientists created a baby seal robot to provide comfort to residents in an old people's home and built in the need for the seal to be 'fed'; they inserted a dummy tit that was actually a recharger for its batteries, so that recharging became a part of the robot's story.

In one of my projects, when the batteries in a robot dinosaur ran down it would 'go to sleep' and transfer itself to your mobile phone, where a virtual image of it could continue to play with you (while someone recharged the actual robot), then it would go to sleep on the phone and wake up in the robot body remembering what you had done with it on the phone. Can you think of a story for a robot?

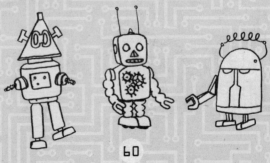

60

How long will it be before we have robot politicians? After all, robots can make decisions based on all the facts, and they can't be corrupted, can they? When should we have robots flying our planes, driving our trains and cars, teaching in our classroom, helping us in our homes and offices, performing surgery on us or fighting on the battlefield making the decision to shoot by themselves? Well, we already have basic forms of these sorts of robots, but always at present there is a human somewhere in control. Should that always be the case? After all, people make mistakes all the time. Could robots do better?

New advances in nanotechnology will allow us to create microrobots that can be injected into our bodies to perform repairs or even update us, linking our bodies and minds with external technology, building a new species of humans – transhumans: robot human hybrids. Is this the stuff of nightmares or a way to improve the life of the disabled and give humanity exciting new abilities? Who knows? It might be you who builds these future robots.

I too started by reading books, having ideas and dreaming about robots. When I was about seven, I built 'Billy' the robot from boxes and string (and I still have him), then I dreamed a lot. I'm now about fifty, and have been lucky enough to be involved in building robots that dance, help kids learn chess, assist the elderly in their homes and work as part of the team with people in their offices. None of my robots wanted to rule the world!

I have worked with loads of amazing, creative scientists and engineers to help turn my childhood robot dreams into reality. The cardboard and string have been replaced by maths, electronics and computers, but they are all proud descendants of 'Billy'.

They are my robots and I'm still having fun.

What will *your* robots be like?

Peter

The Antikythera mechanism

Part of one recovered from a shipwreck found in 1900

Babbage calculating machine

Part of his machine built by his son

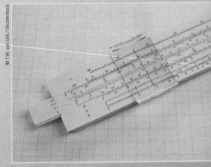

Pic of a slide rule

Babbage's brain is on display at the Science Museum apparently!

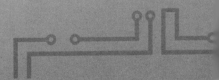

Enigma machine

Turing

Colossus (at Bletchley)

Early computers

Zuse Z3

ENIAC main control panel:

Vaccum tubes

Stephen Hawking and staff
Stephen Hawking (Cosmos PI), and left-to-right
Andy Barrington (SGI), John Scarborough (SGI),
Simon Appleby (SGI), Paul Shellard (COSMOS@DiRAC Director)
and Andrey Kaliazin (COSMOS System Manager)

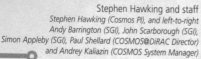

Old-fashioned computers

Modern computers

Early automata

Duck automaton

Windmill and soldiers automaton

Henri Maillardet automaton

Car factory robots

Milking robots
on farms

Japanese android

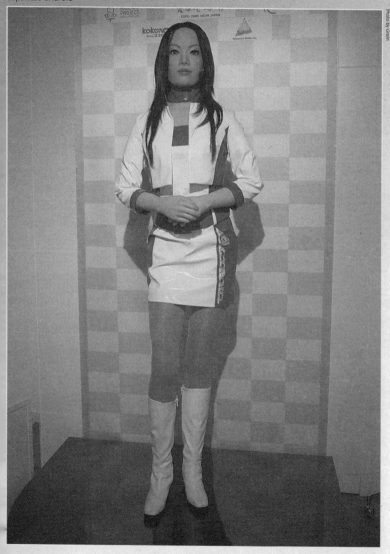

Photo by Grisin

Seal robot

Bio-inspired Big Dog quadruped robot

Bomb-disposal robot

Medical robot

NASA's Curiosity Rover

UIG via Getty Images

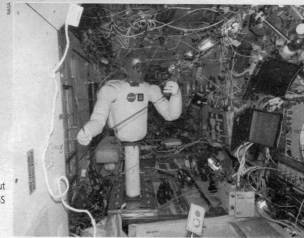

NASA

Robonaut
on the ISS

Chapter Five

'Real Dad!' cried Annie.

'As opposed to . . . ?' asked Eric.

'Fake Dad!' she said tremulously, pointing at the android, now sprawled at a crazy angle across the armchair, still clutching Annie's bear. The light in his eyes had gone out, which seemed to mean he had switched himself off.

'My personalized robot!' said Eric, his own eyes lighting up instead. 'He's arrived!'

'Your what?'

'He's my helper-bot – or Ebot, if you like,' Eric told Annie, going over to where the robot sat, unmoving. 'I ordered him ages ago. He's me in robot form. He even has all my biometric measurements, so in certain situations it would be quite tricky to tell the difference between us. When did he get here?'

'He just arrived!' chipped in George. 'We got back from the market square—'

'What were you doing there?' Eric stopped examining his robot and looked round sharply. 'Why were you in the middle of town? Why weren't you safely at home?'

'We saw the commotion from my treehouse,' George admitted. 'So we just went to see what was going on. We didn't realize it would be like that.'

Annie gave him a grateful smile for not including the part about her wanting to see her favourite boy band.

Eric's eyes widened. 'But that was the most dangerous afternoon there's ever been in the whole history of Foxbridge!' he said. 'I can't believe you kids were in the middle of it! When I left the office, I had to take the long way round because the centre of town is still blocked off – all those people fighting and rioting over the money that came out of the banks. You're not hurt, either of you?'

George and Annie shook their heads.

'It's not just Foxbridge!' Annie checked her phone again. 'It's happening everywhere! All over the world!'

'I know,' said Eric seriously. 'Look at this.' He produced an iPad from his messenger bag. He showed them a video clip of people rioting, the Eiffel Tower clearly visible in the background. Above their heads floated bits of blue, green and brown paper; rioters were leaping up and trying to grab them.

'And New York . . .' He showed them another video clip: yellow taxi cabs were hooting furiously in the avenues between huge skyscrapers as the same scenes played out, only all the bits of paper were green. The streets were overrun by people frantically trying to catch the banknotes as they drifted about on the breeze.

Eric tapped the screen, and the two friends saw another city jammed between a white beach and tall green mountains, a huge figure with outstretched arms perched on the highest one. 'Rio,' he told them, 'South

America. But watch . . . ' This time they saw how the whole process had begun. They watched as a bank machine on an ordinary street in Rio suddenly started to spew money, notes pouring out of it. On the video, a passer-by doubled back in astonishment as the money just kept on coming. He looked around furtively, and then started stuffing his pockets with notes. But within seconds, more and more people had appeared, attempting to push each other out of the way to get the cash. The view shifted, and they saw how, all over the densely packed city, cash machines were behaving in the same inexplicable and bizarre way, spitting out banknotes . . . unnoticed at first – until some passer-by saw what was happening and then, a few minutes later, a fight broke out.

'It's the same the world over,' said Eric. 'Here's Beijing.' They saw red yuan notes floating above the Forbidden City; euros trodden into the ground in St Peter's Square in Rome; purple Turkish lira being chased by thousands of eager hands in the Grand Bazaar in Istanbul; and rupees whirling like a cloud of insects through the narrow streets of Delhi.

'There's money everywhere,' he went on. 'There seems to have been some kind of massive global glitch in computerized banking systems which has caused ATMs everywhere to start giving out cash.'

'Wow, but that's really cool!' exclaimed Annie. 'I bet loads of those people don't even have enough money to buy food to eat or get shoes for their kids. But the banks have squillions to spend: it's all just sitting in their vaults while people go hungry. Now they've shared their loot with the world, which is brilliant. Don't you think that's how it *should* be?' Annie appealed to George and Eric.

George thought about it. Unlike Annie, he had actually grown up without all sorts of things that kids around him seemed to take for granted – new clothes, computers, skiing trips or meals in restaurants – because his parents couldn't afford them. But even though part of him would love to be given money to spend on anything he wanted, he couldn't quite agree that it was a good thing. It seemed as if someone somewhere had taken a radical decision about how people should live their lives, without actually asking them whether this was what they wanted. After all, whose money was it that the banks were giving away? It might belong to a bunch of very rich people . . . but what if it was the savings of old people or really poor people who would now find themselves with nothing? Was that fair?

'I do agree,' chipped in Eric, 'that wealth should be shared out across the world in a better way. Right now, we've got billionaires spending more on snacks than other people will earn in the whole of their lives. But I am not at all sure that what went on today is the way to fix it.'

'But how could it have happened?' George asked in

amazement. 'How could all those machines have gone wrong at the same moment?'

'I have no idea! I don't think anyone knows. One thing is for certain – I'm going to have to find out. Because this seems to be a computer-based problem – and as I'm the government's "Information Technology Czar", it looks like I'll be drafted in to solve the problem.' He looked at his robot and sighed. 'I won't have time to get old Ebot here working properly, which is a shame. Where's the box he came in? There should be some other bits and pieces with him.'

Annie jumped up and ran into the hallway. They heard the noise of her rootling around in the big cardboard box; then she returned carrying a sleek black bag, which she handed to her father.

'Oh, wonderful!' Eric pulled out a lilac-shaded pair of glasses with a strange attachment at the side. He put them on and wiggled his eyebrows, which caused the robot in the chair to come back to life with a start.

'Remote-access glasses,' said Eric happily. 'I ordered them specially! When I put them on, I can give commands and see through Ebot's eyes!' He searched around in the bag and found a pair of gloves. 'Haptic technology,' he murmured, putting on the gloves. He waved his hand, and Ebot waved his hand in exactly the same way.

Just then, Eric's mobile rang. He reached into his pocket for it – which caused Ebot to mimic his move-

ments, reaching into his pocket for an imaginary phone, which he also pulled out and pressed to his ear. As Eric spoke into the phone – 'Yes . . . Really? Oh, no! I'll come straight away' – Ebot imitated his movements perfectly.

Eric hung up and turned to Annie and George. 'OK, kids,' he said. 'You're in charge of Ebot. Here are the glasses . . .' He passed them to Annie. 'Here are the gloves . . .' He gave them to George. 'Now, I have to dash.'

He already had the absentminded look that appeared whenever he put his enormous brain into gear and started thinking about a new problem.

'What's going on?' Annie jumped up and down with the glasses on. 'Ooh, these are really weird,' she said. 'I can see me, but I can see me as Ebot sees me! It's so strange . . . It's like I'm seeing myself on TV or something. This is soooo cool!'

George had quickly put on the gloves and was making Ebot lift up first one hand and then the other. It was brilliant to have a machine that did exactly what he commanded! This was much better than dealing with people, who behaved in random and weird ways just when you least expected it.

'I've been asked to go to a meeting with the Prime Minister,' Eric informed them as he gathered his things together.

'The Prime Minister?' squeaked Annie. 'Why?'

'She wants me to help her understand how all those banks could have decided to give away money at the same moment,' said Eric. 'She's worried it might be a cyber-attack. We've got to look at what happened to the financial systems and stop it from happening again.'

'Is it a cyber-terrorist?' George wondered. 'Like Beryl was saying last night, maybe someone has worked out how to read the secret messages and use that information . . . ?'

'That could be it,' Eric agreed. 'But it's very strange. How did all those different banks in different countries come under attack at the same moment? To do that would be a huge job, and I didn't think anyone had the computer power to do that. Anyway, I've got to go – the PM doesn't want me to communicate with her by internet or phone: it has to be in person. Be good!' With that, he whirled out through the front door and was gone.

George, Annie and Ebot all waved goodbye to his departing back. Silence fell, but only for a second.

'So what shall we do now?' asked Annie. 'We've got robo-Dad to look after us, so we should be allowed to go and see what's happening in Foxbridge!'

'But he's not a *real* adult, is he?' said George doubtfully. 'And if we lose him in the crowd, your dad isn't going to be very pleased.'

'Dad'll never know! *We've* got the remote glasses, so it's not like he can look through Ebot's eyes and see where we've gone.'

'Hmm . . .' George scratched his chin, causing Ebot to do the same.

But at that moment a new sound reached their ears: fat little feet were thumping along the hallway, accompanied by high-pitched squeals. A few seconds later, two very grubby small girls burst into the playroom. Spotting their big brother, Juno and Hera crowed with delight and ran to give him sticky hugs and sloppy kisses, which he fought off as tactfully as he could while Ebot mirrored his movements behind him.

'Urgh,' he muttered as he wiped drool off his cheek.

HACKING

A hacker is someone who tries to find weaknesses in the software or setup of a computer to obtain unauthorized access.

- 'White hat' hackers may do this with the permission of the computer's owner as a test of its security.
- More commonly, a hacker is a 'black hat' – someone with only mischievous or criminal intentions. And if you have a computer connected to the internet at the moment, it is quite possible that a black hat somewhere in the world is trying to break into it!

A bot army

A hacker can use or develop software to target automatically many internet addresses. The attack may even be coming from another computer in your street, which – totally unknown to the computer's user – is already controlled by the hacker and has joined what is known as their 'bot army'! The hacker directing this army of compromised computers may be in another country and be difficult to trace.

Malware

An attachment to an email – or a link posted on a social media site like Facebook – could be a piece of malware – this is hostile software that is a help to the hacker when run on your computer. For example, it could be:

- a computer virus which inserts itself into files and tries to spread to other computers. Early viruses could do things like delete any photo you look at, or replace text with rows of gibberish. Imagine losing all your school coursework as a result of a virus!

- a program which starts recording your key presses and activity and sends them to the hacker, in order to capture passwords and credit card numbers used to buy goods online.
- a program which directly connects to the hacker and gives him or her remote control (your computer just joined the bot army!).

Why do hackers hack?

It's illegal but hackers may like hacking because . . .
- They enjoy the challenge or thrill.
- They may disagree with the policies of an organization and want to embarrass it by getting hold of and publishing private data, or by vandalizing their website. It is possible, for instance, to make all the computers they control try to log on to the same website, so that the website crashes. This is called a 'distributed denial of service' attack.
- And many are serious criminals who just want your money! These people want to trick you into giving away your passwords and secret information so that they can buy things with your money, or simply steal money out of a bank account. They may also want to pretend to be you online, to hide their own identity while they do something illegal. Or use your computer in their bot army to attack someone else.

How do hackers hack?

1. Physical attack
The computer itself might be stolen, and then you have to assume that the thief will get access to all your files on

72

it, even if you used a strong password. Everything on the hard drive is at the mercy of the hacker who can play your music, look at your pictures – even read your blogs and email messages to your friends!

Stop the hacker! If you own a laptop, take great care if keeping data you wouldn't want to lose – or have read by someone else – on its hard drive, because a laptop can easily be stolen. And keep backups at home.

2. Software attack

If your computer is connected to the internet, there can be vulnerabilities (mistakes!) in its software that could allow a hacker to gain access remotely, through the network. Some of these mistakes could allow a hacker to run programs on your computer without even having to trick you into doing something first, and if hackers find out about these security holes before the people who write the computer software do, they can exploit them before anyone has time to fix the problem: these attacks are known as 'zero day' exploits because they take place on day zero of the vulnerability becoming generally known.

Stop the hacker! Updates (patches) are made available by the software company to fix vulnerabilities. Nowadays, your computer will usually let you know if a patch is available, and you should always install these – ask your parent or guardian to do so, or help you to do so, if it is their computer - otherwise the computer, the data on it, including any of your private information, may be at risk. Additionally, make sure any computer connected to the internet has its firewall turned on - a firewall is a barrier that can block uninvited connections to the computer from the internet.

3. User attack

A hacker may try to trick the computer user into doing something for them. For example, you could receive an email asking you to click on a link, or open an attachment, or a link might send you to what looks like the genuine web page of your favourite site. But email is totally insecure – in fact, anyone can send a message which claims to be from someone else, and can attach a link that looks genuine. So an unexpected message like this could be from a hacker, and the attachment could be a nasty piece of malware.

Stop the hacker! Never open a strange attachment - even if the message appears to come from someone you know and looks like it would be a lot of fun to look at! Would your friends really just send you a link without a message too? Watch out too for fake web pages and never enter your username and password on any site unless you are positive it is the genuine site. Don't even click on a link that comes out of the blue, because the link itself may contain malicious code that your web browser will then execute. Beware!

Don't make it easy for hackers! Passwords are really important. Weak passwords (less than ten characters long, or containing obvious words like part of your name, or no punctuation characters), can often be easily found with modern computers. So always choose a good password – never just use 'password', for instance, and don't be guilty of using the same one for everything!

Annie looked on in amazement. 'How did they get in?' she wondered.

'I told you,' said George, who had given in and collapsed back into the armchair, where he was being warmly embraced by his two little sisters. Ebot was copying his movements in a very awkward manner: the poor robot had no one to hug and no chair to sit on, which made him look most peculiar. 'They get *everywhere*.'

Annie's mum stuck her head round the door. 'Hello, everyone!' she said cheerfully. 'My goodness! What *is* that robot doing? What a funny way to stand.'

'Don't ask, Mum,' said Annie. Susan wasn't an enormous fan of science and technology: they seemed to have taken over her life more than she had bargained for when she married Eric as a graduate student.

'How sweet of you to bring your sisters round, George,' she said. 'But don't you think it's getting a bit late for little ones? Perhaps you should take them home now . . . And, Annie, don't you need to get on with your half-term project?'

George tried not to look too disappointed. He had been really looking forward to working out how to operate Ebot – and having a chat with Annie about what had happened in Foxbridge earlier. Now, thanks to his sisters, it didn't look like he'd get the chance to do either. He stood up, holding one sister under each arm, their fat little legs kicking wildly, while behind him,

Ebot produced an exact copy of his actions.

'Gracious me!' said Susan, noticing Ebot properly this time. 'That robot looks just like your father!'

'We know,' sighed Annie. 'Seriously, Mum, please don't ask me to explain.'

'Well, it's not my fault that I'm always the last to know,' she said huffily. 'No one in this house tells me anything!'

'C'mon, George,' said Annie. 'Let's take the little ones back to yours.'

'Straight back when you're done,' her mother warned. 'You need to get that chemistry project under way. You know why . . .'

Annie sighed again.

George plonked his sisters down on the ground, and he and Annie set off for his house, each holding a small hand; Ebot followed behind, guiding an imaginary child as he did so.

Annie was quiet as they walked through the garden. She looked a bit glum at the prospect of going home alone to work on her project.

'At least you've got Ebot to keep you company now,' said George, trying to cheer her up. 'I'd rather have a robot in the house than twin sisters.'

'But a robot is just a machine,' said Annie sadly. 'It's not like Ebot will grow to love us, is it?' As she spoke, she heaved Juno through the hole in the fence and hopped through after her.

'Unless you program him to,' said George. 'You could see if your dad could get Ebot to have feelings. You can probably download "robot emotions" from the internet.'

'But it wouldn't be the same as being loved by your sisters. They aren't programmed to love you; they just do it naturally.' Annie caught Hera as she stumbled through the hole in the fence and hugged her before setting her gently down on the ground. 'Look, babies!' Annie pointed up to the clear evening sky where two stars blazed. 'That's Castor and Pollux, the twin stars. That's you, if you were stars.'

The twins gazed upwards, plump hands outstretched as if they could grasp a star each and bring it down to Earth. 'Reach a star?' they asked Annie hopefully.

'Sorry, girls,' she said. 'Even I can't make a star fall to Earth for you. You just have to look at them in the sky.'

The duo toddled towards their house, followed by Annie and George.

'It's spooky,' said George, turning to look behind him. 'Ebot really *does* look just like your dad.'

'Except that he's not alive,' said Annie. 'He's just like Dad, except that Dad is living and Ebot isn't . . .' She paused. 'I know!' she exclaimed, jumping up and down in excitement. 'That's what I'll do!'

'What?' asked George.

'For my project!' She was bouncing around on her toes. 'Why is Ebot not alive when Dad *is* alive? What's the difference between the two of them? What is Life? That's my half-term project.'

'Your half-term project is "Life"?' asked George. 'Are you serious? It's Monday already.'

'Yeah!' Annie looked absolutely delighted, her earlier gloom forgotten. 'But not just that,' she said. 'I already know the first bit – how life developed on Earth and how Charles Darwin sailed on the *Beagle* and found all that out. Now I'm going to do how life came to Earth from space! I'm going to do the Cosmic Chemistry of Life! Ha! Take that, Karla Pinchnose . . .' she muttered.

George stared at her in amazement. 'Isn't that, like, a bit overambitious?' he hazarded.

'Have you forgotten about my outstanding IQ?' she asked him. 'C'mon, Ebot, we've got work to do . . . Can

I have those gloves back, George?'

He handed them over and, with a cheery 'Ta-ra!' Annie headed back towards her house, Ebot following, leaving George to babysit the twins.

Great, he thought to himself. *Annie's off to do a super-exciting science project without me. That's just great. When I grow up*, he grumbled, *I really am going to live only with robots – no people whatsoever . . . except perhaps Annie occasionally. But no one else.* Muttering under his breath, he turned and walked back into his house.

THE HISTORY OF LIFE

When we look at the animals and plants around us, the sheer diversity of life seems amazing. Even in a busy city a single walk brings us into contact with dozens of species, from insects so small we can hardly see them, to trees and large animals like birds and mammals. In the countryside there are literally thousands of species in even a small bit of forest, grassland or marsh.

We still don't know how many species there are in the world. About 1.2 million have so far been carefully identified by scientists, described, classified and given a name – but the total figure is much bigger than that. The best current estimate is that there are about eight or nine million species in all, though some biologists think the figure could be much higher than this. This means that the great majority of species on our planet haven't even yet been given a name. They could go extinct and we wouldn't even notice!

Where do all these species come from? This is a question that humans have often asked. Many of the world's religions have an answer. They talk about God creating life. This answer isn't enough for scientists, though. Even if God did make species – including us – we want to know when and how!

It was Charles Darwin in the nineteenth century who provided the answer that we still think is correct. Darwin was a wealthy man and was happily married. He and his wife Emma had servants and his wife ran the household. That gave Darwin time to do his scientific work, even though he and Emma had ten children, most of whom loved nothing more than to rush into their father's study and try to get him to play with them.

Darwin realized that just as farmers can produce new breeds of farm animals by selectively choosing to use only certain individuals to produce the next generation, so nature can produce new species by what he called 'natural selection'. Suppose, for example, that a widespread species of seed-eating bird occurs in some places where plants produce mainly *small* seeds and in some places where plants produce mainly large seeds. Suppose too that there is inevitably some variation in the size of the birds' beaks and that how large a bird's beak is partly depends on the size of its parents' beaks, so that birds with small beaks tend to produce offspring with small beaks and birds with large beaks produce offspring that typically also have large beaks.

Nothing very surprising, so far. But Darwin realized that if beak size is important for a bird's survival and reproduction – for example, because food is sometimes in short supply – then natural selection would gradually lead to changes in beak size. Over time, birds that live where the plants have large seeds would come to have large beaks, and birds that live where the plants have small seeds would evolve small beaks. Given enough time, the original single bird species might evolve into two new species, each one well adapted to its food source.

Darwin published his theory in 1859 in a book called *On the Origin of Species* (the full title is *On the Origin of Species by Means of Natural Selection*, or the *Preservation of Favoured Races in the Struggle for Life* – the Victorians liked long book titles). This is one of the most important scientific books ever written. It changed the way we see our world and has never been out of print. It is a long book but still very worth reading.

Darwin was the first to admit that his theory didn't explain everything. In particular, how did the first species come into existence? After all, his theory may explain how species can change over time and evolve into new species but doesn't say anything about how the whole process gets going.

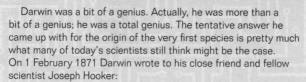

Darwin was a bit of a genius. Actually, he was more than a bit of a genius; he was a total genius. The tentative answer he came up with for the origin of the very first species is pretty much what many of today's scientists still think might be the case. On 1 February 1871 Darwin wrote to his close friend and fellow scientist Joseph Hooker:

It is often said that all the conditions for the first production of a living organism are now present, which could ever have been present.— But if (& oh what a big if) we could conceive in some warm little pond with all sorts of ammonia & phosphoric salts,—light, heat, electricity &c present, that a protein compound was chemically formed, ready to undergo still more complex changes, at the present day such matter wd be instantly devoured, or absorbed, which would not have been the case before living creatures were formed.

We still don't know for sure how life started. It might well have been in one or more of Darwin's warm little pond's, much as he suggested. But once it got going, there was no stopping life. As millions of years went by, life gradually reached more and more of the Earth's surface. Species got bigger and hardier.

They colonized the land and took to the air. Eventually, three to four billion years after the process started we have whales and hummingbirds and giant redwood trees and beautiful orchids and all the other eight or nine million species there are today, including us.

And we are still discovering some of these species. Maybe you too might one day find yourself journeying to a part of our wonderful Earth and being the first person to identify a new species!

Michael

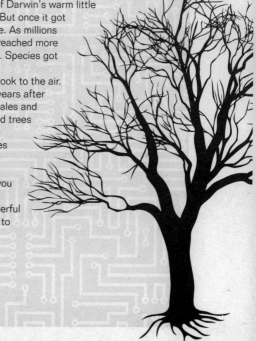

Chapter Six

The next morning George woke late, to an unusually quiet house. He could hear none of the normal angry screams as the twins acted out their morning pantomime of outrage and horror that anyone could expect them to eat breakfast. He stretched and wiggled his toes under the warmth of his duvet. And then he remembered! Annie and the Cosmic Chemistry of Life – how life came to Earth from space . . . And then he also remembered the bank machines going crazy and spewing out money all over the world. He had to find out what was going on! He leaped out of bed, threw on his clothes and ran downstairs.

The scene that greeted him was surprising in its normality. The twins sat meekly in their high chairs, placidly eating their breakfasts without spattering food on the walls and floor; George's mother and father smiled at him. He was bewildered by this change of pace – breakfast was usually an infant war zone – and startled to find his sisters looking angelic rather than demonic.

Catching his shocked expression, his mother said, 'We told you they'd grow up one day, didn't we?'

'Overnight?' queried George. Surely that wasn't actually possible . . .

'Kids,' said his father smugly. 'They change so fast!' He sighed. 'You were the sa—'

But at that moment a home-baked muffin hurtled through the air and thwacked him squarely on the jaw. The impact sent crumbs flying across the kitchen while the twins dissolved into peals of laughter. One muffin was followed by a second, until George's poor father was being bombarded, like a young solar system full of colliding debris.

George used that moment to escape out of the back door. 'Off to Annie's!' he shouted back to his parents.

He hopped through the hole in the fence, and sprinted up to the back door of the next-door house. As usual, it was open, so he let himself in with a cheery 'Hallllooooo!'

A second later, a corresponding 'Halloooooo!' told him that Annie was in her father's study – the room which housed Cosmos, the extraordinarily intelligent computer that Eric used to help him with his work. The sound of a violin drifting down from upstairs – the same phrase over and over again – also told him that Annie's mum was at home, practising for a concert. When Annie was younger, her mum had worked as a music teacher, but recently she had returned to her original career as a concert musician and was away from home more and more often, performing with her orchestra.

Sure enough, George found Annie perched on several cushions in front of Cosmos, who had been their friend and helper on so many adventures now. It hadn't always worked perfectly – on one occasion, Cosmos had struggled to make their homeward journey possible alone, and needed to be linked up with another supercomputer in order not to leave the two friends stranded in a distant exosolar system, that is a planetary system which orbits a star other than our Sun. On another, Cosmos had nearly exploded with the effort of rescuing Annie's dad when he fell into a black hole. The computer could still be unpredictable and erratic when he chose . . . And today looked like it was one of those days.

'He's being really tricksy,' said Annie, wrinkling her nose.

Cosmos said nothing, which was unlike him, but sneezed instead.

'Has he got a cold?' asked George.

'He's being really off,' said Annie. 'He says he feels ill, but that sounds really weird to me.'

'Yeah, not like Cosmos at all! What were you trying to do with him?' George pulled up a chair to sit next to her.

'Well, I'm working on my project!' Annie explained.

'Let's see!' said George immediately.

'OK – here it is . . .' She brought up a screen which showed pictures of Eric, side by side.

'One of these is real Dad, aka Eric,' she said, pointing.

WHAT IS A SUPER COMPUTER?

What is a flop? Or a megaflop?

As time goes on, more and more powerful computers become available. One way (not the only way!) of measuring the power of a computer is to measure the maximum number of *floating point operations per second* (usually abbreviated to *flops*) that it can perform.

One big system

Whatever the power of today's processors may be, there is a simple idea for making a much more powerful machine – put lots of them together! A supercomputer is a computer specially constructed to achieve exceptional performance by linking many processors together into a single big system. Each processor can then work on a part of a task simultaneously – *in parallel*.

Linking multiple processors means connecting them to some sort of network, and often it is enough to have computers connected across large distances through networks like phone networks, or via the internet.

An embarrassing problem?

If the work can be broken up into separate pieces, each processor working completely independently of the other pieces, the problems to be solved are called embarrassingly parallel problems. In these cases, the network is only really needed to tell each processor what it should be doing and to collect the results at the end.

But this would not give you a supercomputer, because most big problems aren't *embarrassingly parallel*. Instead, the processors need to send intermediate results to each other and a supercomputer must be able to parallel-process general problems and solve them faster, as well as being able to process many independent, little problems at once. This is what makes it different from a loose network of computers, and from a mainframe computer.

How good is the network?

The parallel performance is limited by the quality of the network, in particular two features:

- *bandwidth* – the amount of data it can carry per second, which we would like to be big
- *latency* – the delay between sending and receiving, which we would like to be small.

87

'And one is robo-Dad, or Ebot.'

'So one is alive and one isn't,' said George, catching on quickly.

'That's right,' confirmed Annie. 'But what's the difference?'

'Erm . . .' said George, baffled. 'One of them can choose his own actions and the other can't?'

'Nope,' said Annie. 'Ebot's got a control panel, but he can also learn from previous commands in order to determine his own movements.'

'One needs food, sleep and water, the other doesn't?'

'Ebot needs energy too,' said Annie. 'And you can't say that my dad really sleeps.'

'True . . .' mused George. Eric was famous for only needing about three hours' sleep a night – a fact that all his neighbours were only too well aware of: he played loud opera music in the small hours while he was working. 'Where's Ebot now?'

'Recharging,' said Annie.

'One of them breathes,' George suggested, 'and the other doesn't? One has things like a stomach and a heart and the other has wires and stuff inside?'

'Yeah, that's what I thought!' said Annie. 'I'm taking a look at what each one is made of. I'm making a list of the elements of life.'

'What's number one?'

She scrolled down past the pictures of the two Erics to a banner headline that read *CARBON*.

'*Everyone knows*,' George read out loud, '*that carbon comes from stars*. Hmmm . . .' He paused.

'What?' said Annie, self-conscious now that George was reading her work out loud. 'Have I made a mistake? I spell-checked it.'

'No, the spelling is fine,' he told her. 'But I just don't think everyone *does* know that about carbon.'

'Oh, OK . . .' She erased the line on Cosmos's screen and started typing: *Az most peoble no*—

'You've put a "b",' said George. 'It should be a "p".'

'I thought it was on autocorrect!' exclaimed Annie. She pressed a few keys to switch the function on.

'But the point is,' continued George, 'I don't think people know much about carbon at all. I mean, you and I know that carbon comes from stars because your dad got Cosmos to show us what happens when a star reaches the end of its life: there's a great big supernova explosion. But I don't think most people know that the elements are made in stars.'

You might not know, Annie wrote, the computer now correcting her spelling as she went along, *that carbon comes from stars. One of the important elements made in a star while it is burning is carbon, and when the star dies, the carbon gets sent out across the Universe and can become other things, like you and me. We are 'carbon-based' life forms. Carbon*—

'Are you going to say what carbon actually *is*?' interrupted George. 'Otherwise people are going to read this

WHAT IS A SUPERCOMPUTER?

Using computer memories

There are several different ways today of connecting processors together to create supercomputers.

Symmetric Multiprocessor (SMP) systems

This system connects all processors *equally* to all the memory inside the supercomputer. They are also shared memory systems because the memory is shared between all the processors. It is difficult to do, and very expensive for large systems.

Nonuniform Memory Access (NUMA) systems

These networks become slower when the processor and the memory it wants to read or write to are further apart. As they also have *shared memory*, the programmer has to be careful to keep data as close as possible to the processor which needs it. They are cheaper to run than SMPs.

An interconnect

This is a special, high quality network that can connect a group of separate computers (referred to as *nodes*). The processors in one node cannot see the memory in other nodes at all as the memories aren't shared; these are *distributed memory* supercomputers. The programmer has to program the transfer of data as messages between the nodes. When the nodes are just ordinary computers rather than special modules, such supercomputers are often referred to as *clusters*.

Modern computer systems

It is common for modern computers to contain some of the parallel features once found only in supercomputers. For example, a single processor may now contain several cores, each of which functions as a processor in its own right – the processor becomes a SMP system, with multiple cores connected to a block of nearby memory. More expensive computers have more than one processor socket, so that each becomes a NUMA system, with a set of cores and a block of memory associated with each socket.

Graphics Processing Units (GPUs) for supercomputing.
This is a recent development – perfect for anyone who likes
gaming on their computer. They are very fast at creating pixels
to send to your screen during a PC game. And the same design
makes them very fast also at certain types of computation.

> ## From flops to exaflops!
> - 1 megaflop = 1 million flops
> - 1 gigaflop = 1 billion flops (1,000 megaflops)
> - 1 teraflop = 1,000 gigaflops
> - 1 petaflop = 1,000 teraflops
> - 1 exaflop = 1,000 petaflops

Using this measurement and looking over just the past few
decades, it is easy to see how computer performance has
improved:

- 1998: a computer with one processor might have a peak
  performance of 500 megaflops
- 2007: lots of single processors were rated at around 10
  gigaflops
- 2013: single computers with two processors are available,
  each with eight cores, with a theoretical peak performance
  of 20 gigaflops per core, giving a total peak performance per
  machine of 320 gigaflops. This is actually a NUMA, shared
  memory, sixteen-core parallel machine in its own right - but
  today we wouldn't call it a supercomputer unless we connected
  several hundred similar units together.
- The Top500 (www.top500.org) is a list of the world's five
  hundred most powerful supercomputers, updated twice every
  year. At the time of writing, most machines on the list give a
  measured performance of a few hundred teraflops – but the
  top machine achieves a massive 33,862.7 teraflops (33.8627
  petaflops). This is *massively* more
  powerful than the computers
  available at the end of the 20th
  century!

> In a few more years, it
> is probable that the first
> exaflop supercomputer
> may appear. How
> powerful is *that!*

and think they're made of lumps of coal.'

'Yeah, yeah, I'm getting to that bit,' protested Annie. 'I *do* know what carbon is, by the way!'

'Then what *is* it?' asked George, who genuinely wanted to know.

'Well,' she said. 'It's like this . . .' She stopped typing and just talked. 'Carbon,' she said, 'has the atomic number six, which means that it has six protons and six electrons. The bond that carbon forms with itself is very strong: compounds containing bonds like this are very stable. It also allows it to form long chains and rings, better than any other element. This means that there are more known molecules containing carbon than all the other elements put together – apart from hydrogen. And it's the fourth most common element in the universe,' she added.

'Wow!' said George. 'You weren't kidding.'

'I can't be a chemist and not know about carbon,' replied Annie. 'That would be like Mum trying to play the violin without doing her scales. Or baking a cake without eggs. It just wouldn't work.'

Up until that moment, the music from upstairs had been melodic and beautiful. It stopped for a second when a distant phone beeped with a message. Then the kids heard a great squawk as Annie's mum played a horribly tuneless chord.

'Annie!' A few moments later Susan appeared at the study door, a look of shock on her face. 'What do you know about the free aeroplane flights?'

'What free flights?' exclaimed Annie.

'All flights are free!' Susan held out her phone so the kids could read the message.

G'day, rellies! Whole gang on way. Got free flights. Cya soon, my darlings. Harroo!

'But what does it mean?' said Annie, checking her own phone. 'I don't believe it but it's true! All flights are free! Can we get one? Can we go to Disneyland?'

'No, we can't! Because my whole family' – Susan looked rather green – 'are now coming over from Australia.'

'When are they arriving?' asked George.

'I don't know!' she said in panic. 'My sister only said "soon"! It could be any time. All of them! Oh my goodness! In the next message they say they've decided to come as quickly as possible in case the free flights were a mistake and get cancelled.' She flicked on the small TV in the corner of Eric's study. It was tuned to the news channel.

'*International chaos at airports around the world,*' said the announcer, looking worried as, behind her, footage showed airports deluged by people trying to push their way into the terminals with their baggage, '*as airlines sell tickets for nothing. Major world airlines were surprised to find that their websites had taken overnight bookings for all international flights, all charged at the same price: zero. Passengers have raced to snap up the free tickets and are now attempting to travel on the cheapest flights the world has ever seen . . .'*

'How many of them are coming?' asked George. He'd only ever associated Annie's family with peace and quiet; with learning, music and technology. It was a surprise to find that a whole new branch of them was arriving from the other side of the world.

'Mum's sister has seven kids,' explained Annie. 'I've never met them, but they sound really fun,' she added longingly.

'Oh dear, oh dear!' fretted Susan. 'This is going to be very difficult. And your father's not here. I suppose it will take them at least a day to arrive, so perhaps he'll be back by then . . .'

'Perhaps they won't notice that Ebot isn't him?' said Annie.

'Don't be silly, Annie,' her mother snapped. 'Of course they'll notice. They're hardly going to mistake a robot for the real thing!'

'But Eric said that Ebot is very nearly the same as him, except for not being actually alive: lots of types of technology wouldn't be able to tell the difference between them,' George supplied helpfully.

But to judge by Susan's expression, he hadn't said the right thing. 'I think they'll notice,' she said firmly.

At that moment Cosmos sneezed again.

'And what is wrong with that computer?' demanded Susan.

'He's been a bit slow this morning,' complained Annie.

'I don't feel well,' said Cosmos miserably. 'I think I've caught something.' He sneezed three more times and then gave a feeble cough.

'I hope he hasn't picked up a virus on the internet,' said George, worried. It wasn't like Cosmos to be this listless.

'Should you be using it when your father isn't here?' Susan fretted.

'Oh please, Mum!' begged Annie. 'I need Cosmos to do my chemistry project. I really really really have to get it done this half-term, and it has to be amazing! It's super-important to me – I can't fail!' She was pleading now.

George was taken aback to see that she had real tears in her eyes. He wondered why school was suddenly so important to her. With all these exciting relatives arriving from the other side of the world, he thought she'd forget about her project and get swept up with making plans for her family.

'Oh, all right . . .' Annie's mum wouldn't usually have agreed to let George and Annie have free rein on Cosmos, a computer she considered dangerous and subversive. But the prospect of so many of her relatives showing up in the near future meant she wasn't thinking straight.

'Where am I going to get enough sleeping bags?' she worried as she headed back into the hall. 'And I've got a whole new symphony to learn . . . These airlines have really messed up everyone's lives. How are we going to fit another nine people into this house?'

'At least you won't be lonely any more,' George pointed out. 'That's good, right?'

'No – and hurray!' said Annie cheerfully. 'Not lonely, for sure. Lots and lots of friends to play with! You can hang out with us, George.'

'No thanks,' he said. 'Sometimes I'm not sure I like people that much. I think I prefer machines.'

Cosmos sneezed again.

Annie's mum put her head back round the study door, looking flustered. 'Now, Annie and George . . . I know this isn't how we usually do things, but this is a sort of emergency. I'm trusting you to be very grown up. I'm going out and I want you to promise me that you will be responsible and good while I am gone – especially with everything that's happening. I want you to stay in the house. You can get on with your chemistry project, Annie. I'll be back as soon as I've bought bedding and supplies. Do you promise?'

'We promise,' chorused George and Annie.

'I don't think they can possibly turn up while I'm

out, but if they do . . .' Susan shouted back over her shoulder as she ran towards the front door. They heard it slam behind her.

'If they do . . . what?' said Annie, looking at George.

'Feed them on dinosaur toenail and take them for a nice spacewalk,' he suggested with a wicked grin.

'A spacewalk!' cried Annie. 'That's what we should do!'

'Oh no – hang on a minute,' said George. 'I didn't mean . . .'

They both looked at Cosmos, snivelling on the desk.

'I'm sure it would make Cosmos feel better,' wheedled Annie. 'I expect he's feeling bad because we haven't used him lately. After all, he *is* a super-computer, not just any old ordinary computer.'

George reflected that this was one of Annie's more unlikely explanations. They hadn't been allowed to go on any space expeditions for quite some time now: Eric had introduced some new super-rules over the use of Cosmos after Susan had been very clear that she would not tolerate any more perilous adventures.

'And we would be working on my chemistry project, after all,' said Annie. 'My super-important chemistry project, which has to blind everyone with its brilliance when I go back to school next week.

97

It's got to be the most incredible piece of work I've ever done – we have to make it truly fabulous!'

'Do we?' asked George. 'Why?'

'Well, I know I'm very clever and everything, but even so, it's time for me to prove it. Now that I've done carbon, I've got to do my next entry, and I want to write about water in space. So we have to go and investigate or I won't have anything to say! And we wouldn't actually be leaving the house . . .'

'Well, we would really,' said George, 'if we went into space . . .' He was longing to go, but he still needed convincing. He was naturally more cautious than Annie, and he didn't want to be banished from her house for misusing the space portal, either. It was all very well for Annie . . . she lived in the same house as Cosmos and would always, one way or another, have access to him. The same could not be said for George himself.

'No we wouldn't!' said Annie. 'Mum meant don't go out into the street. She didn't say don't go out into space!'

Before George could object any further, she started typing rapidly on Cosmos's keyboard.

'What if your mum comes back and we're in space?' he asked. 'How would we know?'

'Good point!' Annie jumped up and ran out of the room, returning quickly with the haptic gloves, and Ebot following behind.

'He's working now,' she said. 'Say hello to George.'

Ebot raised a hand in greeting. 'Hello, George,' he intoned.

Annie took off the gloves and handed them to George. He was quickly coming round to her idea. 'Shall I put these on under my space gloves?' he asked her.

She grinned. 'Good idea! You never know when we might need to operate Ebot remotely. Ebot, sit there . . .' Annie pointed to a spare chair from where he would be able to see both Cosmos and the door. Then she grabbed the remote-access glasses from the table by Cosmos.

'While we're in space,' she explained to George, 'I'll be able to see through Ebot's eyes. So if Mum comes home, we'll get an early warning and come back to Earth *tout de suite*!'

As she talked, Cosmos was already creating the space portal. Two narrow beams of brilliant light shot out of his screen, picking a point in the room from which they moved in opposite directions to outline the shape of a doorway.

Meanwhile Annie rifled around in the large cupboard where her dad kept the spacesuits.

'Here's mine!' She came across a suit which she had customized with ribbons, glitter and badges. 'But where's yours . . . ?' She threw a few others out of the cupboard. 'I can't find it! Here – take this one.' She chucked him one of the random suits.

'That's your dad's!' said George. 'I can't wear that! It's got his insignia and call sign! If I use the voice transmitter, it will look like Eric is in space!'

'Stop wasting time!' Annie was impatient to get going. 'We're only going to nip out to space for a few minutes. It's not like NASA will notice.'

The space door Cosmos had created was now swinging open very slowly. Annie and George could just see a faint glimmer of the world that lay beyond.

'Where did you ask Cosmos to take us?' asked George.

'I told him' – Annie was now speaking through the voice transmitter in her space helmet – 'to take us to see water in space.'

'But where *is* it?'

The door swung back, just as it had so many times before. Through the doorway, they saw what looked like a black and primrose-yellow world: a dark sky behind a pale, empty landscape with large soft flakes drifting down towards the surface.

'What is this?' Annie breathed softly into her transmitter, her voice emerging from the receiver in George's space helmet as though it was right in his ear.

'Welcome,' said Cosmos, sniffling a little as he spoke, 'to Enceladus, the sixth largest moon of Saturn. Please go through the doorway. Add additional space weights to your boots so you will be able to cope with the effects of Enceladus' lower gravity.'

Annie ran back to the cupboard, grabbed the space weights and attached them to their boots.

'Here we go!' Moving heavily in his weighted boots, George approached the doorway and crossed the threshold. He thumped down onto the distant moon. His heart was pounding so loudly that all he could hear was a sound like bongo drums. This was so cool! He had assumed that half-term would be the most boring holiday ever, but it was suddenly turning out to be a blast.

Annie followed, and as they both stood by the portal on Saturn's moon, they realized that the glass on their visors was quickly becoming covered with thickly falling snowflakes.

'I don't believe it!' George laughed. 'We're on Enceladus! And it's snowing!'

Chapter Seven

The light on this faraway moon was a strange yellowish colour, casting deep shadows through the gloom that surrounded them.

'Watch your step!' warned George. He was thrilled to be back in space; he had waited for ages for another cosmic adventure – and now it was actually happening! But during his time at home, dreaming about space, he'd forgotten how dangerous it felt to be out in the Solar System, just him and Annie against the great backdrop of space itself. Inside his two pairs of gloves, his fingers felt tingly with excitement and nerves. He knew he had to be careful though, in case he made movements on Enceladus which caused Ebot to react on Earth and knock something over in Eric's study. He tried to keep his hands as still as possible. This time, there was no real Eric to help them if they got into trouble, and George realized he would have to make sure they were super-careful. He couldn't imagine Ebot being able to rescue them if they had an accident on Enceladus.

ENCELADUS

It's just a tiny white dot, orbiting the enormous frozen gas planet, Saturn, within the densest part of Saturn's rings. It's only one out of Saturn's 60 moons. It's not the biggest or the most visible in the night sky. And yet scientists now think that Enceladus, named after a giant in Greek legend who was buried under the volcano Mount Etna, may be one of the most habitable places in our solar system! Why? The answer is simple . . .

Water

This snooker ball of a moon – white, round, with an icy smooth surface – seems to have liquid water, one of the most important ingredients for life as we know it. Discovered as long ago as 1789 by the famous astronomer William Herschel, Enceladus remained pretty much a mystery until two Voyager spacecraft passed it in the early 1980s. Voyager 2 revealed that despite the small size of this little moon, it had all sorts of different landscapes. In some parts, Voyager 2 saw ancient craters; in others, ground that had recently been disturbed by volcanic activity.

Enceladus endures frequent eruptions. But whereas Mount Etna sends hot ashes, lava and gas into the Earth's atmosphere, on Enceladus, cryo volcanoes shoot out plumes of *water ice* into the atmosphere, some of which float down to the surface as snow. The Cassini space probe which has been flying past Enceladus since 2005 has taken many photos of the ice fountains of Enceladus. So if you could visit there, you could build a real snowman in space!

A very special place

As well as liquid water, Enceladus may boast all sorts of other useful ingredients for life such as organic carbon, nitrogen and an energy source, and scientists who study Enceladus recently stated this makes this moon a very special place. Could it mean there are extra-terrestrial life forms on Enceladus? Could there be aliens living deep within this secretive world? Maybe one day you will design a robotic spacecraft which can visit Enceladus and find out if an alien giant is sleeping under the surface of this distant and fascinating little moon!

'Those craters don't look easy to climb out of – not even the tiny ones,' he commented.

Around them lay hundreds of small craters and one enormous one, the bottom covered in some kind of mysterious bright substance which glowed in the amber light. Nearby stood a ridge which overlooked the pock-marked ground, while running under their feet was a thin line, like the crack in a pavement – only it went on and on into the distance in both directions, as far as they could see.

However many times George travelled in space, he never got used to it. He would always be amazed by the incredible cosmic scenery. There would never come a time when he was bored of space – it was so extraordinary, enormous and beautiful . . . And there was no one there: just him and Annie and the whole empty, perfect world that lay around them, waiting to be explored.

'Awesome!' breathed Annie as she looked at the view.

George followed her gaze. On the horizon, he could see a sharp curve of brilliant light across the empty void of this weird little moon; it was creeping very slowly towards them.

'That's the light of the Sun . . .' Annie pointed. 'Over there, it's daylight.'

'Then what's this funny yellow glow?' asked George. 'Where's that coming from?'

Above the horizon on the other, dark side, away from the Sun, hung the giant frozen ball of gas that was the planet Saturn. Saturn's rings, made up of dust and rocks, encircled the magnificent planet.

'It's the light from Saturn,' said Annie in a whisper – she wasn't quite sure why. 'Light from the Sun reflects off Saturn and illuminates the dark side of Enceladus. And look!' She pointed to a dot in the sky. 'That must be Titan! Hey!' She fumbled in the pocket of her spacesuit. 'Do you think I could get a photo of Saturn?'

'You could try,' said George. He wished he'd thought to bring a camera. Annie's photo of Saturn was going to be much better than the one he was trying to take from Earth. Saturn seemed so close here; it was almost as if they could reach out and touch it.

But Annie was clicking and clicking her camera without any success.

'I think it might have frozen,' George realized. 'It must be pretty cold up here.' Perhaps after all, he thought, he was going to be the one who ended up with a photo of Saturn. That made him wonder what was happening back on Earth.

'Have you checked Ebot's field of vision?' he asked.

'I've got the remote-access glasses on,' said Annie. 'I can switch frames by moving my eyeballs and it gives me . . . Ebot! Here we are. I can see home – wow! That's weird. But no – no sign of Mum yet. I expect she's still trying to buy a bazillion pillows or something.' It seemed really odd to be talking about Annie's mum doing her shopping back on Earth. It felt like all those things were happening not just on a different planet but in another Universe.

George reached out a hand, wondering if Ebot was making the same movement. 'The snow's slowing down,' he observed. He had never seen such huge snowflakes before. They made him want to dance across the pristine surface of this strange little moon.

'Ohmigod, look in that crater!' Annie had taken a few steps forward.

George edged gingerly after her and peered over the edge into the vast bowl.

107

LUCY & STEPHEN HAWKING

'It's full of snow!' continued Annie. 'If we went down there, we could make the most amazing snow angel ever!'

'But we don't know how deep it is,' warned George. 'It might have been snowing for millions of years – we could sink in and never come up.'

'It would be like swimming – but in snow!' squeaked Annie.

'Don't try it!' George didn't believe she would really sprint down into an unknown crater, but he decided to take no chances. 'I might never get you out!' Suddenly, as though from far away, like distant thunder, he felt a rumble.

'Did you feel that?' he asked Annie.

She nodded.

Then he felt a harder jolt, right under his feet, as if it was coming from the thin crack in the surface. 'Cosmos?' he asked the supercomputer via his instant messaging device. But he got no reply. Cosmos's silence was starting to make him feel uneasy.

Annie checked in again to see the view from Ebot's eyes back in her father's study. 'Nothing happening on Earth,' she said. 'Cosmos is just sitting on the desk, and Ebot's keeping an eye on the door. No reason why he shouldn't answer.'

'Cosmos!' George tried again. 'Are you sure you've landed us in a safe location?'

The ground lurched beneath their feet, and they

bumped into each other. For a second George felt as frozen as Annie's camera, unable to move or react. Pure terror glued him to the spot. He looked around for some kind of escape: there was no sign of the space portal, and no way for them to escape – except by . . .

'Move!' Annie grabbed George and dragged him after her as fast as she could. He stumbled along, roused from his petrified state by her urgent voice in his ear. 'Come on, George! I can't carry you! We've got to run – *faster*!'

At last, his limbs started to propel him away from the place where Cosmos had brought them, which was now shaking continually, the ground shifting and buckling.

'It's a fault line!' panted Annie. 'You know – the ones where earthquakes happen. It must be. I think it's going to erupt!'

The two friends struggled over the rupturing ground. George followed Annie in a desperate bid to avoid tumbling into the abyss opening up as the sides of the fault line moved apart.

'This way!' Annie pointed at the ridge above the cratered ground, from which little jets of water vapour and gas were now spewing forth.

Staggering onward, George wondered if he would ever get back home. Would he ever again know the happiness of being cross with his baby sisters or eating his mum's strange food? A lump came to his throat as he pushed himself forward. Perhaps planet Earth wasn't so bad after all.

Annie had chosen a good route. Together, they scrambled up the ridge, finding hand- and foot-holds, clambering up the near-vertical incline, their hearts pounding with fear. The low cliff face seemed to mark the edge of the moving ground – it seemed to form a natural border to the moonquake.

Once they reached the top, Annie threw herself onto her front, pulling George down next to her. Inching forward, they gazed over the edge of the ridge at the spot where they had been standing.

As he lay there, George felt his heart rate slow a little. They might just be safe after all, he thought. But looking back, he realized that if Annie hadn't been so quick to spot the danger, they really wouldn't have been going home again.

In the exact place where Cosmos had positioned the portal to drop them off, they saw the fault line widen and the ground finally split apart entirely. A huge belch of steam flew up into the air, twisting and curling as the vapour hit the freezing atmosphere. A second later, an enormous jet of water exploded out of the ground, rising many metres above the surface of the planet. Against the pure blackness of the sky, the spray made a beautiful lacy pattern as the droplets of water shot up into the atmosphere, froze, then drifted down as an ice fountain.

'Wow, it's a cold-water geyser!' said Annie in wonder. 'Cosmos *has* found us water in space!'

'Yeah, but he nearly got us killed too,' said George in horror. Annie didn't seem to realize that she had just saved their lives. 'Annie, if we hadn't moved, we'd be dead by now. Either we would have fallen into that hole or we'd have been blasted into space or frozen into ice statues. This isn't good.'

'I'm sure Cosmos didn't do it deliberately.' Annie

watched the play of water and ice against the dark starry sky, with the curve of Saturn's pale globe in the background. 'He wouldn't do that! Would he?' She suddenly sounded less sure. 'It *must* have been a mistake.'

'I don't know!' George was puzzled too. 'Perhaps it's because he's not feeling well . . . but that was really dangerous: he put us on top of a cryovolcano just minutes before it erupted!'

'Ew – horrible!' Annie sounded shocked. 'You don't think . . . ?'

'I don't know what to think,' said George. 'But we defo need to get out of here before anything else blows up underneath us.'

'I'll summon Cosmos,' said Annie. 'Yoo-hoo! Cosmos!'

'Hell-air!' Cosmos checked in suddenly, using a very unfamiliar, smarmy-sounding voice. 'How it's going on Enceladus?'

'That doesn't sound anything like him,' George whispered to Annie. Inside his spacesuit, he was nice and snug as it was perfectly temperature controlled, but all at once his blood ran cold. Why was Cosmos turning into someone they didn't recognize?

'Er, terrific, thanks,' replied Annie bravely. 'A great view of the geyser erupting from a cryovolcano – so says my friend Factoid George over here.'

'A view?' Cosmos sounded surprised. 'What do

you mean, a *view*? Weren't you — ?' He stopped very suddenly.

'Uh-oh,' said George quietly. It was as though his worst fears had been confirmed. Cosmos had purposely put them in danger!

'Yes, a lovely view,' continued Annie. 'But we've seen water in space now, and we'd like to come home.'

The two of them reached out their space gloves and grasped the other's hand with a squeeze of solidarity. They were in this together. It might have been Annie's idea to come on this adventure, but George knew that he had gone along with it because he really wanted to take a moonwalk. They could never have known that their great friend and ally Cosmos would let them down like this. But now they were right in the middle of this awful adventure, with no one to help them out.

'But you haven't really,' insisted Cosmos. He seemed to be speaking fluently now – no sign of his cold – only with someone else's voice; and he was saying none of the things they expected. It was very odd and very mysterious, as though a friend had become an enemy and no longer wished to look after them.

'There's lots more water in space,' Cosmos continued in his new strange voice. 'Why don't I take you to a super-massive black hole which has so much water vapour around it, it would fill up all the lakes and oceans on Earth trillions of times over? You can't want to come home already.'

'I do, actually,' said Annie. 'I've been as close to a black hole as I ever want to be.' She and George had once rescued her father from a black hole, using Cosmos. An evil scientist had sent him on a journey with the wrong coordinates – and he had plunged into the heart of the darkest place in space. 'I'd like you to take us home.'

'No,' said Cosmos flatly. 'The Earth return portal cannot be activated until I am convinced your mission has been accomplished. You need to visit another location in order to investigate the phenomenon of water in space before I can authorize your homeward journey.'

'What?' whispered Annie. 'I've never heard that rule before . . . This is bonkers.'

'Even if he won't take us home,' muttered George, 'perhaps we could get closer.' Clearly, they could no longer trust Cosmos as they used to, and needed to manipulate him into doing what they wanted rather than asking him outright.

'What about the Moon?' he suggested. 'There's water on the Moon!'

'The *dark side* of the Moon?' asked Cosmos rather unpleasantly.

'No!' said Annie sharply. 'As you know perfectly well, it isn't called the dark side of the Moon. We call it the 'far side'. But we want the near side, please. Or at least, wherever the water is.'

'Opening up the inter-solar-system transportation portal now.'

THE DARK SIDE OF THE MOON

It sounds like it should always be night on the dark side of the Moon, but that's not true as any friendly astronomer will tell you. First of all, astronomers don't talk about the dark side. They call it the far side of the Moon, because the far side of the Moon has night and day, just like we do on Earth.

When we look up at the Moon in the night sky, it looks familiar to us, no matter where we are on the Earth. We see the same features each time because we are always looking at the near side of the Moon. So how come we never get to see the other side of our old friend the Moon?

Why can't we see the far side?

The Moon orbits around the earth while rotating on its axis. It takes the Moon the same amount of time to complete one orbit of the Earth as it does for our rocky satellite to rotate – 29 days. If the Moon didn't rotate, we would see all of its faces or sides, near and far, as the Earth rotates while orbiting around the Sun. But because the Earth is turning and the Moon is turning – and the gravity of the Earth has slowed down the Moon's rotation to its current speed – it means we always see the same face of the Moon.

Phases of the Moon

The positions of the Earth and the Moon in their orbits around the Sun give us the phases of the Moon.

- When the Moon is between the Earth and the Sun, we call it a new moon. The Moon looks dark to us from Earth as it is lunar night time on the near side of the Moon (the side nearest to us).

- When the Earth is between the Sun and the Moon, that's a full moon. If you were standing on the near side of the Moon, we might be able to see you from Earth as you would be standing in the midday sunshine of a lunar day!

Even though we can't see the far side of the Moon, it has been visited by astronauts, one of whom said it reminded him of his kids' sandpit!

The familiar doorway appeared in front of them, shining in the odd burnished glow of Saturn's reflected light. The door swung back and the two friends could see beyond it the dimly lit greyish-white surface of the Moon, with a clear black sky behind the mountain range.

'Quick,' said George, who was keen to get moving: anywhere would be better than here. 'Let's leave before Cosmos changes his mind and decides we should stay on Enceladus for ever.'

They both jumped through onto a patch of lunar ground, and found themselves in the polar region of Earth's friendly little satellite.

'Whoa!' said George as he stepped onto the Moon itself. 'This is amazing!' For a moment he forgot that he'd escaped terrible danger on Enceladus only to be denied passage back to Earth by a computer which had suddenly developed a bad attitude and a control fixation. Just for a few seconds, the pure pleasure of standing on the Moon overwhelmed him. He spread his arms wide and experienced the wonder of space travel and the joy of discovery.

Despite having endlessly pestered anyone who would listen about her wish to visit the Moon, Annie wasn't quite as rapt as her friend. She was still focused on the practicalities. 'Where are we now?' she radioed Cosmos.

'You are at the lunar pole, where a series of craters

contain water ice,' said Cosmos, still using the unpleasantly smarmy voice.

'Thank you, Cosmos,' said Annie quietly. 'Even
though I've always wanted to stand on the Moon,
I have to say, this isn't going to be my number one
favourite space trip ever. And I think I've seen enough
for my chemistry project.' She scuffed the ground with
her boot, and dusty, icy fragments drifted upwards. 'I
now know without a doubt that there is water in space
and I have plenty to write about. Which means that
you can take us home! Please,' she added, knowing
that Cosmos – at least in his former incarnation –
appreciated politeness.

'*In ten minutes*,' said the computer, now in a tinny,
mechanical voice. '*Nine minutes fifty-nine, nine minutes
fifty-eight . . .*'

'What are we going to do for ten minutes?' George
wondered. He knew it didn't sound like a long time, but
when you were trapped in space and unable to get home,
even a few seconds could start to feel like millennia.

'Override him so we get home faster!' Annie sounded
panicky. 'Wait! Look behind you!'

George wheeled round and gasped. Just moments
before the dusty lunar landscape had been totally
empty, but now he saw what looked like a small car
perched on a distant outcrop, outlined against the black
sky in the faint glow of light that touched the ridges of
the Moon mountains.

'It's a lunar exploration rover!' exclaimed Annie. 'It must have been left behind by a mission to the Moon. But why is it moving? And WHO is driving it?' She sounded nearly hysterical now.

George was rooted to the spot, his mouth wide open inside his space helmet. 'It's OK,' he tried to reassure her. 'They must be miles away. If Cosmos sets up the portal, we can get out of here before they reach us. It'll take them for ever to drive round all those craters without crashing into one.'

But he hadn't anticipated what came next. The doors of the rover opened, and two large, sleek robots jumped out; they immediately headed towards the two friends, covering the ground with long, purposeful strides.

Back on Earth, Cosmos didn't seem bothered. '*Eight minutes thirty*,' he was still intoning. '*Eight minutes twenty-nine.*'

'Hurry up, Cosmos!' shouted Annie.

The robots were advancing quickly; they were silver with very long legs and arms attached to a short but powerful looking body. Their heads were square and even from a distance, there was something menacing about the expressions on their robotic features. As they moved, their arms swung in time with their strong legs. They didn't look like the sort of robots that anyone wanted to meet when they were out for a walk on the Moon. On and on they marched, shattering moon rocks under their boots as they did so.

But Cosmos just casually replied: '*Eight minutes twenty-eight . . . eight minutes twenty-seven . . .*'

'He's ignoring us!' cried Annie in frustration. 'I think he *wants* those robots to get us!'

'I don't know what they are,' said George, 'but I don't like this. Annie, can you think of another way to get us out of here?'

'No, I — Hang on, I've got an idea! Ebot!' Using the special glasses, Annie tried to summon the android. 'Rats!' Inside her space helmet, she was frantically swivelling her eyes and wiggling her eyebrows, trying to activate the eye-gaze technology that alerted Ebot and got him operational. She managed to change to his field of vision, but he seemed to have gone back to sleep.

'Why isn't this working better!' she cried in frustration. 'It was easy before!'

'*Eight minutes and two seconds*,' said Cosmos unhelpfully.

George realized that, given the speed with which the robots were now approaching, they would easily reach them before Cosmos had opened the return space portal. If Cosmos opened it at all. There was, he reasoned, nowhere left to run, so only one option remained. He would have to stand and fight. George drew himself up to his full height and prepared to face down the robots.

Having made his decision, George felt surprisingly calm. If this was his time to show courage, he figured, then that was what he would do. He would stand here until they arrived, and then he would take them on in boy-to-robot combat. He was ready.

Behind him, Annie was still attempting to contact Ebot. In front of him, one of the robots slipped as it tried to bound over a massive hole in the ground, crashing into the crater. But the other one kept going, arms outstretched. It was still a long way away, but every stride brought it closer.

A second later, however, Annie managed to wriggle her eyebrows and get control of Ebot: she sparked him into action. Using the command menus on the glasses, which Eric had had customized to include a long list of useful commands, she managed to make Ebot stand

up in Eric's study and walk over to Cosmos. But once he reached the computer, Annie found that she had run out of options. She couldn't persuade him to do anything else. She had a terrestrial android standing in front of a sulky, unhelpful computer, but no way of connecting the two pieces of technology.

'I don't know what to do!' she said to George in despair. 'I don't know how to work Ebot's hands!'

'I do!' George had the haptic gloves under his space gloves. He waved a hand in front of his face while Annie watched through Ebot's eyes, as the android copied the movement. 'Do you know how to override Cosmos?' he asked Annie, casting a fearful glance at the robot, which was advancing inexorably.

'Not really,' she admitted. 'But if you try pressing a random combination of keys, it might be enough to jolt Cosmos out of the auto-function he seems stuck into now.'

'I'll try it,' said George. He wriggled his fingers as though tapping a computer keyboard. 'It would help if I could see what I was doing.'

'I can't take off my helmet to give you the glasses!' said Annie. 'My head would explode if I did that!'

However, she could see the scene in her father's study. And she could see that George and Ebot's combined efforts with Cosmos's keyboard had come to nothing. Ebot's fingers had just skimmed across the surface without having any impact.

'Try again,' Annie instructed. 'Go more slowly! Pretend you are pressing one key at a time, but keep them down.'

Holding his hands in mid-air in front of his chest, George moved each finger and thumb with deliberation.

As he did so, 360,000 kilometres or 225,000 miles away on Earth, Ebot depressed a series of Cosmos's keys.

In the distance, the strange robot continued to advance, using the low gravity of the Moon to help it cover the ground.

Meanwhile this time, amazingly, it seemed as though George and Ebot's random movements on the keyboard were having an effect. '*Time lock cancelled,*' announced Cosmos, still speaking in his mechanical tinny voice but at least saying something they wanted to hear. '*Portal command has been reinstated.*'

'Whoa!' said Annie as a familiar shape started to materialize in front of them. 'It's the portal! We did it, George! We're going to get out of here just in time!'

They glanced round at the approaching robot; they had just enough time for the portal to stabilize and let them through before it reached them.

Annie hugged George in triumph, but as she did so, over his shoulder, she noticed something and yelped in horror, 'Ohmigod! There's a red light on the back of your spacesuit. The robot's got you in its sights!'

Suddenly the robot sped up. 'It's locked on to you!' she shrieked. 'If it tries to shoot you, it can't miss!'

Closer and closer the robot came; now they could see that instead of hands, it had huge pincers at the end of its arms, one of which it was aiming straight at George, as though it could fire something from it. They could see the set expression of anger and determination that its robot features had been forged into. They could see how the ground shook each time a heavy robot foot slammed down on it. Meanwhile the portal doorway gradually solidified out of beams of light.

Just as the robot was stretching towards George, the portal door swung back; through it they saw Eric's study, Earth – and safety.

'George!' screamed Annie, shoving him ahead of her before the robot could grab him. She tumbled after him, doing a forward roll through the door, which started to close behind her as the robot attempted to barge its way through.

As George turned and caught a last glimpse of the robot's ugly, menacing face before the door swung shut, he noticed something they hadn't seen before. Emblazoned on the side of the robot's face were three letters: IAM. Not only that . . . as they passed through the doorway, George heard a strange robotic voice through the voice transmitters in his space helmet:

'*QED, Professor Bellis. QED.*' And then the door on space closed, leaving the robot on the other side of it.

Saturn

NASA/JPL/Space Science Institute

Enceladus

NASA/Science Photo Library

Enceladus Hubble

Enceladus showing
ice fountains

NASA/JPL-Caltech/Space Science Institute

Its surface

NASA/Goddard/Arizona State University

Two sides of the moon?

Jupiter with Ganymede

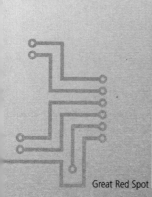

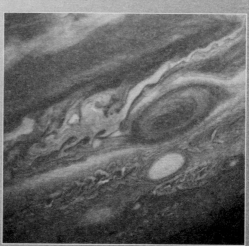

Great Red Spot

NASA, ESA, and the Hubble Heritage Team (STScI/AURA)

Comet ISON

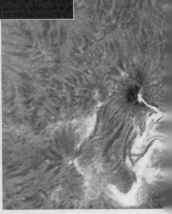

Sunspot

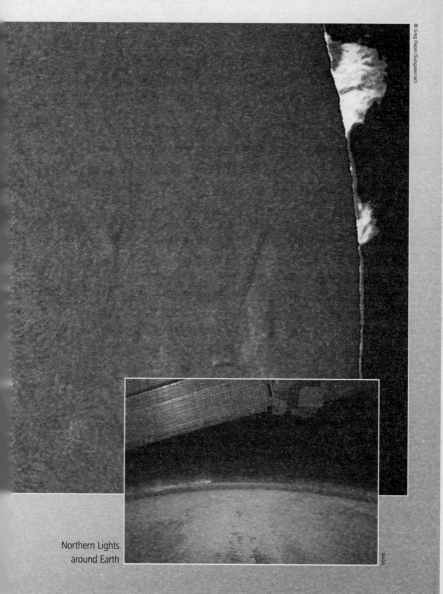

Northern Lights
around Earth

NASA

Space Oddity

NASA

Expedition 35 Crew members

Chapter Eight

The two friends lay on the floor, panting with the sheer terror and excitement of their expedition. Finally they managed to drag themselves up, not only out of breath but also readjusting to Earth's gravitational pull, so much stronger than that of the Moon. Each time they returned to Earth from space, they experienced the shock of coming back to the Earth's gravity; yet each time they forgot about it until it happened.

'Well, I think we found out all we needed to know about water in space, don't you?' said Annie as she wriggled out of her spacesuit. She was trying to sound normal, but once she had taken off her helmet, George saw that her blue eyes were wide and staring.

She went straight over to Cosmos, opened up a new file and started to type: *WRATE*.

'That was super-scary!' said George. 'Annie . . . just before the door closed, I heard a voice say "QED, Professor Bellis"! What does that even mean?'

'Um, it means something like "That is proved",

doesn't it?' she told him. 'I think I've heard Dad say it. But why would a robot on the Moon say that to you? It doesn't make sense. None of this makes sense.'

But suddenly they both had the same thought: their eyes swivelled towards Cosmos, who sat innocently on Eric's desk, as though nothing in his Universe had changed since the days when they were such great chums.

George was paranoid. Was the computer actually listening to their conversation? Was it safe to talk in front of him? They both went very quiet. It was hard to believe that Cosmos had tried to . . . George couldn't even begin to think what he might have been trying to do to them. Surely it wasn't possible? But reviewing the evidence, he reflected that not only had Cosmos deposited them on top of an erupting cryovolcano, he had then transferred them to a location on the Moon governed by aggressive robots who seemed to bitterly resent intruders.

'What now?' he asked cautiously.

Cosmos supplied the answer. 'Don't you want to write up your research notes about water in space?' he suggested to Annie. 'Your project is time-sensitive, after all.' It still wasn't his old voice; it was now silky smooth again, but somehow rather threatening. On the screen, he changed Annie's *WRATE* to *WATER*.

'Yes, of course I do,' said Annie rather faintly. She looked like she couldn't decide between continuing with her beloved project and running from the room screaming.

George was astonished that they were talking about a school project so soon after nearly being poached in volcanic water on a moon of Saturn. It was hard to adjust to life back on Earth in Eric's office, chatting away with Cosmos as though everything was normal.

'Affirmative,' agreed Cosmos. Ebot had gone back to sitting quietly in the corner, looking like an abandoned giant doll.

Annie and George exchanged baffled looks.

'We'd better do what Cosmos says,' whispered Annie. 'It might give us an idea about what's going on with him.'

She started to talk, and as she did so, Cosmos wrote her words out on the screen. 'Water,' she said, 'is a molecule made up of two hydrogen atoms and one oxygen atom. It is made when—' She stopped. 'How *is* water made?' she asked.

'It's made by stars, isn't it?' said George. 'Is that right, Cosmos?'

If he started up some kind of conversation with the supercomputer, they might be able to work out what had happened to the Cosmos they knew and loved. It was like the scene in a horror movie where the kids try to pacify a dangerous lunatic in order to buy time and come up with some kind of rescue plan.

'Yes,' agreed Cosmos, who sounded slightly more

friendly now that they had him on his own specialist topic: the Universe and everything in it. 'Most of the water in the Universe is made during the formation of stars, where high pressures and temperatures in the surrounding cloud force hydrogen and oxygen atoms together. Water makes up seventy-one per cent of the surface of Earth; there is so much water that we never have to make any ourselves, but no one is exactly sure how it got to be here.'

Suddenly George had an idea. He wasn't entirely sure if it would work, but he figured it was worth a try. If Annie could keep Cosmos occupied, he might be able to run a check on the computer's systems, see what had happened to him and find out whether he could make a repair. George wasn't as IT-gifted as their friend Emmett, who had come to stay one summer, but he had learned a lot from Emmett and from IT lessons. It was worth a shot. Rootling around, he managed to find a piece of scrap paper and a pen which sort of worked. He scribbled a message and showed it to Annie:

Keep him talking! And give me your phone.

'Erm, Cosmos . . .' said Annie gamely, slipping her phone to George. 'Why is water so important?'

'Ah – water,' replied Cosmos enthusiastically, 'is one of the most important molecules of all, as far as you humans are concerned, because life as we know it would not be possible without it. Around sixty per cent of the body is made up of water, and people cannot survive more than a few days without it. This is because a lot of the chemistry that happens in the body needs water in order to work. Plants also need water to grow.'

'Yes, that's right.' Annie was at her most charming. 'A good point, Cosmos, our clever friend.' While the computer had been talking, George had discreetly plugged a backup hard drive into the laptop and was now connecting Annie's phone to the Bellises' home wireless network – trying to log into Cosmos remotely and search his system for signs of a problem. He motioned for Annie to keep the computer talking, in the hope that this would distract him from noticing what George was up to.

'Cosmos, what is the link between water and life?' asked Annie, gazing at the screen with rapt attention.

'I'm glad you asked,' replied the computer. Very fortunately, Cosmos seemed so intent on his explanation that he didn't react to what George was doing. 'In fact, water is so important to life that people looking for life on other planets first check for evidence of the existence of water. If there is no water, it is almost certain that there will be no life there. The chemistry to make the building blocks of life happens in, and uses, water; without water, the molecules of life cannot easily be made.'

'Thank you.' Annie looked over at George, hoping he might have been successful by now. But just as she did so, there was a commotion in the hallway. Suddenly, the two of them realized that it was already evening! Neither of them could have said how long they had spent in space but the day on Earth seemed to have finished while they had been out exploring.

'Why is the car outside full of duvets and bottled water?' Eric asked.

'I have some news,' they heard Susan reply. Her voice was rather more high-pitched than usual, as though she didn't believe the words she was saying herself. 'You'll be so excited, I know . . . My family are coming to stay.'

'Your . . . family?' Eric's disbelief was clear even through the walls. 'How many of your family?'

'Well . . . all of them.' Susan broke into hysterical laughter. 'They got those free flights on the internet, and now they're all on their way here from Australia!'

'Oh no, you are *kidding*!' cried Eric in horror. 'Your whole family! What have I done to deserve this?'

As they talked, the pair of them burst into the study where Annie and George sat meekly in front of Cosmos, her chemistry project displayed on the screen.

Ever the scientist and teacher, Eric couldn't help reading out a few lines:

'One oxygen bonds with two hydrogen to form H^2O . . . Excellent,' he murmured approvingly. 'Well done, you two – it's good to see you working so hard. Thank goodness for you – the rest of the world seems to have gone bananas and I'm at my wits' end trying to sort it out.'

'Oh yes, well done,' said Annie's mum, admiring the onscreen project. 'At least I don't have to worry about you and George. That's such a relief. I think I'd go crazy if I had anything else to stress about right now! It's chaos out there. I had a horrible time doing the shopping. I can't believe anyone else has nine family members arriving from Australia, but people were buying up supplies as though they did. Someone accused me of being a hoarder!'

Annie and George exchanged glances and sighed. Clearly the adults were going to be of no help whatsoever.

'Dad . . .' said Annie. Eric was busy rifling through various drawers in his study. 'What's going on?'

'Annie, honestly, we don't know,' he said. 'Computer systems all over the world are sporadically malfunctioning and nobody can find out why. Our best guess is that somehow, all internet security protocols have been breached, messages intercepted and rogue commands are being given – with some pretty extraordinary results.'

'Like what?' said Annie. 'The free flights?'

'Yes, but also a dam opened in the desert,' said Eric. 'Its computer systems caused the gates to open, so all the water has now flooded out. Drones – you know, those computerized aircraft the army uses – are refusing to take off. A whole bunch of computer networks have gone down too – the ones that let people chat to each other online. That's probably not so bad, compared to everything else. But food deliveries are being affected, and we're worried that power supplies might be next.'

'Do you think someone is hacking into all the computers in the world?' asked George.

'We don't know!' Eric burst into stressy-sounding laughter – the sort of laugh grown-ups use when things aren't really that funny. 'It is literally unbelievable. But it looks like every system in the world has been hacked into! Speaking face to face is the only safe form of communicating now!'

'Even mobile phones?' said Annie.

'Yup,' Eric confirmed. 'Everything. It seems that every system in the world is vulnerable.' He unplugged the spare hard drive from Cosmos – the one that George had been using to check Cosmos's systems. 'I'll take that with me, just in case I need to reference anything from Cosmos while I'm away.'

'Who could be doing this?' George wondered.

'We don't know,' said Eric soberly. 'It could be an individual, it could be a rogue state, it could be a corporation. Some people think that, given how random the targets are, it might actually be space weather. One or two people are speculating that this is alien interference – we're not able to trace any signal to a location on Earth.'

'What do *you* think?' said George.

'*Me?* I'm afraid my hypothesis is not very popular.' Eric grimaced. 'I think that someone has managed to develop a quantum computer and is using it to break into every system on Earth. But who it is and how they could have managed it when we can't do it ourselves, I can't tell you, because I simply don't know. But I don't like it . . . not one little bit. And now I have to go.'

'But where?' cried Annie.

Eric sighed, ruffled her hair and kissed her on the forehead. 'I can't even tell you that. There's a car waiting for me outside.

QUANTUM COMPUTERS

Computers have become an integral piece in almost all aspects of our daily lives. Today's computers are in our homes, our cars and most of us carry one with us everywhere we go in our mobile devices. This technological revolution was made possible by our understanding and harnessing the properties of the world around us. At the heart of that understanding is mathematics.

A challenge for mathematicians

In 1900, a German mathematician – David Hilbert – posed a list of 23 problems for mathematicians to solve. When British mathematician Alan Turing worked on one of the problems, which asked mathematicians to find out if we could always discover if a mathematical proposition was true in a finite amount of time, he tackled it by proposing to build a hypothetical machine that would derive theorems in a mechanical way. This machine became known as a *Turing machine*, and was a blueprint for today's classical computers.

Classical vs quantum

Scientists like Galileo, Newton, Maxwell and others described the world around us to high accuracy, coming up with the theories of *classical mechanics*. But when scientists began working at the scale of atoms and molecules, classical approaches broke down and they needed a new set of theories and rules: *quantum mechanics*.

These rules are very different from those of classical mechanics. For instance, the *superposition principle* states that if A is a solution of an equation of quantum mechanics and B is also a solution, then A+B is also a solution. What does that mean? In the case of an electron, it means that if we have one solution with an electron here, and another solution with an electron there, we can have a solution with a single electron being here and there *at the same time*. Pushing this possibility to its limits led the physicist Schrödinger to show that at the quantum level we could see a cat alive and dead at the same time – something we certainly don't see at our scale!

134

Using quantum principles with computers

1. First we transform a bit of information into a quantum bit, or qubit for short – and this can be encoded in the superposition of the state 0 *and* 1 *at the same time*!

2. If we have two qubits, they can therefore be in the superposition of *four* states: 00, 01, 10 and 11. Now imagine three qubits: 000, 001 . . . 111: a total of *eight* states.

3. You can see that the number of states grows exponentially with the number of qubits. Just by changing the classical *or* (0 or 1) to a quantum *and* (0 and 1), we can have exponential increase in our computing power!

4. This means that if we change the rules with which we compute, we can develop new algorithms and drastically change the type of problems we can solve too, though quantum computers would not necessarily have an advantage on *all* problems.

5. For some problems, quantum computers therefore are formidable devices. An example of a quantum algorithm is factoring large numbers which are the product of two primes – a hard problem of classical computers and the basis of most of today's cybersecurity. A quantum computer would be able to solve factoring problems with ease and break encryptions. Quantum algorithms will also be applicable in other complex disciplines such as materials science (where we want to create new quantum materials and understand their performance), chemistry (to predict the behaviour of large atoms and molecules and apply it to drug design, for example), health care (by constructing new types of sensors) and much more that we have not yet imagined. These principles have allowed us to develop a new language which is the proper one to talk to and listen to quantum particles such as atoms and molecules.

> Quantum mechanics has provided a key to understanding the very building blocks of our world. Quantum information science gives us an incredible opportunity to harness the power of quantum mechanics for the development of mind-boggling technologies such as the quantum computer, quantum cryptography, quantum sensors and more that have not even been imagined today.

Raymond

But I'm sure you're safe here – we'll get this sorted out within the next few hours.'

'But what are we supposed to do?' asked Annie.

'Um . . . write your chemistry project!' replied Eric. 'You finish that off, and when I get home, I'll look forward to reading it.' He paused and typed a few commands on Cosmos's keyboard. 'I've given you permission to use Cosmos for your chemistry project . . . but just to make sure you're safe, I've cut your access to any other function. He will only operate for you on matters related to your homework. I can't imagine that will generate any interest from a malicious computer hacker, if that's really what this is.'

George felt his spirits sink.

'Wait!' said Annie. 'So you're not taking Cosmos? Or Ebot?'

'No, I don't think so,' said Eric. 'I'll travel without my digital footprint.'

With that, he charged out of the study, hot on the trail of another great scientific mystery that he hoped to solve before anyone else. As he shot down the hallway, he cannoned into his wife; he tried in vain to hug her – she was carrying armfuls of spare bedding so his arms didn't reach round her. Instead, he just managed to kiss the top of her nose and then disappeared through the front door.

'Annie!' called Susan. 'Can you help me? We need to make up lots of beds.'

'Why don't they camp in the garden?' said Annie. 'It's not cold and they're always telling us on Skype about their adventures in the Outback.'

'Brilliant idea!' said her mum. 'Can you find the tents and start pitching them?'

'Yes – leave it to me!' Annie replied.

George said to her quietly, 'We didn't get to ask your dad about IAM and the robots. Or QED. Or Cosmos. We didn't get a chance to ask him *anything*!'

'I know!' She sounded annoyed. 'But what could we do? He was here and then he was gone – and we couldn't really start talking to him in front of Cosmos.'

'*And*,' said George, 'he's taken the hard drive that I was using to check Cosmos. We would have been able to tell if he had been hacked into, and if that's what's making him so weird. But now we can't know for sure . . . '

'You'd better go,' said Annie. 'Unless you want to help canvas over my garden. Let's meet later and I'll see if I can find anything out while you're gone.'

When George got home, his mum and dad were looking perplexed. On the table was a loaf of Daisy's bread, which they were studying earnestly. He waited for an explanation, but they just stood there, gazing at the burned and very solid-looking rectangle sitting on the table.

'Er, Mum and Dad . . .' said George; from the lack of noise in the house, he realized that the twins must

already be in bed. "'Scuse me for asking, but why are you standing staring at a loaf of bread?'

'We're wondering,' said Terence, 'why someone offered us a thousand pounds for this loaf of bread earlier today.'

'And you didn't sell it?' cried George. 'That's got to be a once-in-a-lifetime opportunity!'

'I'm not sure about that,' said his mum gently. 'We took our turn at the cooperative today, and people kept coming in with whole wheelbarrows of money to spend on buying our food.'

'But the cooperative doesn't accept money!' said George. It was a venture his parents were involved in: people exchanged goods and services without any money changing hands.

'That's what we said,' replied Terence. 'But it looks as though there's no food anywhere!'

'So now people have got lots and lots of money from the bank machines,' added Daisy, 'but nothing to spend it on! So we've decided to keep our bread and not to sell it, because money doesn't seem to be worth anything any more.'

'We just can't get over someone wanting to spend a thousand pounds on a loaf of your mother's bread!' said Terence with a rare glint of humour.

At that moment, with a gentle fizz and a plop, all the lights in the house went out.

The three of them stood there in the gloom. 'The babies!' cried Daisy, trying to fumble her way towards the stairs.

'They'll be fine,' Terence reassured her. 'It's just a power cut. Or perhaps my wind panels have come unstuck.' George's family tried to use only the energy they could produce themselves from their own wind generator, but they were still connected to the mains as well.

Blundering about in the darkness, George found the back door and peered out. The only light was coming from the stars in the sky. He realised how late it must be. 'It's everywhere!' he exclaimed. The lights had gone out all over Foxbridge. George reflected that this would be an amazing night to take a photo of Saturn: there would be no light pollution at all. But he didn't have much time to dwell on this idea as his dad decided it was time to become a man of action.

'George,' he announced, 'I'm going to head up onto the roof, but I'll need your help. I want to check out our turbine. It should have kicked in, but it hasn't, so there must be a problem. We should be able to generate enough power to get our lights back on, even in a power cut.'

Finding their way through the dark house with George's pocket torch was a surprisingly spooky experience. In the darkness, even familiar objects were scary. The cupboard where George's dad kept his toolkit looked like it would open its jaws and swallow his dad whole. The stairs were a flight of steps in Dracula's

castle. A chest of drawers on the landing had turned into a looming tombstone, and the ticking of a clock sounded like the chimes of doom. George was glad that his dad had gone ahead and that he could hide behind him, in case anything really scary jumped out at them. Even the gentle snores of his baby sisters had started to sound like the heavy breathing of zombies lying in wait for their prey . . .

Upstairs, they tiptoed through the twins' bedroom, climbed out of the window and onto the roof. George saw that his dad was right – one of the wind panels had come adrift.

Most of the time the generator worked quite well. George and his dad were rightly proud of their efforts: the turbine used wind power to move a magnet around an arrangement of copper wire, generating a modest amount of electricity. It was just a shame it seemed to have fallen apart when they really needed it.

George balanced on the broad window ledge, holding onto the toolkit, while his dad climbed up onto the roof above the attic window, where the wind panels lived. Suddenly he saw a flashing light coming from his tree-house. He squinted over to try and make out what it could be. Why would there be a light on there? It didn't make sense. He stared at it again – it looked like a torch being switched on and off.

'Hammer,' instructed Terence, perched on the sloping roof.

George obligingly handed it up to him. He didn't dare tell his dad to look over at the treehouse: if he twisted round, he might fall off the roof. So George watched in silence as the flashes came and went, some quick, some slow. After a few moments he realized that there was a pattern to them: slow, slow, slow; quick, quick, quick; slow, slow, slow.

'Dad?' he said cautiously as his father thwacked himself on the thumb with a hammer.

'*Youch!*'

George heard noises from the other side of the house: some passers-by were hurrying along the road. 'I read on a website that someone captured a werewolf,' one of the unknown people said to another, his voice carrying very clearly on the still night air.

'What is it?' Terence now had his thumb in his mouth.

'What does three slow, then three quick, and then three slow flashes with a torch mean?'

'That's Morse code,' said his dad through a mouthful

of damaged thumb. 'It means "SOS".'

Who would be sending an SOS from the treehouse?

'Dad,' he said casually, 'do you know any more Morse code?'

His father, preoccupied with the wind panel, didn't seem to think this was an odd question. 'I'm putting on my head torch,' he said, switching on the small bulb attached to his forehead by a band of elastic. 'Your torch is wobbling all over the place. Yes, I do know Morse code. Learned it years ago. It was the kind of thing your grandfather was very keen on.'

'Can you do D-I-K-U?' George asked eagerly as Terence hammered away.

'Hmm . . . Dash-dot-dot . . .' His dad aimed the hammer at the innocent nail, his strokes keeping time with the dots and dashes. 'Dot-dot.' (*Tap-tap.*) 'Dash-dot-dash.' (*Long tap – short tap – long tap – sharp hard tap at the end.*) 'Dot-dot-dash.' He finished hammering with a flourish. 'What are you doing?' he asked as George transferred his instructions to flashes on his torch.

'Just practising,' said George earnestly. 'How's the generator looking?'

'Nearly there.'

The reply from the treehouse came quickly. 'Dot-dash. Dash-dot-dot-dot,' George repeated out loud. 'Dad, what does that mean?'

'Erm, let me think . . .' Terence was now holding

two nails between his lips but speaking at the same time. 'That makes *AB*. *Arrgh!* I think I've swallowed a nail! I'm choking!'

George reached up to thump his dad on the back, and a tiny tack popped out of his mouth.

AB. Annie Bellis. *SOS*. From his treehouse.

'Dad, are you done?' George swiftly shone the torch on the wind panels, which had started moving again.

'Are you in a hurry?' Terence was surprised.

'I've got to go to my treehouse and take a photo of Saturn,' explained George. 'Before the lights come back on.'

With that, he nipped back through the open window, past his sleeping sisters, down the stairs, out of the back door and up the ladder to his treehouse.

Sure enough, the SOS was waiting there. Even in the darkness, Annie looked panicky.

'What were you doing on the roof?' she asked.

'Mending the wind generator,' replied George. 'With my dad. He hit his thumb and then swallowed a nail – that's why he was shouting.'

'Wow, your family are weird.' Annie was huddled into George's beanbag, arms wound tightly around her knees.

'Er, I don't think *you* can talk,' said George. 'Who's

got a fake robot dad? And loads of relatives arriving on free flights from Australia?'

'OK,' said Annie. 'You win. We are way weirder. Anyway,' she added as the lights came back on in George's house, now the only one in the row that wasn't dark, 'you guys win in another way. You might be the only people in Foxbridge with electricity.'

'It's just a power cut,' said George. 'Isn't it?'

'I don't know! Dad said not to use the internet, so I can't check what's going on in other places. D'you remember, he said we shouldn't use mobile phones, either, but I don't know if we even could – my signal keeps cutting out.'

'Is that why you're sending messages to me in Morse code,' asked George, 'from my own treehouse?'

'Yeah,' said Annie. 'I thought it would be like WhatsApp, old skool! Enigma-style texting. I didn't know if you'd crack it, but you did!'

George peered out of the treehouse. Not a single streetlamp or house (apart from his own), office or restaurant was lit up. The whole town was in darkness.

'Seriously?' he said. 'We are the only house in Foxbridge with power?' In other houses, lights were now gradually going on, but they were dim – the flickering glow of candles rather than the blaze of electric light bulbs. 'What's happening, Annie?' He turned to her in the darkness. 'What's going on?'

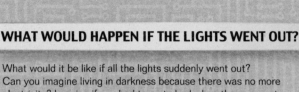

WHAT WOULD HAPPEN IF THE LIGHTS WENT OUT?

What would it be like if all the lights suddenly went out? Can you imagine living in darkness because there was no more electricity? Imagine if you had to go to bed when the sun went down – in some parts of the northern hemisphere, you would be tucked up by 4 p.m. in the winter! Astronomers might be thrilled that a lack of electric light would mean no light pollution spoiling their view of the night sky – but they might find day-to-day life a bit more tricky than usual!

Why we might lose power

There are all sorts of reasons why a huge power cut could strike the Earth.

- Terrorist acts – or events in a war – could knock out power stations.
- We are likely to face problems with supplies as more and more people on Earth want to use lots and lots of electricity.
- Already bad weather on Earth also regularly causes thousands of homes to lose their power supply.

The importance of the Sun

But it's not just Earth weather that could make your home go dark – experts now think that *space weather* could drastically affect our electricity supply over the next few years. We get our light, of course, from our Sun. But the Sun can also disturb our weather. A Coronal Mass Ejection (CME) – when the Sun throws out a great bolt of solar matter and energy – can cause magnetic storms or a rise in radiation levels. These can disrupt electrical power grids and radio communications on Earth.

CMEs happen most often during a solar maximum – the time of greatest solar activity during the Sun's 11-year cycle. Scientists who study the Sun believe that the Earth is in a solar maximum between 2013 and 2015. This is great for viewing the Northern Lights, a spectacular night-time show of coloured lights in the northern sky, caused by electrons and protons from the solar wind interacting with gas in the atmosphere. But the solar maximum could cause problems on Earth with our power supplies.

So . . . what might life be like if the lights went out?

Light

Human beings existed on the Earth long before the invention of the electric light bulb! So we should be fine without electric light. We could light our homes with candles or lamps. Modern technology has also provided us with battery or solar-powered lamps which we could use in a power cut. But we would have far less light than we are used to once the sun has set. And we would have to be careful not to run down our supplies, especially if we had no idea how long the power cut might last.

Heat

Many of us rely on electricity for warmth. Even people with gas boilers, which need electricity to ignite, would find themselves with no heat in their homes. Many of us use electricity to cook – so we'd have to think again about how to make a hot meal. And keeping food fresh, even in cold temperatures, would become a challenge without a working fridge or freezer. With a wood-burning stove and plenty of logs, we could huddle around it to keep warm. We would have to wear more clothes and go to bed much earlier . . .

Water

You might not have any water at all! And even if you did still have running water, very quickly that water would not be clean enough to drink. Without electricity, the vast water purification plants and sewage plants would stop working. So you would have to filter and then boil water before it became pure enough to drink. You would have to heat water to wash yourself and your clothes – which you would have to do by hand as machines won't be working.

Entertainment

We could play Scrabble (the board game, not the online version) by torchlight, wearing our winter coats, sitting around a wood or coal fire in the evenings, eating tinned food that we've heated up over the fire! But we wouldn't be able to watch television or play computer games. Your mobile phone would lose its charge quite fast, unless you have a solar-powered charger. You might be able to use the landline as the telephone system works off a different grid to mains electricity. And if you have a wind-up radio, you could listen to it, which would be a good way of getting news and updates.

> Life without electricity would be very different for most people on Earth! How do you think your life would change if electricity didn't flow at the flick of a switch?

147

'I don't know . . .' she said, looking very serious. 'But I don't like it. That robot on the Moon as well . . . What was it? And who did it belong to?'

'That was so *not* good!' said George. 'It wasn't friendly, that's for sure. And it was super-weird that it seemed to want *me*. Why would a robot want *me*? I'm just a kid! And who – or what – is IAM, and what is it doing in space?'

'Cosmos said something after you went home,' said Annie. 'That's what I wanted to tell you . . . The mission report for our space trip came up on his screen – good job Dad had already left! Anyway, it showed that I'd been on a spacewalk. But when it came to you, it didn't list you as George Greenby. The report said that Eric Bellis had been in space.'

'Because I was wearing your dad's suit, it looked like he'd been into space, right?' said George. 'Like I said in the first place.'

'Yup,' said Annie. 'But get this – even Cosmos didn't seem to realize it wasn't Dad. So if anyone was watching through Cosmos's system, they would have seen that Eric Bellis went into space.'

'So when the robot fixed its sights on me,' George mused, 'it was actually after your dad? We need to tell him!'

'Yeah, but how?' asked Annie. 'How we can do that? He's told us not to use any communication devices.'

'He said he would only be gone for a few hours' –

George sounded doubtful – 'so perhaps when he gets back, we can tell him then?'

'If he hasn't been captured by a mad "IAM" robot in the meantime,' Annie muttered darkly.

'Perhaps the robots can't come to Earth,' said George. 'Perhaps they are only allowed to live on the Moon; that means they can't get your dad, provided he doesn't go into space . . .'

'But we don't know that! You're just making stuff up now!' Annie argued. 'And anyway, who put those robots on the Moon in the first place?'

George puffed out his cheeks. 'Who is doing this?'

'And how is Dad going to find out who it is if we don't tell him what we know?' said Annie. 'That the Moon is now home to some super-angry robots who want to kidnap him. They must be operated by some kind of technical genius – just the sort of person who might mess around with all the computer systems on Earth. Don't you think that's a pretty vital clue, as far as Dad is concerned?'

'Yes, I do!' George wondered why he felt like he was arguing with Annie when in fact he agreed with her.

'Then that's who we need to find,' said Annie in a determined voice. 'We need to find out who owns those robots in case it's the same person who's hacking into systems on Earth. We can't contact Dad to tell him to follow up on IAM, so we'll have to do it ourselves.'

At that moment they heard another screech from

George's house. The Moon had now risen behind the roof, where Terence stood outlined against the glowing white orb. George reflected that even more people would now think there were werewolves about!

'Ouch!' Terence was crying. 'Ouch, ouch, *ouch*!' Suddenly they heard a wail from inside the house as George's sisters were woken by the commotion.

Annie peered out of the treehouse at him. 'What *is* he doing?'

'I think he must have hit his thumb again,' said George. 'I'd better go.'

'Tomorrow, George . . .' Annie told him. 'Tomorrow, we have to sort out a plan. I don't know how much worse things can get, but I don't really want to find out, do you?'

George nodded. Annie was right: they couldn't just leave this situation in the hope that Eric would work it out and save the day. Eric didn't have all the right information – he knew nothing about the robots on the Moon or their attempts to capture him, or that they bore the IAM insignia – the same marking George had seen on the mysterious spaceship he had accidentally photographed. And if Eric didn't know that a scary robot was on his trail, it might be far too easy to catch him. George couldn't let that happen – not on his space watch, anyway . . .

Chapter Nine

The next day Annie appeared bright and early at George's back door, carrying a laptop bag messenger-style across her chest. But she wasn't alone. Behind her lurked Ebot, a benevolent smile on his robot face. He seemed to be wearing a spacesuit and was carrying a space helmet under one robot arm.

'Oh! Come in, Annie,' said Daisy, opening the back door. She was much more subdued than usual. 'Come in, Eric! Eric . . . ?' She looked startled. 'Is that really your dad? Why is he wearing a spacesuit?' she whispered to Annie. 'And why does he look so odd? He looks rather . . . plastic!'

It was still quiet in George's house: he was eating breakfast with his mother while the twins slept on upstairs after their disturbed night.

'Hi, Annie!' said George, who was still in his pyjamas. 'Hi, Ebot!'

'No, it's a personalized robot that Dad customized to look like himself,' Annie explained. 'But he's very convincing – I just took him for a walk to the end of the road and back. A couple of people said "Hi, Eric!" as they passed. Mind you, everyone was in a massive hurry! So many people are rushing around this morning. Can we put on your radio, Mrs G? We haven't got any power at my house so we can't check the internet or anything. Nothing is working!'

'What about your experiments in the fridge?' asked George. 'Are they going to be wrecked if they warm up?'

'Probably,' said Annie sadly. 'Some of them have defo died already. But one of them seems to be growing even faster than before. It's not very nice – the fridge looks pretty yucky inside already.'

Ebot looked around the room, still smiling pleasantly, and then pulled out a chair and sat down.

George's dad arrived, looking pleased with himself. He stroked his beard, one thumb now heavily bandaged. 'Well, young Annie,' he exclaimed, 'we are one of the few power spots in Foxbridge now. I know your father didn't think much of my home-made wind generator, but at least we still have electricity.'

George was already winding up the radio. 'We don't even need power to get the radio working,' he said smugly as he turned the handle and then flipped the switch.

153

'*There are worldwide food shortages,*' came the radio newscaster's voice. '*A complete breakdown in the travel network after airlines accidentally gave away flights for free, combined with a sudden upsurge in the availability of cash globally, have meant that supermarket prices have risen sharply while their stocks have fallen. Reports of hopeful shoppers arriving with wheelbarrows of banknotes to try and buy a sack of potatoes or a loaf of bread . . .*'

Daisy and Terence looked meaningfully at each other.

'*. . . have resulted in fierce fighting over meagre supplies as hoarders attempt to buy up all remaining food stocks in case of a worsening situation over the next few days.*'

'Daisy,' said George's dad urgently, 'what about all our produce at the cooperative?'

'*Break-ins to food warehouses,*' continued the announcer, as though answering Terence's question, '*have become common: supermarkets and shops are emptying too fast to provide enough food in these increasingly desperate times. But government officials have begged people not to panic. Blaming an as yet unexplained series of computer glitches worldwide, the Prime Minister has appealed for calm and told the public that she is working with other governments and expects the networks to be restored within the next twenty-four hours. However, in some locations, community leaders have clubbed together to provide food and shelter for*

*people in need. Safe houses are being set up in schools,
churches and mosques, and local people are trying to
help each other deal with this crisis. A group of young
people, separated from their parents and unable to get
home, have started their own refuge – our reporter
is with them but, for reasons of safety, cannot reveal
where they are located—'*

At that moment the bulletin was interrupted as a new
voice, completely unrelated to the broadcast, emerged
from the radio.

'*I am coming to save you . . .*' it said.

The hairs on the back of George's neck stood up as a
chill ran rapidly down his spine.

'*I am the answer . . . I am giving you what you
need . . . I am your salvation . . . I am . . .*'

As abruptly as it had started, the voice disappeared
and the radio news started again. But George and
Annie were both mesmerized by the interruption to the
broadcast. What did it mean? And where had it come
from?

'*Apologies for the break in service,*' the news reader
resumed, sounding a little panicky now. '*We have no
idea where or whom that transmission came from.
We now have an official message from the National
Broadcasting Service – please do NOT come to our
offices! We do not have much power left from our
generator! We have closed our doors now and will not
be admitting anyone to the premises. Please do not try to*

force the doors – we will not be opening them! We don't have any more—'

The broadcast stopped very suddenly, breaking the spell that had been gluing George and Annie to their seats. George grabbed the radio and wound it up again, but there was nothing to hear on the airwaves.

'Daisy,' said Terence urgently, 'we must get to the cooperative and collect the food supplies that we delivered there yesterday. We have to get our own food back again – we're going to need it! We should go now before people break in and take everything!'

'What about the kids?' said Daisy. 'Shouldn't I stay here with them? What about finding a safe house and taking our food there? Shouldn't we do that?'

'You and I will get the food,' Terence insisted. 'Then we'll look for a safe house, and then we'll come home to get the kids. Otherwise we won't have enough in the house to survive until the crisis is sorted out.'

'Annie, where are your parents?' asked Daisy.

'Dad's with the PM,' replied Annie. 'And Mum went out really early to stock up at the supermarket – but she went ages ago, so she'll be back soon, I'm sure.'

'Can you two look after the little ones while we dash out?' said Daisy.

Terence was collecting canvas bags so that they could carry their own food back from the cooperative where it was now stored.

George was thinking about what they had just heard

on the radio. There was a clue in those strange state-
ments – the ones that had interrupted the broadcast – he
was certain of it.

'Of course!' said Annie, kicking George.

'What? Oh yes! Of course.'

'No time to lose, Daisy.' Terence was halfway out of
the door already. 'Let's go!'

With that, George's parents disappeared into the
outside world, leaving George, Annie and Ebot alone
in the kitchen.

As soon as they heard the front door close, Annie
reached into her messenger bag and produced a flat
silver laptop.

'That's Cosmos!' said George. It always surprised
him how ordinary the little computer looked. 'What's
he doing here?'

'There's no electricity next door,' said Annie. 'He
needs to be charged up, so I brought him over. Anyway,
I thought he might be useful. I am thinking—'

'Stop!' cried George. 'Say that again!'

'There's no electricity next door . . .' Annie repeated
slowly.

'No, the next bit!'

'I thought he might—'

'NO! The next thing . . .'

'I am thinking—'

'*I AM!*' cried George, having a Eureka moment.

'You're what?' said Annie, totally confused now.

'I AM . . . like the weird interruption to the radio broadcast,' said George. '*I am your salvation.* It's the same as IAM on the spaceship. It's the link.'

'I-A-M,' said Annie. 'It's not an acro-thingy. It's "I AM"!'

'But what does it *mean*? We still don't know!'

'No,' said Annie. 'But we do know that I AM is in space. And we think that an I AM robot may have tried to capture you when you were wearing Dad's spacesuit on the Moon. And now we know from the radio that I AM thinks that he is giving everyone on Earth what they need. Which means . . .'

'Which means . . .' said George, trying to piece it together, 'that we guessed right! Someone in space called I AM is messing around with all the computer systems on Earth.'

'Hang on – all that stuff is encrypted,' said Annie. 'It wouldn't be possible for someone to just walk into absolutely every system on the planet . . . would it? Unless . . .'

'Unless they had a quantum computer,' finished George.

'Ohmigod!' said Annie. 'Are you saying that I AM – whoever that is – has made a quantum computer?'

'Maybe. So what are we going to do? How are we going to find I AM? We can't just go into space to look for him – the Universe is infinite! We'll never find him. Or her. Or it. Or whatever I AM really is.'

'I've got an idea,' said Annie. 'Ebot – right? He's like Dad – right? According to Dad, certain technological systems wouldn't be able to tell the difference between him and Ebot. So if I AM was fooled into thinking that Dad was you when you were wearing his suit, Ebot could easily pass as Dad – at least, well enough to send a robot army after him. I don't know about you, but I don't want these bots to trace Dad to Earth and kidnap him – the one we saw didn't look at all nice to me.'

'No, it didn't. But how would we do that? How would we use Ebot as an Eric decoy?' asked George,

'We send Ebot into space!' said Annie triumphantly. 'There's a good chance – or at least *a* chance – that I AM will think he's Dad and use a robot to pick him up!'

'Which helps us how?' George was perplexed. He prided himself on being able to keep up with Annie, however many imaginative leaps she made. But this time he couldn't track her thought processes.

While he was talking, Annie was busy unravelling a cable for Cosmos. 'Which plug connects to your wind generator?' she asked. George pointed to a plug in the corner. As he did so, he realized what Annie was driving at.

'The glasses!' he cried. 'That's what you meant, isn't it? Ebot goes into space, and when he gets kidnapped – or robo-napped – we can see through the special glasses and find out who or what I AM is! And maybe even where!'

'Well done, Einstein!' said Annie, pressing the power button on Cosmos's keyboard.

The dull screen changed to a bright rectangle as the supercomputer woke from his deep sleep. Unfortunately Cosmos was not the only person in the house to wake from a slumber at that moment. The sound of heavy thumping announced that the twins had clambered out of their cots and, like evolution itself, were advancing inexorably.

'How may I assist you today?' purred the world's cleverest computer.

'He sounds like an automatic lift, not a cranky genius supercomputer,' George whispered to Annie.

'Ew!' she said. 'Creepy, isn't it? I don't like him when he's polite. It's so not him! Yikes – look out, George, here come your sisters!'

Juno and Hera threw themselves down the final few stairs and toddled merrily into the kitchen. They spotted Ebot standing there and squealed with delight, imagining that he was some kind of enormous toy. They ran towards him with outstretched arms – in a way that must have triggered an alarm system in Ebot's robotic circuits as he backed away from them, heading towards the playroom, the girls in hot pursuit.

'Hello, Cosmos,' Annie continued cheerfully as the trio disappeared. 'We've got a mission for you.'

'How fascinating,' said the supercomputer in his silky voice. 'However, I am currently commanded to

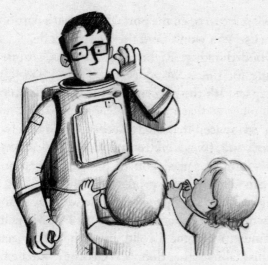

only help with your chemistry project.'

'Ah,' said Annie, remembering what her father had done. 'And is it possible to override that command?'

'If you know the access code to perform the newly installed override function,' replied Cosmos, 'then please go ahead.'

Annie glared at the computer and then glanced at George, who was looking frustrated. 'I could try hitting all the keys, like Ebot did . . .' she whispered. George nodded and she struck a random selection of keys just as Ebot had done when George had been directing him from space. But nothing happened.

'Think of something in space that we need to do for your chemistry project!' hissed George. 'And then

Cosmos will *have* to open the portal because it's part of your project so you won't need the override code.'

'OK! Good thinking! Right, well, Cosmos,' Annie said, playing for time. 'We . . . need . . . to . . . find . . . protein in space! It's the next subject for my chemistry project!'

'Protein in space,' repeated George. 'Absolutely. That's exactly what we have to do. We've got carbon and water – now we need you to find us a location where we can identify space proteins, Cosmos.'

Obligingly, Cosmos opened up the doorway to space, drawing a rectangle with beams of light, which then filled out to become a solid, door-shaped object hovering just above the floor in George's kitchen. When the door swung back, the view was not of anywhere inside George's house – or even any location on planet Earth.

Over the threshold, once again, lay space itself – enormous, unexplored, mysterious and mostly empty, apart from events of extreme violence or patches of terrifying beauty. In some parts, you might land safely on a distant exoplanet in orbit around a star other than our sun. In others, you might drift through the great clouds of a nebula. Or you might find yourself battling against the explosive, angry forces of a quasar, one of the most luminous, energetic and powerful objects in the Universe. The Universe itself was dangerous enough, and their previous space journeys had been fraught with peril – but at least on those adventures they had been able to rely on Cosmos to help them out of danger. Now it looked like the supercomputer was all too keen for them to walk straight into it. It was a terrifying prospect.

'Wow!' Annie breathed as she and George looked out through the doorway onto the seemingly endless landscape of space. But as Cosmos zoomed closer into his chosen spot, the view grew darker and murkier – until it looked as though the portal led into a sand storm, with rocks and dust whistling by at great speed.

'Where is this?' George asked Cosmos in amazement and horror as he watched the chunks of debris flying past, so close that he could almost have reached out and caught one – though they were moving at such a speed they would have snapped off his hand if he'd tried it.

'This is a disc of dust around a young proto-star, around 375 light years from Earth,' said Cosmos calmly. 'In the interior of this disc, you will find some of the basic materials needed to make the kind of proteins that Annie seeks; the sort that are found in the building blocks of life itself.'

Through the doorway, they saw larger lumps of rock smashing into each other, swirling around in the chaotic and violent environment of a young solar system. Everything was travelling in the same direction, but within the stream of material there were still sizzling crashes and mighty impacts.

THE BUILDING BLOCKS OF LIFE

Life (plants, animals and humans) is based around the element carbon. This is because it is better at forming very complex and stable molecules than any other element. There is also a lot of it in the Universe, carbon being the fourth most abundant element. These facts mean that, apart from hydrogen, there are more known molecules containing carbon than all the other elements put together.

However, you need more than just carbon to create life. Another essential piece is water. Around 60% of the human body is water. It is so important because it is involved in many of the processes that make the body work and also it is involved in, and makes a very good solvent for, the reactions that are needed to make the complex molecules that life is made from.

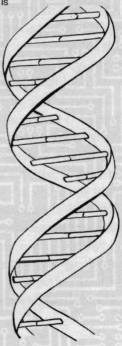

A very important set of these complex molecules that life is made from are called amino acids, which contain carbon, hydrogen, oxygen, nitrogen and sulfur. There are only 20 different amino acids in the human body but they combine in lots of different ways to make much larger molecules called proteins. These are found throughout the body and have many different jobs: they help make hair, muscles and ligaments; they help provide structure to the cells in your body; they are in blood; they help you digest your food and do all sorts of other important jobs in your body.

So, you can see how in just a few steps, very simple things like atoms can become something as complex as life.

Toby

'This is how the Earth was formed,' murmured Annie. 'Cosmos is showing us how a solar system comes into being and how it gets the ingredients to create life.'

'Please step through the doorway!' ordered Cosmos.

'No thanks,' said George quickly. There was no way he or Annie were joining that swirling high-speed soup. 'C'mon, Cosmos! We can't go through that portal – we need a destination in a nearby solar system where we can safely go for a little spacewalk. Can you change the portal location, please?'

'Negative.' Cosmos sounded quite unpleasant now. 'I can't open the portal for no one to go through. That's against my operational rules.'

'Is it?' said Annie in surprise. 'I've never heard you say that before.'

'I'm running a new operating system now.' Cosmos confirmed their fears that he was no longer the same computer they had known and loved.

Annie and George looked at each other in horror, wishing they had never thought up this plan. If only they could time-travel back by half an hour and change it.

'Such an action – opening the portal with no passenger to transport – will cause me to crash, with fatal errors,' Cosmos went on.

'*We'll* have a fatal error if we step out into that,' said George, viewing the dangerous scene beyond the doorway. Even Ebot would only last seconds if he was sent into that roiling cauldron. George could see that Annie was glancing around frantically as she tried to think of a way out of this predicament. His heart sank – he could tell that she had no more idea what to do now than he did.

'Someone,' said Cosmos nastily, 'has to go through the portal door.'

At that moment someone – or three someones; or rather, two someones and an android – came back into the kitchen: the twins were dragging a rather ruffled-looking Ebot with them.

'Breakfast,' said Hera in a very determined voice as she unglued her sticky hand from Ebot's.

'Oooh,' said Juno, pointing at the doorway. 'Sand!'

'We can't,' George told Cosmos firmly. Perhaps he just needed to stand his ground. Maybe he would be able to win the computer over by rational argument. 'We can't send anyone or anything through the portal into that place – as you know perfectly well, Cosmos.'

Ebot was smiling in a kindly fashion as Hera jumped up and down on his foot. He must have put the space helmet down somewhere as his hands were now free. Juno was still transfixed by what lay through the doorway.

'Build sandcastle?' she asked Annie hopefully, pointing to the place where the spinning rocks hurtled past.

'No, Juno,' said Annie, gathering the little girl up

onto her lap and holding her very tightly. 'No babies in space. That's not allowed.'

'A space passenger has to go through the portal,' said Cosmos in a threatening voice. 'If nothing physically passes across the threshold, the system will explode!'

Annie looked sadly at Ebot, who was now entertaining Hera with a tap-dancing routine, whisking his feet out of the way as she tried to trip him up.

'It's funny,' she said to George. 'When I thought about sending him to space before, I wasn't bothered what happened to Ebot. But now it makes me feel really miserable. It's like we'd be sending him to his death, and that just isn't fair.'

'Well, he isn't alive, so he can't actually die,' reasoned George. But he agreed with Annie. 'We still can't let him go through the portal. To start with, it would be wrong; and if Ebot is destroyed, we'd have even less chance of working out what's going on.'

'*Who* is going into space?' Cosmos's voice sounded really horrible; it was the sort of voice that sent chills down the spines of all who heard it. Even the two toddlers shivered; Juno hugged Annie even more closely and Hera hung onto Ebot's leg.

'If no one goes into space, I will explode, and take this whole house with me. None of you would survive such a calamitous event.'

Annie's jaw dropped and George's eyes were as round as marbles. He gulped. 'Blow up the whole house?' he said in disbelief. 'You wouldn't – you couldn't – do that!' For a minute he imagined what that would look like: if the house exploded, all the other houses in the street would go up with it, creating a domino effect. The whole road would be destroyed.

'There's one way to find out,' said Cosmos. 'Let's put me to the test, shall we?'

'But you would annihilate yourself as well!' said Annie in a high-pitched voice. 'Why would you do that? Don't you want to survive?'

'I'm not a living being,' said Cosmos. 'I just do what I'm ordered to do by the rules that govern my operating system. This is a rule, and I will be forced to follow it if you don't send someone through the portal.'

There was a moment's silence.

'Are you *sure*?' asked Annie slowly, as though she was giving the supercomputer the chance to back down. 'Are you sure this is what you have to do?'

'Yes,' replied Cosmos. 'I can – and will – auto-destruct any time I like. In fact, it's a security feature your father recently fitted me with in case I was captured by hostile hands. And I can do it in a very spectacular fashion. Would you like to see some fireworks? Oh, sorry . . .' The computer sniggered. 'Would you like to *be* a firework?'

'I'll unplug you,' said Annie, who sounded close to tears.

'I can't allow you to do that,' said Cosmos. 'If you

try, I will blow the system anyway.'

'Annie,' said George decisively, 'there's only one thing for it. We're going to have to send Ebot into space or we are all going to be reduced to dust rather than life forms!'

'Ebot . . .' Annie called softly.

The android turned round, giving her a smile that was so exactly like her father's that her heart turned over.

'I can't do it,' she wailed to George.

'I'll take over,' he said. 'Ebot!' He was sitting on the other side of the space doorway, and now gently but firmly called the robot and motioned him forward. 'Hang on.' George turned to Annie. 'He's not wearing his helmet!'

'It's not like he's going to need it,' said Annie grimly.

'True,' said George. He realized this space trip was not going to help them understand the situation in the world at large. Right now, they needed to concentrate on saving their own lives before they could save anyone else. 'Ebot,' he continued. 'We need you to come here. Step forward through the space portal.'

But George didn't see until it was too late that Hera was still attached to Ebot's leg. The android limped forward, carrying Hera along on his left foot, until he stood facing the doorway to space.

Suddenly Annie noticed George's sister and gave a loud scream, pointing at her.

George had a moment of blood-curdling terror when he realized that his stubborn little sister was facing certain death. Ebot was still edging forward . . . any minute now he would cross the threshold to space and be gone.

'C'mon, Hera,' said George urgently. 'Let go.'

'Shan't!' She held onto Ebot's leg, her favourite doll tucked under her arm.

'Hera' – George used his deepest voice, hoping he sounded a bit like his dad – 'you have to let go!'

'Won't!' she yelled, clinging on even more tightly.

The android was moving ever closer to the threshold; he looked as if he might step into the maelstrom at any moment, taking little Hera with him.

'Careful, George!' Annie was wide-eyed with alarm now. Juno had buried her face in her shoulder, frightened by the tone of panic in her voice. 'You might make him fall over and he'll take Hera with him. Ebot, STOP! Don't go any further!'

But either Ebot hadn't heard or he was still working on fulfilling the earlier command. He stood on the threshold, silhouetted against a backdrop of shattering collisions and explosions around the dusty young star.

'Hera!' ordered George. 'Let go of Ebot's leg! He's going to jump and you MUST LET GO!'

'NOOOOO!' wailed Hera, gripping Ebot's robotic calf with all her might. George tried to prise her little fingers open but couldn't budge them. But Hera

was so focused on hanging onto Ebot that her doll, usually clamped to her side, was dangling loosely by a single foot. Taking advantage of the moment, George grabbed the doll and threw her  into the storm beyond the doorway. It was a desperate move, he knew, and he could only hope that the action of propelling something through the door would be enough to force Cosmos to shut down the space portal.

He acted so quickly that he didn't have time to wonder if his sister might attempt to rescue her favourite doll; and in truth, Hera might well have done so if she hadn't been so transfixed by watching what happened next.

For a nano-second they saw the doll's bright yellow hair against the backdrop of dust as she spun through the portal. Swept along, she seemed to turn and wave, and then disappeared for ever, torn into tiny pieces . . . perhaps to be reassembled, many millions of years later, as part of a planet.

George just had time to insert himself firmly between Hera and outer space, pushing her and Ebot backwards, away from the threshold, with all his might.

'There!' he yelled to Cosmos, holding tightly to Hera while Ebot continued to inch his way forward.

'Someone has gone through the portal. You never said it had to be someone human or something alive – you just said it had to be a passenger! We've done it! You have to close the door.'

'Cosmos, close the door!' screamed Annie. 'Close it *now*! We've done what you commanded. You told us that something had to physically pass across the portal, and it has! You *have* to follow your own rules! That's what you told us!'

With a slam, the space portal closed, leaving George lying on the floor, a bulwark between his sister and Ebot, and space. Ebot toppled over backwards, Hera still attached to his ankle.

Just as the space doorway evaporated into thin air, leaving no trace, two other doors burst open: the front and the back. George's mum and dad rushed in through the front door; while Annie's mum came in through the back. All three looked as though they had had the shock of their lives.

'You'll never guess!' they gasped in unison.

'Oh, try us,' said Annie. 'You never know . . .'

Chapter Ten

Annie's mum, Susan, and George's parents, Terence and Daisy, looked boggle-eyed with surprise.

George and Annie did a quick scan of the scene in the kitchen, to check there were no telltale signs that would lead their parents to suspect a near-fatal space adventure had just taken place. But apart from a faint sprinkling of dust where the space doorway had opened and a few beings such as Ebot and Hera lying on the floor, there were very few clues. The grown ups would surely never notice that anything was amiss. Just to be on the safe side, Annie tried to grind the space dust into the floor with her foot.

'Annie!' her mother complained, noticing what she was up to. 'Did you bring that dirt into George's house on your trainers?'

'Oh, sorry – I'll sweep it up,' she said quickly. It was so like a mum, even when a national emergency was erupting, to notice that the floor was dirty.

'Door,' said Hera, pointing at nothing while still hanging onto Ebot. 'My dolly!' She burst into tears. Letting go of the android's leg and leaping up, she flung herself at George and started hitting him, small fists flailing wildly.

'Whoa . . . Hera!' George grabbed the pudgy little hands and gently restrained her.

Juno joined in. 'Dolly went through door,' she explained helpfully, pointing to where the space portal had been; but for once, no one was listening.

'Yes, yes,' said Terence vaguely, clutching a couple of empty canvas bags, obviously thinking they were talking gibberish. 'Door, dolly – whatever. Kids, I don't want you leaving the house. Things are even worse than we thought.'

Ebot sat up from his prone position on the floor and Hera installed herself comfortably on his knees.

'Why, what's happened now?' asked Annie. What else could *possibly* happen?'

'You know that the price of food rocketed yesterday,' said Daisy, 'because everyone had lots of free money but the food deliveries got held up?'

'Well, now' – Annie's mum suddenly sounded just like her daughter – 'the supermarkets can't charge for their food! Every time someone tries to ring an item through on the till, it comes up as zero pounds and zero pence!'

'But no one is trying to put things through the till

any more,' added Terence. 'They gave up and just started grabbing stuff off the shelves – anything they could get their hands on. We saw folks arriving with bags, suitcases, even a wheelie bin, to take free stuff home with them.'

'And they started fighting!' said Daisy. 'It was horrible – people were punching each other to get to the food and water. Nothing costs anything, so everyone just wanted to take as much as they could. It's a free-for-all – literally!'

'It was terrifying.' Susan shuddered. 'It wasn't like being in Foxbridge at all; it was like being in the middle of a war zone. The police weren't doing anything – they were helping themselves as well.'

'Right, kids,' said Terence. 'This is a very serious situation. We couldn't get anywhere near the cooperative to rescue our own food stocks, we couldn't find out about any nearby safe houses, so we need to dig up whatever we can from the garden.'

Everyone's heads swivelled to look through the window at the vegetable patch.

'There isn't much there,' said Daisy regretfully. The moment for self-sufficiency had arrived and, to her chagrin, it was not the season of abundance. 'It's not really harvest time of year, you know. We've only got lettuces and radishes.'

'George, Annie . . . in a minute, I want you to go into the garden and pick what you can,' ordered Terence. 'It may not be much but it's better than nothing. It will still provide us with vital nutrients while we sit out the siege.'

'What about Dad?' Annie asked her mum before she followed George out to salvage what they could from the vegetable patch. 'Where *is* he? And when's he coming back?'

'I think he's still stuck in some nuclear bunker with the Prime Minister, advising her on what happens when all computer systems break down . . .' Annie's mum wrung her hands with worry. 'I wish we could contact him and find out how long he thinks this will go on for! I know we're not supposed to phone, but in the circumstances, I think we could—'

177

LUCY & STEPHEN HAWKING

'We can't. My phone's not working!' said Annie. 'What about yours, Mum? Have you got any signal?'

'I'll have to look for it . . .' Susan was always losing her mobile. 'It must be around somewhere . . .'

'Stop chatting! Actions, not words,' ordered Terence, who seemed to have assumed the role of leader. 'Supermarkets will be entirely emptied by now. Farmers have probably locked their gates. Food banks will have been looted and all suppliers will have barricaded their warehouses.'

'What are we going to do?' Susan fretted.

'We are going to need to lie low until the crisis has passed,' Terence went on calmly. 'And we need to stay safe. We will all take up residence in the basement.'

'Does that include us?' Susan wondered out loud.

'Women and children will always find a safe haven when I'm in charge.' Terence, whose father had been in the army, saluted her crisply.

'I know!' she said. 'I've got a whole pile of sleeping bags and duvets next door! Goodness knows if my family will be coming now. I haven't heard from them . . . I'll go and get the bedding – we can use them to make the basement more comfy.'

'Dad?' questioned George. 'Don't you think someone should stay above ground, as a lookout? I mean, what if the crisis passes and we don't realize because we're all in the basement? Should we take it in turns to keep watch from the treehouse?'

'Excellent idea, George.' Terence was no longer the quiet pacifist vegan recycler they knew and loved.

'Me and George should take first watch,' Annie jumped in quickly. Just like George, she had realized that if they got stuck in the basement with their parents, they would be powerless to intervene in events in the world outside.

'No – I've got a better idea,' piped up Annie's mum. 'Didn't you say you've got some special glasses which you can use to see through that robot's eyes? In that case, we can put him on lookout and you can watch through the glasses.'

'Rats,' muttered Annie. She hadn't expected her mum to be so quick to come up with a solution.

Susan went back next door to retrieve her unusually large stocks of bedding while Annie and George grabbed buckets and started raiding the vegetable patch for anything they could find to help their two families survive the emergency.

Chapter Eleven

As they grubbed around in the thin earth of the back garden, everything seemed to have gone unnaturally quiet, as if in anticipation of some kind of massive impact. Their little corner of Foxbridge was always quite peaceful, but right then, it felt as though the Earth was silently waiting for some catastrophic event. The skies were empty; not even a tiny plane buzzed overhead. Traffic seemed to have come to a halt, and there was almost no sound of human habitation. Just birds chirping their melodies, and insects busy pollinating the spring flowers. No music blared from radios, no phones rang, no television shows played on large flat screens. The hubbub of human life had stopped abruptly – as though people themselves had been totally erased, leaving the Earth to be taken over by other life forms.

But something about the sinister quality of the silence made George think it wasn't going to last. The minutes ticked by, and the longer he waited for it to break, the more worried he grew.

Daisy and the twins had come out to help in the

garden, but they were all just standing there quietly, watching George and Annie fill their buckets with leaves and roots.

'Daisy,' ordered Terence, coming out into the garden, 'I want you to take the twins inside and start packing whatever supplies we have to carry down to the basement. We need dry food, water, wind-up torches – anything you can stash down there. We may need to stay underground for days on end – we can't risk coming back up. We'll take the radio and hope that transmissions will resume to let us know that the chaos is over.'

Daisy nodded, ushering Juno and Hera inside with her. Even they seemed intimidated by the strange atmosphere.

Susan returned from next door, bringing with her not just armfuls of bedding but a person; a very elderly and dishevelled-looking person who was just recognizable as the former code-breaker George and Annie had met with Eric a few days earlier.

'I found her on the doorstep,' said Susan, sweeping past them and heading for the basement with the bedding.

'Beryl!' exclaimed Annie in astonishment. 'What are you doing here?'

'I didn't know where else to go,' she admitted. 'And I thought that if anyone could explain what in heaven's name is going on, it would be Eric.'

'He's not here,' Annie told her. 'He's the "Information Technology Czar" so he had to go and meet the PM.'

'Tsk! What silly titles they give people these days!' said Beryl, who despite her appearance seemed remarkably bright-eyed, almost as if she was enjoying herself. 'Well, isn't this fun. Reminds me of the good old days!'

'You'll have to go down to the basement,' said Annie. 'I don't think George's dad will let you hang around up here.'

'Oh, marvellous!' enthused Beryl. 'It will be just like the Blitz all over again! I do hope there's some sherry down there!' With incredible agility, she headed down the steps into the basement, humming a favourite wartime tune as she went.

'What are we going to do?' Annie hissed to George as she picked up her bucket.

'Where's Cosmos?' he asked urgently.

'Still indoors. Shall we just leave him there?'

'I think we should get him,' said George.

'But he's evil!' squeaked Annie. 'He's turned to the dark side!'

'I know that . . . But we might be able to use his own rules on him, to help us out. I think we should get him.'

'OK.' Annie slunk inside with her bucket and returned a few moments later, showing George that she had stashed Cosmos, the world's greatest computer, under a pile of salad leaves. 'But I still don't get what 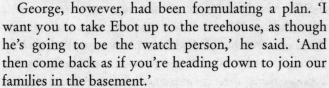 we're actually going to do,' she whispered.

George, however, had been formulating a plan. 'I want you to take Ebot up to the treehouse, as though he's going to be the watch person,' he said. 'And then come back as if you're heading down to join our families in the basement.'

'What do you mean?'

'We'll pretend we're going to live in the basement with them,' said George. 'But then we'll lock them in and stay outside ourselves.'

'Lock them in?' gasped Annie in horror.

'We have to! If we don't, there's no *way* they'll let

us crack this. Our parents will make us hang out with them and eat thermoses of soup and sing stupid songs, while outside, the whole world will fall to pieces! And we won't be able to do anything about it.'

'What can we do?' asked Annie. 'Isn't this all getting a bit big for two kids?'

'No, Annie!' said George firmly. 'I thought that before, but there's no one else here to do it, and we have to try. Even your dad isn't having any effect. We've got to do something, Annie. Like Beryl – if she hadn't helped to crack that code during the war, millions more people would have died. So even if we just do something small, it might make a difference.'

'You're on,' said Annie, squaring up her shoulders, impressed by his words. 'In that case, I'm with you. I'm not going to hide in a basement. I'm going to help. We can do this. We *can*.'

Soon the little back garden was as bare as on a winter's day. No edible leaf was left on a stalk. Every shred of vegetable life had been plucked, pulled, dug up or cut, then bundled down the stairs to the basement to form part of their supplies for what could be a long stay.

By now Daisy had taken the twins safely downstairs, and they were listening to her read them their favourite book about a caterpillar who couldn't stop eating on Saturdays.

As she read by the light of her torch, Terence and Susan were busy arranging the final details of their hideaway, while Annie passed snacks, water bottles and comic books down through the trapdoor.

'You two go down there,' she insisted bossily. Terence wasn't the only one able to summon his inner tyrant at will. 'That's it! Right down. And I'll pass the rest of the stuff to you. Oh look, here's George! He can finish off.' She gave him a very meaningful look. 'I'll take Ebot up to the treehouse and install him,' she said very clearly. 'And then, when I come back down, George and I will follow you down to the basement. Capish?'

The adults nodded solemnly, too focused on their own plans to turn the basement into a comfortable and cosy living space to suspect the pair of treachery.

Annie rescued Ebot, who had been left forlornly deactivated in the sitting room. She found and jammed Eric's space helmet onto the robot's head and, half supporting him, staggered over to the treehouse ladder, which was fortunately lowered. She propped the android Eric against the tree while she felt around in her pockets for the remote access glasses, put them on and used the eye-gaze control to wake Ebot out of his sleep.

He came alive with a jerk and a squawk.

'Climb the ladder,' Annie instructed him.

Stumbling and awkward, Ebot started to ascend the swaying ladder, like an ungainly spider in a spacesuit

scaling a wall. Annie shimmied up after him with the bucket containing Cosmos. Ebot fell rather than climbed onto the platform; Annie leaped over him, setting the bucket down, then went over to look through George's telescope. The town still appeared quiet and sleepy, but a frisson in the air told her that thunder, of one sort or another, was on its way.

'Wait here,' she instructed her robot friend, before shinning back down to the ground again and running over to where George was hovering by the double trap-door that led to the basement.

Looking down, she gazed at the upturned faces: her mother, George's parents and the two small girls. Suddenly she knew that George wouldn't actually be

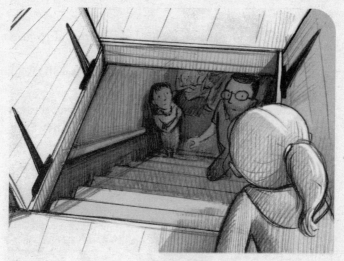

able to do what was needed. And in that second, she also realized that it was her turn to be brave and act on her words.

'I'm sorry,' Annie mouthed. And then she flipped both doors down and shot the bolt across before the people in the basement had a chance to stop her. She just had time to see the look of shock on their faces. And then they disappeared from view, sealed into the underground hidey-hole.

But they were not sealed for sound. 'Hey!' Terence banged loudly on the door from below. 'What do you think you're doing? You can't stay up there. Open the doors! *Open the doors, I say!*'

'Sorry!' Annie shouted down towards the basement.

'We'll explain. Later.'

She grabbed George and wheeled him round to face the back door. 'Run!' she said.

A lone voice floated after them: it was Beryl. 'Well done, you two! Good luck!'

Together, they pelted towards the treehouse, scrambled up the ladder and drew it up behind them. They both automatically lay down on the platform, out of sight from below. As an afterthought, George reached up and pulled Ebot down beside them. Now anyone looking up from the ground  would just see an empty treehouse, inaccessible to anyone but the birds and the most sure-footed of climbers.

At this point neither George nor Annie could have said exactly why they behaved as they did; their instincts for survival seemed to have taken over, prompting them to take cover.

Their instincts were sound: they had reached their treetop hideaway with only seconds to spare. As they lay there, panting and breathless, they heard a noise in the distance which got louder and louder as it approached George's house. At first it was just white noise; they couldn't differentiate individual sounds. But soon they could make out shouts, crashes, yelps, explosions and thuds.

'What is it?' Annie was trembling. George's idea of remaining outside the sanctuary of the basement had been a brave one, but she wondered now if it had been sensible. This was seriously scary.

Annie didn't need to wait for an answer. Underneath the treehouse, the ground shook as a gang of looters invaded the back garden, flattening the fences and churning up the ground as they charged across. They smashed windows and doors, rampaging through the

LUCY & STEPHEN HAWKING

houses in their search for food. From their hideaway the pair heard dogs barking, then screams as people got hurt. As they peered out of the treehouse, they saw the mob fighting for possession of the few items left behind by householders who had already fled the area. Luckily they passed through quickly – although it felt like hours to Annie and George. Within minutes the gang had moved on down the row of houses until they were out of sight.

'Yowza!' whispered Annie. 'That was nasty. Your dad was right about the danger.'

George breathed out heavily. The pounding of his heart had almost blocked out the noise of the rioters. 'Good call,' he agreed, 'to get everyone into the basement.' He couldn't bear to think what might have happened to his little sisters and parents, to Beryl and Annie's mum, if they hadn't hidden. He hoped that Eric really *was* in some kind of uber-safe location with the Prime Minister, and not out on the streets, but he thought it was better not to mention this to Annie. Things were bad enough without adding other fears as well.

'Do you reckon they're OK?' whispered Annie, her voice trembling.

'Yup, they're fine,' said George confidently. To his surprise, once his heart rate dropped, he started to feel much better. While the riot was going on, he'd wondered if he was going to stay frozen to the platform

190

with fear for ever. But now that he knew it was time for him and Annie to leap into action, he suddenly found within himself a whole extra stock of bravery. 'Probably a bit dusty, but I don't think anyone found them. They just ripped straight through the kitchen and out the other side.'

'What now?' asked Annie quietly.

Below them, in the ravaged garden, a few stragglers charged across the flattened fences, pausing to hurl the odd stone through the few remaining unbroken windows, before taking off again.

'They're just smashing anything they can.' Annie was disgusted.

'That's why we need to be quick,' said George. 'If anyone sees us up here, we could be in big trouble. I mean, big-like-the-Universe trouble.'

'Be quick with what?'

'We've got to try again,' George replied. 'You know, if at first you don't succeed . . . ! Your idea about getting Ebot captured so we could see who this I AM is and what it is up to is the best we've got. But this time we need to give Cosmos more specific instructions so that he places Ebot somewhere he'll be found.'

'So we've got to carry on doing my chemistry project?' asked Annie in amazement. The world was falling to bits and she was still doing her homework! It was so normal and yet so weird all at once that she couldn't quite take it in. 'Even though it's apocalypse time?'

'Yup.' George was amazed at his own confidence. 'We'll tell Cosmos we need to work on the next element of life, and then we'll send Ebot through the doorway . . . Ebot is wearing your Dad's spacesuit already so the fact that your dad is travelling through the space portal should be broadcast out there. Isn't that how I AM found us before?'

'You're right!' Annie got Cosmos out of the bucket, brushed off some lettuce leaves and a small slug, opened him up and pressed the power button.

'Do we need our suits?' asked George.

'Um, we might do,' Annie realized. 'It depends. But they're in Dad's study.'

George was already letting down the rope ladder.

'You can't!' she squeaked. 'It's too dangerous! What if they come back?'

'I'll be very quick,' said George confidently. 'Get Cosmos working and open up the portal. I'll be back in a nano-flash.'

'Okey-doke,' said Annie as he disappeared from view. 'Let's get this show on the road . . . Cosmos!' She took a very deep breath as the computer came to life. 'I want to carry on with my chemistry project. I want you to look for amino acids in space. I want you to summon the space portal and open the doorway onto a comet in the Solar System where I can find amino acids, which are the building blocks of life.'

Chapter Twelve

George scrambled back across the empty vegetable patch and went through the fence into the mysterious dense jungle of Annie's back garden. He ran up the path, but suddenly stopped in his tracks. The back door of the Bellises' house had been ripped off its hinges and thrown to one side. All the windows had been smashed. George picked his way across the broken glass and into the house, and found the furniture overturned, the fridge door hanging open and the cupboards ransacked. Bags of flour and sugar, which had clearly burst when they'd been snatched out of the cupboards, lay on the floor, spilling their contents all over the terracotta tiles. Someone had stamped on a bottle of lemonade, which had sprayed across the cupboards and floor, mixing with the flour and sugar to form a gooey mess. Nearby lay a row of empty plastic tubes which looked like they belonged in a lab, not in a domestic fridge. The contents of these tubes seemed to have leaked out and joined the sticky lake on the floor, giving it a greenish glow. It looked as though Eric and Annie's experiments had met an untimely end.

'Urgh!' George to pick his way across the slimy floor but he slithered on broken egg mixed with jam – which catapulted him across the kitchen, into the cold arms of the open fridge.

'Ow, ow, ow!' he muttered to himself, rubbing his nose, which had collided with a shelf. All the food had gone, even the old pots of unwanted jam and mustard that usually lived at the top. Someone had reached into the fridge – and the freezer and all the cupboards – and swept out the contents, leaving behind only the damaged items, which had been thrown on the floor to make a horrible soup of nasty fizzing sticky chemicals and food.

George gingerly edged his way across the kitchen, but stopped when he noticed Susan's phone surfing on a pile of gunk in the corner. Somehow, in all the chaos, her lost phone had managed to reappear – if he could reach it, he could try calling Eric!

Eric never knew what to do in normal situations – there was no point in asking him how long you should boil an egg for or who was number one on iTunes. But he was at his best when great cosmic accidents happened, or when the world was threatened by evil, or when an alien appeared. In those circumstances, he was more useful than anyone else in the whole world. Right now, it would be really handy to know what Eric thought was going on.

George tried to make his way across to the phone to find out if it still worked. But almost immediately he

skidded, his arms flailing, looking like a surfer trying to negotiate a huge wave. As he crashed into the kitchen cupboards on the other side of the room, he realized that he was wasting precious time. In the distance he heard a roar – the same sound they had heard before the looters swept across the gardens, plundering each house as they went. It might only be minutes before they returned, desperate to scavenge any scraps they'd missed the first time round. George slithered his way round the room, feeling as if he was ice skating, and decided to give up on the phone. This time, he teetered into the hallway and headed towards Eric's study.

Of all the rooms in the house, the study seemed to have suffered the least damage. It must have been ignored by the mob. A few books had been pulled out of the shelves, but otherwise the room was untouched. George quickly found what he was looking for: a couple of spacesuits, along with all the clobber that went with them. But how could he carry everything? He decided to put on the spare suit and boots. The space boots were so big, he could fit them on over his ordinary shoes. Zipping himself in, he tied the arms of the other suit around his neck, looking as if he was carrying a very floppy person on his back. Then he put on a pair of space boots and clipped another space helmet around his wrist along with the other pair of boots. He stomped out of the study in the heavy space boots. They had far more grip than his trainers, and he

crossed the slippery kitchen floor easily, without falling over once. He marched out of the house and back across the garden, a spacesuit fluttering behind him like a flag, not noticing that some of the chemical ingredients from the kitchen floor had decided to come with him.

Up in the treehouse, Annie had switched Cosmos off to save power, and arranged things on the platform so that Ebot could step through the space portal without falling out of the tree. While she was doing that, she kept a worried eye out for George. There were no grown-ups around now if anything went wrong. Cosmos was more like an irritating know-it-all older cousin, and could now no longer be relied on to help them. She and George really were on their own in a strange and hostile world. The only person – and he wasn't even a person – on their side was Ebot, and in the end, he would do whatever he was ordered to do, no matter what that might be. He wasn't able to distinguish between what he should and should not do.

While she was waiting, Annie heard a scuffling noise, which made her draw in her breath sharply. Screwing up all her courage, she peered over the edge of the treehouse. As soon as she saw George climbing the ladder in his spacesuit, with the other one flying out behind him, she gave a deep sigh of relief.

George stomped across the platform and threw down the space gear.

But Annie was perplexed. 'What's that on your space boot?' Annie was pointing to a glistening blob of glowing slime.

'It must be from your kitchen floor. But – hang on . . . it looks like it's moving!' George realized. 'It's like it's alive!'

'What slime? Where did it come from?'

'What does your dad keep in the fridge at the moment?'

'Dunno for sure,' Annie replied. 'He had some experiments sealed in test tubes in the fridge door, but he said I wasn't to touch them – ever.'

'I'd just like to know what this weird stuff is, and why it seems to be spreading,' said George.

'It's probably those protein crystals that Dad grew in space,' Annie told him. 'He does that – he goes to space to grow stuff that doesn't grow as fast on Earth. Now, listen, can we get on with things here?'

'OK, then . . . what now?' George turned to gaze anxiously across Foxbridge. It seemed quiet and still again, but they knew from experience how quickly that could change.

'Amino acids,' said Annie decisively. 'They're the next ingredient in my recipe for life.'

George looked down at his boot. He was sure the slime had moved again, but it didn't seem the moment to mention it; in terms of priorities, it wasn't number one.

'Where do we find them?' he asked.

'I've given Cosmos the command' – with the computer turned off, she was able to talk freely – 'to find a comet in our solar system. Comets are just the kind of place where we might find tiny amounts of amino acids. And it's the ideal location for Ebot to be kidnapped, especially if we dress him in Dad's spacesuit and make him use Dad's space call sign. He'll be obvious, just sitting in the middle of a comet! If I AM is monitoring all computer activity, Dad or Ebot's presence in space should be noticed straight away.'

'Brilliant!' said George. 'But will they be able to pick him up from a comet, rather than the Moon?'

'Well, how would I know?' Annie sounded tense. 'We've just got to try it; if it doesn't work, I'll have to persuade Cosmos that we need to look for amino acids on the Moon. That would be a bit awkward, as I don't think there are any. Let's put ours on too!' she added.

'Annie, are we actually going into space?' asked George. 'We can't use Cosmos's space portal again – it's not safe.'

'No, I agree.' She nodded. 'But do you remember last time we were on a comet? It didn't have that much gravity. If Ebot lands there, he might just fall off and drift through space.'

LUCY & STEPHEN HAWKING

'Yeah, good point,' said George. 'What are we going to do about that?'

'We put on our spacesuits,' said Annie decisively, 'and just kind of reach through the doorway so we can peg him down onto the comet without actually stepping through ourselves. How about that?'

'OK, I get it!' said George. 'It's good.'

Annie quickly got dressed in the spacesuit George had brought for her. 'Let's get that portal open,' George instructed Annie.

She pressed the command on Cosmos's keyboard.

'Greetings,' said the great computer; it sounded as if he was smirking. 'How may I assist you?'

'We're ready for you to open a space portal onto a comet in our solar system so that we can investigate amino acids in space for my chemistry project,' Annie reminded him, shoving her feet into the space boots. 'We – that is me, my friend George and my father Eric, who is just over there – would like to use your space portal for our research.'

'Eric?' said Cosmos in some excitement. 'Eric is going into space?'

The friends glanced at each other – would this work?

'Yes, that's right,' Annie confirmed. 'Can you make that happen for us?'

'Affirmative,' replied Cosmos. 'I have already located a comet in the region of Jupiter.'

'OK.' Now entirely encased in her spacesuit, Annie

200

saluted George. She propped up Ebot and held him at the ready.

George wondered about the probability of their plan working. Now, instead of a normal half-term holiday, he was about to push an android through a space portal onto a comet near Jupiter as a decoy for his best friend's dad. It was all so strange . . . better not to think about it too deeply or he would begin to freak out entirely.

'We won't be long,' said Annie. But she sounded very nervous too. 'We just have to collect the amino-acid sample and then return to Earth, OK? There's no need for you to even close the portal door behind us. In fact, I'd like you to leave it open. My father might walk out onto the comet, but George and I won't. Will this work with your rules? You won't try and blow us up again, will you?'

'Provided one passenger passes through the portal,' said Cosmos, 'there will be no errors of that description.'

The portal glowed, and gradually became a solid object through which the three of them could walk. The door opened and they saw a greyish-white, rocky expanse. On either side of Ebot, George and Annie prepared themselves to step through.

'Remember, the gravity will be lower!' Annie whispered out of Cosmos's hearing. 'So push Ebot through and we'll hold him down on the comet, hammer in the space pegs and let go.'

'Got it!' said George. 'Good luck in space!'

With that, they shoved the android in front of them, through the doorway and onto a comet. A comet in orbit around Jupiter, the most magnificent planet of all.

Chapter Thirteen

The last time George and Annie landed on a comet, they had fallen through space towards it, travelling in great circles until they touched down on the surface with a bump. That was on their first ever space journey together. Annie had opened up the space portal in a fit of pique, to prove to George that she knew how to fly in space. It had been the start of George's cosmic journeys; an amazing beginning to a series of strange and wonderful adventures.

But this time the space doorway didn't deposit them above the comet; it opened right onto the comet itself – and to George's relief, they were able to push Ebot through, exactly as planned, onto the crunchy, rock-strewn ground.

As soon as the android passed through, they felt the effects of the much lower gravity. He immediately flew up into the air, and they had to drag him down to the surface. The robot looked at them, a quizzical expression on his face visible through the space helmet. They knew it was impossible, but they wondered if it was an expression of betrayal; if he knew what they were up to.

'Here – quickly.' Annie passed some space pegs, a tiny space hammer and a length of space rope, which came as standard issue in each spacesuit, over to George. 'You jam a couple of pegs into the surface – try and tie him down so that he doesn't float away.'

It reminded George of helping his father mend the wind turbine. He carefully let go of Ebot and knelt down to thwack a couple of pegs into the crumbly surface of the comet, one on either side of the portal, waiting for the back kick of the reaction as he hammered. The android's legs were now floating around in the air, while Annie clung onto him from behind.

Neither of them were in the mood for sightseeing, but even so, they couldn't help noticing the extraordinary close-up view of the biggest planet in our solar system. However crazy and dangerous their current predicament had become, Jupiter wasn't something they could ignore. It hung before them, dominating the starry backdrop like a vastly outsize ball on which someone had painted an uneven row of tiger stripes.

'It's so . . . so Jupiter-ish!'  George heard Annie's voice whispering through the voice transmitter in his helmet. 'How did they know, hundreds of years ago, that it would be exactly the right name for it?'

'It's so red!' said George, taking a quick break from hammering in order to study the red spot – the storm that had been raging on Jupiter for over 300 years. Astronomers on Earth had been able to see it through telescopes for centuries, but he and Annie could now see it right before their eyes, and turning like a whirlpool of orangey red, against the distinctive cream and brown stripes of the mighty planet.

As George gazed at the awesome sight, he realized that Ebot was starting to drift away from the space doorway again.

'Hurry up!' Annie whispered, struggling to hold onto the robot.

'Done!' George said, winding a length of space rope around the pegs and then tying it to Ebot's suit loops, as though he was a helium balloon back on Earth. 'You can let go of him now!'

As Annie watched Ebot, silhouetted against the backdrop of Jupiter, she had a strange thought. When they travelled into space, they usually regarded going home as a journey back to safety; to what they knew best. This time things were very different. This time they both felt freer and safer in space than they had on Earth.

She pulled herself back through the space portal.

'Oops – we nearly forgot the main thing!' she exclaimed. 'We have to get Ebot to use Dad's call sign so that anyone who is tracking interspace communications thinks that he's in space. We don't know what Cosmos is passing on, so we need to make sure that I AM knows he is there.'

'I can't believe we forgot about that!' said George. 'Quick – call Ebot and get him to reply.'

'E-Eric,' said Annie. 'Can you reply to my signal?'

'Yes,' replied the robot.

'Are you in space?'

'Yes,' said the robot again.

'Are you on a comet?'

'Yes.'

'How long can we keep the doorway open?' George whispered to Annie.

'Not long,' she admitted. She checked Cosmos's battery life. It was running down fast. She tapped a few keys and zoomed the space portal out, so that Ebot seemed further away.

They watched him through the doorway for a few more minutes, but they were both horribly aware that it was getting much darker on planet Earth now. Even though it was early summer, and the northern hemisphere received much more daylight than it did in winter, the light couldn't hold for much longer; they realized that it was getting dangerous for them to stay outside. Cosmos and the space portal gave off a considerable glow, which, once it got dark in Fox-bridge, would be all too visible and make them a target if the mob returned.

'I think we'd better shut down the portal,' said George reluctantly. 'Anyway, Cosmos has hardly any battery life left. Space travel drains him of energy.'

They took one last lingering look at Ebot, floating gracefully like a tethered kite against the glistening, icy stream of gas and dust behind the comet. It looked like a small person on a jet ski was motoring across the sky.

'Bye, Ebo— er, I mean, Dad,' said Annie sadly. Then, whispering, 'I hope you get kidnapped soon.'

'Bye . . . er, Eric,' said George.

'Rats.' Annie's finger hovered over the keyboard, ready to give the command to shut down the portal. 'I was so sure this was going to work; I was so sure that I AM would be monitoring all space communication channels and that Dad showing up in space would cause him to swoop down on him like the robots did last time.'

'Perhaps we *should* have gone to the Moon,' said George. 'Maybe that's the only place I AM hangs out.'

'But how could we?' asked Annie. 'We can only get Cosmos to take us to a place where there's stuff for my chemistry project – and that's not the place where we needed to be.'

HOW LONG IS A 'DAY' ON EARTH?

Why is a day in winter shorter than a day in summer?

It's because the Earth tilts on its axis as it orbits around the Sun. If the Earth stayed upright throughout its whole orbit, day and night would be exactly the same length on all days of the year. But as the Earth orbits, it is at an angle of 23.5 degrees, and this means that at one point in its orbit, the North Pole and the region we call the Arctic Circle is angled so far away from the Sun that it receives no daylight at all.

In the Northern hemisphere, this happens between the 20 December and the 23 December, otherwise known as the Winter Solstice.

At the same time, in the Southern hemisphere, the South Pole is in full daylight for the whole 24-hour period. (In fact, a solar day is slightly under 24 hours but we round it up.)

As the Earth turns around the Sun, the tilt changes until it is the other way round. At the *Summer Solstice* (between 20 June and 22 June), it is daylight for the full 24 hours at the North Pole. The rest of the world in between the poles receives a varying amount of light, lengthening or shortening the days.

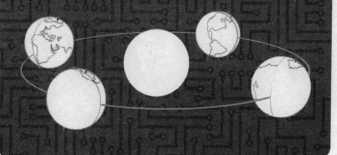

'Your dad said that looking for answers throughout the Universe was like a man looking for his keys under a lamppost,' said George. 'His keys aren't there, but it's the only place where there's enough light for him to look.'

'Yup, this is kind of the same.' Annie sounded sad. 'Well, I don't think we can wait any longer. Shall we try and get Ebot back before I shut it down?' She gave the command to zoom the portal in once more so that they could reach Ebot. But as she did so, George noticed a flash of red light on the comet.

'Annie, stand back!' he cried.

As she jumped back, away from the space doorway, they both saw a dot of bright red light latch onto Ebot's chest. A moment later, robot pincer hands were pulling roughly at the makeshift peg structure they'd used to tether him to the comet.

'They've got him!' George breathed. A second later, the space portal shut itself down as the supercomputer ran out of battery.

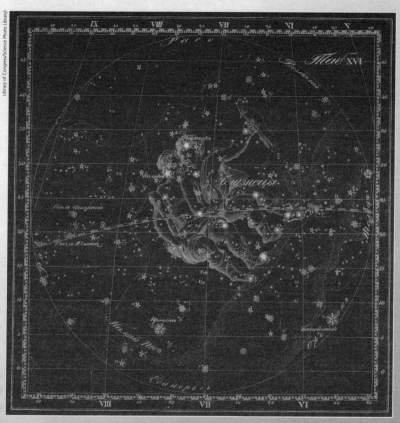

Gemini constellation, 1829

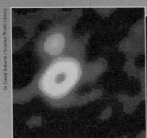

Radio map of the
double quasar

Twin Quasar

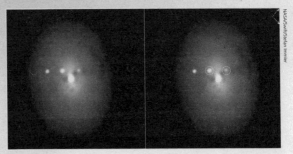

Twin star explosions

Odd galaxy pair

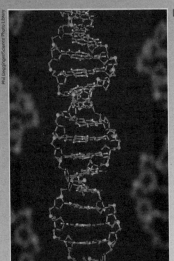

Double Helix

Optical SETI

Roger Harris/Science Photo Library

Space junk

NASA

View of Earth

Cosmic caterpillar

A collision:
June 20 2013

A brown
dwarf –
Jan 2013

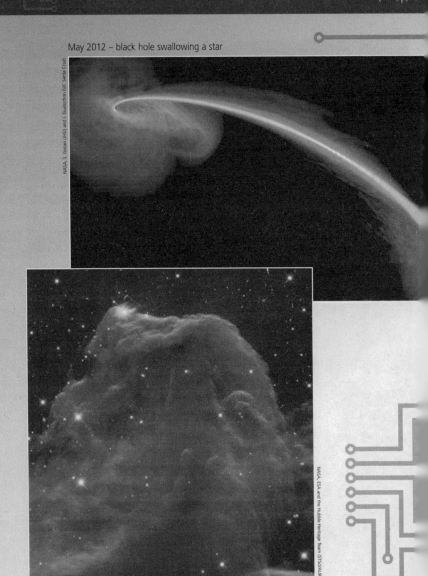

May 2012 – black hole swallowing a star

NASA, S. Gezari (JHU) and J. Guillochon (UC Santa Cruz)

NASA, ESA and the Hubble Heritage Team (STScI/AURA)

April 2013 – a Horsehead

Chapter Fourteen

'Ta-dah! I think I AM has captured Ebot!' Annie crowed.

'So all we need to do is wait for them to take him to the mother ship, and then we can check in with the glasses to find out where it is!' replied George.

Inside their space helmets, they were both beaming. They took them off and wriggled out of their suits.

'We did it! We got our robot captured! Result!' Annie looked very pleased with herself.

'Now we need to wait somewhere safe,' said George. 'I don't think we should stay in the treehouse when it gets really dark.' As he bent down to pull off one of his space boots, he noticed something.

'Annie . . .' he said slowly. 'You know that slime – the stuff that I picked up on my boot in your kitchen . . .'

'Yes.' She gazed at Cosmos's blank screen.

'It's gone.'

'What do you mean "gone"?' asked Annie, without looking up.

'That goo on my boot!' said George, pointing. 'It

was covered in slime, which kind of looked like it was moving! And now it's not there any more!'

'Whoa!' said Annie. 'What if it was actually alive . . . and it's wriggled its way onto the comet!'

'We told Cosmos we were looking for the ingredients for life and said that was why we had to go into space! But instead, we've taken life into space and left it there . . .' said George slowly.

'*We?*' said Annie, turning on her heel to glare at him.

'Well, you're the one investigating the ingredients for life,' he retorted.

'Yeah, but it wasn't me who stood in a great big puddle of living goo and then leant through the space portal – only to find that it had crawled off to start its own colony.'

In reply, George's tummy gave an almighty growl, followed by some interesting gurgles and moans.

The noise released the tension and they both burst out laughing. Quickly they stashed their spacesuits and helmets in the treehouse.

Meanwhile Cosmos was now in his deep sleep, no longer able to hear or communicate with them.

'What are we going to do?' Annie asked George quietly.

'We need to look through the glasses to see if we can

work out where Ebot has gone . . . and find a way to follow him.'

'And we might need shelter overnight,' said Annie. 'George, I'm almost scared,' she added.

'I was,' he admitted. 'But I'm not any more. I was scared when I was wondering about what it would be like if everything in the world collapsed. It was way more spooky when it was all in my head, but now that it's actually happening . . . We've just got to keep going, that's the main thing.'

'Do you think we can use Cosmos to go after Ebot, once we work out where he is?'

'I don't think so,' said George. 'Cosmos is just too dangerous. We have to assume that whoever is messing around with all the computer systems on Earth has also got into Cosmos and is making him behave strangely. And anyway, he's run out of power. Even if we wanted to use him, we couldn't . . . at least, not *that* Cosmos! C'mon, Annie, follow me! I've had an idea . . .'

Even as he spoke, he was already climbing down the rope ladder again. He jumped the last few rungs down onto solid ground and started to make his way across the garden to his back door.

'Careful!' he whispered to Annie, hearing a sharp crunch underfoot. 'Broken glass – smashed windows.'

Together they gingerly edged their way into George's kitchen, stepping lightly over the trapdoor that led down to where their families were hiding. They paused

for a second but could hear only the soothing murmurs of their mothers chatting.

George shook his head violently at Annie, to make sure she didn't say anything. But she just crept on, cat-like, feeling her way towards the front door, with George following close behind. The front door had been torn off its hinges, so it wasn't totally dark inside. A small amount of ambient light, just enough for them to locate and pick up their skateboards, shone through.

'This way,' whispered George, looking out into the empty street. 'And quickly!'

Both Annie and George had learned to skateboard the year before, when they had befriended skateboard champion Vincent, who had not only taught them some

214

basic moves but left behind two of his boards when he moved back to Hollywood with his film-director parents. They would never be as good as him, but they could both skate quickly and safely. However, they'd never tried skating in near total darkness before, and now they stood outside George's front door, holding their boards nervously.

'Where are we going?' whispered Annie.

'Your dad's office at the Department of Maths in town,' said George. 'You know how to get in, right?'

'Yup,' said Annie. 'I can open the front door. But why are we going there?'

'We're going to find Old Cosmos!' said George. 'Your dad's original computer! The first ever supercomputer. That's where he is, isn't it – in the basement at the Maths Department? He's our only hope – if he's still working, that is. But we've got to go and see. Has Ebot come through with any visuals yet?'

'Ooops!' Annie fumbled in her trouser pocket and brought out the remote-access glasses. She put them on and flicked through the screens using the eye-gaze technology.

'Nope, nothing,' she said. 'Hang on – what's this?'

'What?' George wondered if Ebot had suddenly popped into view.

'It's like I'm seeing everything around us clearly,' said Annie, 'but the world's turned a really pukey kind of green.'

'It must be night vision!' George realized. 'You must have night vision on your glasses!'

'Amazing!' said Annie. 'That means I can lead the way. Are you going to be able to see me if I go ahead?'

'If I stay close enough, I can just see the reflectors on your trainers,' George told her.

'Let's go, then. There's no time to waste.' Annie zoomed off ahead of George, but kept checking behind her to see if he was following. She looked right and left through her night-vision glasses as she sped down the middle of the road. There were no cars about, but even so, she didn't follow a direct route. Several times she had to veer off down side roads to avoid groups of people ahead. Fortunately, with her goggles, she could spot them well before they were aware of anyone coming their way. Turned green by the night-vision technology, they looked pretty scary; the sort of people she and George did not want to encounter.

The riots were still simmering; those people who were still out on the streets were searching for anything they could lay their hands on – and they didn't want the booty to be them.

As they travelled through the centre of the ancient university town, past the colleges with their grand columns, arches and courtyards, they came across a sight which showed them how far and how fast Foxbridge had changed. Right outside the gate of one of the larger colleges – an impressive group of buildings with turrets and stained-glass windows, surrounded by sweeping lawns – a group of people sprawled around a bonfire; it looked like they were cooking scraps scavenged from the dustbins they had emptied onto the pavement.

This time Annie figured they simply needed to get past these people as quickly as possible; to avoid them would mean taking a very long way round. She pushed her skateboard along as fast as she could, and hurtled towards them, George following close behind.

As they flew along, one or two people looked up at the sound of the skateboards, but made no move to intercept or follow them. They shot past, curving along the narrow street in a graceful arc.

'That was easy!' said George. 'No one's interested in us!'

But he had spoken too soon.

As they carried on towards Eric's office, he heard a noise behind them, getting ever closer. Turning while skateboarding at top speed isn't easy, but George managed to peer behind him enough to see . . .

'We're being followed!' he shouted to Annie, not caring if whoever it was heard him.

'Who by?' Annie's voice flew back to him on the breeze.

'It's a robot,' yelled George. 'Like the one from the Moon! And it's catching up!'

The robot was still a fair distance behind them, but just as it had on the Moon, it was eating up the ground as it strode along.

'Faster!'

George and Annie were moving so quickly now that the town was a blur around them. Behind them, the robot stumbled on the cobbles, its advanced technology seemingly unable to cope with the uneven surface of the ancient street.

'It's stopped!' said George as they scooted up to the doorway of the Department of Maths. 'Quick, Annie – get the door open!'

'This is so weird!' she panted as she turned towards the entrance, and saw that the building was dark and empty now. 'Were we wrong? Do they want us and not Dad?'

'Don't look round,' urged George. 'Just unlock the door.' Peering through the darkness, he saw the sinister silver figure pick itself up and set off towards them again.

Annie nodded. She concentrated on the combination lock that

would open the Maths Department for them: the small metal wheel protruded through an ancient brass panel next to the front door.

Inside his head, George gave a silent scream. He couldn't risk breaking Annie's concentration as she worked on the lock, but the robot was nearly upon them – they were backed against the door and there was absolutely nowhere for them to go.

Finally she got the correct code, and the lock – a mechanical rather than an electronic device – sprang apart; the grand old door swung open. They both ran through and breathed a sigh of relief as it slammed shut behind them. It was still pitch black inside the offices and, given the way the robot was now battering on the front door, they were far from safe.

'Old Cosmos . . .' whispered George. 'We need to find him.'

Using the night-vision glasses, Annie steered them through the gloom, down to the door that led to the basement, where Old Cosmos was kept. Here they came to a stop. The door was locked.

From upstairs, they heard the sound of breaking glass as the robot smashed the windows around the front door.

'How do we get in?' whispered Annie. On the side of the door, an entry pad glowed faintly.

'What's the entry code?' George asked her.

'Um, we'll have to guess . . .' She typed in a stream of numbers.

'What was that?' George was trying to control his panic. He knew it would ruin everything if he made Annie lose her focus.

'I just tried Dad's birthday,' she said, 'but that didn't work. Then I tried Mum's. And now . . .'

She tapped away – and this time the door slid back, allowing them to enter.

'That was my birthday,' said Annie, nearly crying with relief, 'and it's worked!' The door closed behind them with a satisfying *slurp*.

The robot might still be able to break it down, but at least they had bought themselves some time.

Inside, the enormous, ancient-looking machine was waiting for them. He took up most of the basement with the towers and stacks that contained his extensive circuitry. Looking at him, George thought it 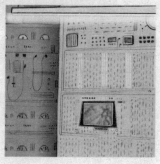 was a marvel that computers were now small enough to carry.

Welcome, Annie, Cosmos said via a ream of old-fashioned computer paper – the sort with a series of punched holes along the edge. This Cosmos didn't have a speaking voice – he had to print out whatever he wanted to say on paper. *I'm glad to see you again.*

WHAT IS A COMPUTER?

Mathematical laws

It is a marvellous feature of the Universe that everything in it seems to follow mathematical laws – anything from a planet to a beam of light or a sound wave – so we can predict what it can do by performing mathematics.

A computing machine turns this around – *we* design and assemble a collection of parts which will behave according to some mathematics of *our* choosing. We allow the machine to then behave naturally (to 'run') and it performs the mathematics and gives us an answer. If the theory behind the machine, the way it is built and our measurements are all sufficiently accurate, we can trust the final answer to be accurate.

Nowadays, we are used to the idea that a computer can be programmed to do almost anything if it has enough memory and processor power, and that the programs themselves are just more data. But the computer you use today is a long way from the earliest designs . . .

A very early analogue computer

Way back in 2nd century Greece, a very early computing machine – the Antikythera Mechanism – was built to simulate the cyclic behaviour of the Sun, Moon and planets using rotating gear wheels. The designer of the machine drew an analogy between the celestial objects moving around the sky and bronze wheels, carefully arranged through a complex mechanism so that they would accurately reflect the arrangement in the sky of those celestial bodies at different times. Since it is based upon an *analogy* with a specific physical system, it is an example of an *analogue computer*.

A slide rule – a ruler with a sliding central strip – is also an example of an early analogue computer. This hand-held device was invented in the 17th century and widely used until the arrival of pocket-sized electronic calculators in the 1970s. It is based upon the mathematics of *logarithms*.

But analogue computers have clear limits. The main disadvantage is that, once created, an analogue computer can only solve one type of problem with a fixed accuracy. A different problem may require different mathematical behaviour, and so a different analogy, a different design, and a different machine.

A human being, on the other hand, approaches calculation differently. He or she might start by writing down a set of equations, then transform these equations into other equations step by step using the rules of mathematics – a familiar process which you will know from school eg: solving quadratic equations.

A new form of computational device was needed to tackle problems in this way.

A computer powered by steam!

Mechanical calculators followed – Pascal's of the 17th century was ground-breaking at the time. Then, in 1837, Charles Babbage designed an *Analytic Engine* which (if it had been built) would have been the first programmable computer – it would have used punched cards for programs and data, used only mechanical parts, and been capable of performing like a Universal Turing Machine – although it would also have been 100 million times slower than a modern computer! And it was powered by steam . . .

From Turing to the first digital computers

A digital computer is a machine designed to automatically follow algorithms (like a human being might follow an algorithm, only much faster). In practice, it turns an *input* whole number (possibly very big) into an *output* whole number.

223

WHAT IS A COMPUTER?

Why whole numbers?

It is easy to turn text into numbers – for example, in the ASCII scheme, 'A' is represented by 65 and 'z' by 122. For actual numbers, in practice we always want to deal with fractions to a certain number of decimal places (or precision), e.g. 99.483. This is the same as 0.99483 times 100 (or 10 x 10, written mathematically as 10^2). So a digital computer only really has to store the *whole numbers* (integers) 99483 and the number 2, which tells us the power of 10 that is used (10^2).

A real computer more normally works with binary digits (bits) which take the values 0 or 1 only – and any data – numbers, text, images, program instructions – can be represented (coded) by integers in binary notation, and put together as one long binary number in the computer's memory.

The mathematics behind digital computers is based on the Universal Turing Machine. A digital computer accepts the program (the list of instructions for a particular Turing Machine, which can be coded into the form of a big binary number) as part of its input and uses this to perform the same job on the rest of the input. So the 'computer', as we understand the idea today, is a single machine capable of computing anything 'Turing-computable', if input with the right program and given enough time and memory to run it.

The first was produced in 1941: the Z3, by Konrad Zuse in Germany. It used telephone relays instead of gear wheels – and was therefore electro-mechanical rather than mechanical – and its input came from punched film tape. It was quickly followed in 1946 by the first electronic general-purpose (Turing-complete) digital computer – the American ENIAC. If you looked inside, though, the electronics weren't on boards studded with chips as today, but consisted of light-bulb-sized vacuum tubes. It was enormous too: 2.4 m × 0.9 m × 30 m, and it took up 167 square metres of floor space!

In 1949, Cambridge University built and started to use another valve-based, electronic and Turing-complete computer, EDSAC, for research, and over the following decades the electronics shrank, first from tubes to transistors, then to integrated circuits and microprocessors with very large numbers of electronic parts etched onto single pieces of silicon.

Computers today

A computer today is a machine we expect to be able to read and store digital data and instructions, and then automatically do what we want it to do at the press of a few keys – or by moving a mouse, swiping, pinching or touching a screen. It is a lot smaller than its predecessors too. And as the electronics shrank, with more and more tiny parts crammed closer and closer together, the speed of a computer increased enormously.

But unlike the Turing Machine, way back in the 1930s, a real computer still only has a finite amount of memory – it might, for example, have 2GB of RAM (Random Access Memory). It also has to perform basic operations at a very high speed – maybe 20,000,000,000 steps or 'floating point operations' per second (20 gflop/s).

For example, when you double-click on an image file on your laptop, the viewer application and the image file are both read into memory from the disk, then the processor runs the application instructions on the image data to decode it into the correct coloured dots to send to the screen so you can see what you asked for. And see it quickly too.

A typical computer today also has permanent storage (a hard disk) which lets you turn the computer off without losing your files. It often has a connection to other computers and most likely is able to log on to the internet.

Many homes now have a personal computer – or more than one – and individual people can even carry one in a pocket on a tablet, or access the internet on a smartphone. New technology is coming out every year, and the computers of the future may look very different.

> • One byte is a group of 8 bits, which is enough to store any letter of the alphabet
> • One gigabyte is 1,073,741,824 bytes

George's Guide to Staying Safe Online.

Give No Personal Information
Stay safe by never giving out personal information when you're chatting or posting online. Personal information includes your full name, email address, phone number and password. If an app or person online asks for this information then check with your parent or a trusted adult if it is OK before you share anything.

Emails aren't always great
Accepting emails, IM messages, or opening files, pictures or texts from people you don't know or trust can lead to problems – they may contain viruses or nasty messages. Be careful!

Online Friends
Meeting someone you have only been in touch with online can be dangerous. Only do so with your parents' or carers' permission and even then only when they can be present. Remember online friends are still strangers even if you have been talking to them for a long time.

Really?

Someone online might lie about who they are and information on the internet may not be true. Always check information with other websites, books or someone who knows about the subject. If you like chatting online it's best to only chat to your real world friends and family.

Get with the Family

Share what you do and who you talk to online with your parent, carer or trusted adult. The internet shouldn't be about secrets. Use your technology in the same room as grown-ups and let them see what you are up to. It will be easier for both of you to talk about any issues that arise.

Explain your worries

Tell your parent, carer or a trusted adult if someone or something makes you feel uncomfortable or worried, or if you or someone you know is being bullied online.

The internet is by far the biggest source of shared knowledge you have access to – you can learn lots about space, technology and new ideas. Don't forget to have fun and stay safe!

Chapter Fifteen

Inside Old Cosmos's lair it was dry, warm and almost cosy – at least compared to what was happening in the world above their heads. A fan whirred gently, keeping the old computer cool and the air moving around what might otherwise become a rather stale underground room. Geo-thermally powered, Old Cosmos was an antique piece of technology with a futuristic energy supply. The previous year, Eric had decided to investigate renewable energy alternatives to keep his power-hungry machines operational. He had suggested that the different parts of the university should use separate energy systems, so that a failure in one place wouldn't affect another. In the current situation, Old Cosmos, who drew his energy right from the core of the Earth itself, was the only functional machine left in the building. The lights on his impressive stacks of hardware shone brightly, a welcome sight after the greyish-green darkness of the outside world.

'Cosmos, the world has gone crazy! The computers are malfunctioning, and now there are robots on the streets! Has anyone tried to attack you?' asked George. 'Little Cosmos has been hacked – we think by the person or organization doing all these weird things.'

Ha, ha, ha, said Old Cosmos. *No one would bother attacking me. They think I'm a relic. It would be like attacking the pyramids.*

'But you're not, are you?' said Annie fondly. 'A relic, I mean. Or a pyramid.'

I am a remarkable piece of technological architecture. Old Cosmos transferred his words onto paper even more rapidly than before. *I may not have all the modern capabilities, but I can still perform extraordinary computational feats.*

'Like sending us into space?' said George hopefully.

I have been portal-modified, replied Cosmos with dignity, not quite admitting that this had not been one of his original functions, *by a former user.*

Annie and George exchanged glances. They knew what that meant. Last year, Eric's old tutor, Professor Zuzubin, had been secretly using Old Cosmos for his own purposes – which included an attempt to blow up the Large Hadron Collider just when the world's physicists were gathered there together. Zuzubin planned to be the only remaining scientist so that his theories, long ago shown by Eric to be entirely bogus, would be accepted. He'd also tried to use Old Cosmos as a time machine: he wanted to go back and edit history, changing his earlier scientific predictions to make himself look like a genius in the present. But he had been unable to change the course of history; the past had protected itself from this kind of cosmic piracy. All the scientists, Annie's dad among them, had managed to leave the Collider in one piece and carry on with their work. However, Zuzubin's legacy was proving to be surprisingly useful in the present crisis . . .

'Zuzubin must have added the space door,' Annie murmured to George.

'Gosh, I never thought we'd say thank you to him!' he replied, remembering the seemingly mild-mannered, white-haired professor who had, it turned out, belied his appearance. 'Dangerous' wasn't really the word for Zuzubin . . . 'deluded to the point of insanity', 'power hungry' and 'reputationally challenged' were phrases that summed him up better.

'But where do we want to go? We don't know where Ebot is yet!'

'Cosmos,' said Annie, 'we've sent our robot into space with a tracking device – using these glasses, we should be able to see where he is. We haven't spotted anything yet, but we're hoping that some visuals will come through very soon. Can you connect to them and tell us where we need to go?'

Easy peasy, typed out Cosmos. *Please attach the hardware device to one of my ports.*

'Ports . . . ports . . . ports . . .' Annie rapidly scanned the enormous cliff face that was Old Cosmos as she unfurled a cable from her trouser pocket. 'If I was a port, where would I be?'

'There!' said George, pointing to a spot just below Cosmos's screen. 'Plug it in there!'

Annie connected the glasses to the cable and plugged the other end into Cosmos. His screen went fuzzy and grey, but then quickly lit up.

At first there just seemed to be random shapes, blurred and colourless, moving in a way that made no visual sense. But Cosmos quickly used the zoom function to sharpen the images, and changed the brightness so it threw them into relief.

They peered at the scene in front of them. It was still hard to make sense of what they were seeing. The angles kept changing, so they still had no idea what they were looking at.

'Look!' said George, squinting at the screen. 'Over there! It's that same robot. It's like the one we saw on the Moon and the one that chased us here – or maybe it's another one and they're all identical!' The robot appeared briefly in front of them, and seemed to somersault, turning a complete circle in the air!

'They're in space!' said Annie. 'That's why it looks weird. Ebot is floating – it looks like he's in some kind of spaceship. Cosmos, can you locate it?'

Old Cosmos chuntered away for a few minutes. They heard his circuits clacking as he tried to trace the exact position of the signal.

'OMG!' Annie exclaimed. 'Look! There isn't just *one* robot!'

Looking through Ebot's eyes, they now saw that he was in a tube-like corridor with pipes and wiring all over the walls. Around him floated a host of robots that resembled those they had seen on the Moon and just now, in Foxbridge. When the kids got used to the fact that Ebot was in a low-gravity environment, they realized that he was surrounded by floating robots, all guiding him in one direction.

'Wow!' said Annie. 'It's like Ebot's got a robot police squad around him!'

'Who do they belong to?' wondered George. 'Who would have so many on a space station? It looks like a robot army.'

'Cosmos, where *is* this?' asked Annie.

They didn't have to wait long for the printout.

Do you want to know where it is, or how fast it is moving? Cosmos needed some further direction from them before he could complete his report.

'We want to know where!' said Annie. 'We don't care how fast it's going.'

Your personalized android's location is a space station which is currently in orbit around planet Earth.

232

'That's not the International Space Station!' exclaimed Annie, who had become very familiar with the inside of the ISS: the commander had broadcast updates and photos every day on Twitter, and she had followed his posts eagerly.

George studied the paper spilling out of the computer and pooling in great rolls at his feet. 'Old Cosmos says here that it's a privately owned space station, but there is almost no information available about it. It's like it doesn't exist . . . except we can see that it does.'

'How is that possible?' asked Annie.

'It may have been "cloaked", according to Cosmos,' George told her, 'to prevent it from being seen. And it may have quantum properties which allow it to change location. Which is why it's been moving around from place to place – like the Moon and then the comet.'

'That's super-weird,' said Annie. 'Does Cosmos think it's linked to what's happened on Earth? Does he *know* what's happened on Earth?'

233

Furious printing followed Annie's question.

Of course I know! Cosmos wrote. *Please address me directly. It is rude to talk about me in the third person.*

'Sorry,' said Annie humbly. 'It's just that we're living in a very strange world where it seems that anything is possible.'

Right at the beginning of the computer age, Cosmos told her, *we pointed out that there was a danger of connecting everything to everything else. It has made it too easy to bring everything crashing down.*

'Well, it doesn't look like anyone listened,' said George.

'Cosmos . . .' Annie directed her comments straight at the old computer. She'd noticed that he could be as cranky as his mini-me, Little Cosmos, used to be, before he got hacked and turned all oily and polite. 'Can you take us to Ebot's location on the spaceship? Not his *exact* location, because it looks like he's with a robot police force who are escorting him somewhere, but close enough to find out what's going on?'

Affirmative, typed Cosmos.

'And can you "cloak" us? Can you make us invisible so that when we get to the spaceship, no one can see us?'

There was a pause.

I can't give you an invisibility cloak ☹. Old Cosmos actually added a sad face emoticon.

'That's so cute,' murmured Annie. 'Cosmos, why

don't you have a voice?' she wondered
suddenly. By now, the whole basement
was filling up with the reams and reams
of paper that Cosmos had used up in
communicating with them.

*Because no one has made one for
me*, he told her. *So I am voiceless.*

'Aw, *I'm* doing a sad face now.'
Annie actually thought she might
cry.

*But I can give you a time
cloak*, Cosmos carried on.

'What's a time cloak?' she asked.

*It means even if someone has managed to pick up
my network activity, they won't know you have space
travelled through a portal until around three minutes
after you've gone. So I can give you three minutes'
head start.*

'Do it,' said Annie decisively. 'Right, let's get
moving. Do we need our spacesuits?'

George looked doubtful. 'It's hard to say,' he replied.
'But most space stations are climate-controlled inside,
so no one wears a spacesuit while they're actually on
board.'

'But this is like a weird, invisible space station,'
explained Annie. 'So who knows what it's like inside?'

'If it's invisible,' said George, 'then how come we
can see it now?'

Because your android is sending us a signal from his tracking device from inside the station, Cosmos explained. *If he wasn't actually there, we would never have found it.*

'But we saw it from Earth!' said George. 'I managed to take a photo of it!'

A glitch in the metamaterial of the invisibility cloak, said Cosmos, *must have produced a brief period when the ship was visible, during which time you took its photo.*

'So that's why Dad has no idea about it!' said Annie. 'That's why all the international governments are unable to find this ship and whoever is on it! Cosmos, get ready to hide us from time itself.'

Cosmos did some complicated computations of his own, with the result that a doorway that George and Annie hadn't noticed until now – concealed as it was amongst all the circuitry and panelling on Cosmos' impressive rows of stacks – started to glow.

'Remember,' said George, 'we need to open the door. It's not like the other portal: we have to physically open it and step through; last time it had a sort of hallway before we reached our destination.'

'What if we fall down the gap and end up in space without our spacesuits on?' said Annie, grimacing.

'Then we'll freeze and boil at the same time; our blood gases will explode while our eyes literally pop out of our heads,' said George helpfully.

'Thanks,' murmured Annie. 'You're sure we have to do this? And that we don't need our spacesuits?'

'Pretty sure,' he said. 'Eric will never find the space station without us – we might be the only people on Earth who have a chance of finding I AM and working out whether he, it or they are definitely linked to what's gone wrong everywhere.'

'Okey-doke,' said Annie. 'Looks like it's just you and me again.'

The door glowed brighter and brighter in a rainbow of colours, until it looked like a lit-up Christmas tree – a beautiful sight in the dim basement.

Without saying anything more, they edged closer to each other. Annie held out her hand, and George took it in his gloved one: while Annie had been talking to Old Cosmos, he had fished Ebot's black haptic gloves out of his pocket and put them on, in case they turned out to be useful.

'Should we take the glasses with us?' Annie asked.

Negative, Cosmos typed out. *I need them to follow the tracking signal so that I can send you to the right location.*

'You will get us inside the spaceship, won't you?' whispered Annie. 'Not floating about in space, outside.'

Unlike later imitations, typed Cosmos snippily, *I never make mistakes. Please step forward. The portal is ready.*

The two of them took a deep breath and stepped

forward. George pulled back the door with his free hand. Through the doorway, they could see nothing but a blaze of multicoloured lights swirling in great green, pink and orange clouds.

'What's through there?' asked Annie nervously.

'We won't find out until we go through,' said George. 'Do you remember? Old Cosmos can't show us what's ahead – we need to step forward; otherwise we'll never know.'

'Wait!' said Annie, tearing a sheet of paper off Cosmos's printouts and scribbling something on the back of it with a pencil she'd found in her pocket.

'What are you doing?' asked George.

'Leaving a note,' she told him. 'Just in case.'

She showed George her message:

GONE TO SPACE. BAK SOON.

'Shouldn't we say where we've gone?'
'You add something,' said Annie, handing George the paper and pencil.

IF NOT RETURNED BY MORNING, PLEASE SEND OUT
SPACE RESCUE MISSION USING COORDINATES HELD
BY OLD COSMOS.
ANNIE AND GEORGE.

'Good note!' said Annie. 'I think that makes it all perfectly clear.'
'Let's go, then.' George stuck the note on a clipboard and took his place next to Annie.
Then they closed their eyes and took a big step forward, still holding hands tightly. They were both wondering if they might be simply walking forward into emptiness; into the massive and unknowable darkness of space itself. Once upon a time, before the world collapsed, they had been to a theme park where there had been a ride just like that – where you couldn't see where you were going and had to trust that you would be safely delivered to the other side. This time it wasn't a game, a ride or a theme park. This time it was for real.

Chapter Sixteen

But they didn't fall through space. Realizing that their feet had touched down on something solid, they opened their eyes and saw the last of the coloured clouds from Old Cosmos's portal drifting away to reveal their new destination. They heard a soft click behind them and whirled round, just in time to see the doorway close and then vanish. At the same time they both rose gently off the ground.

They were in the same sort of cylindrical corridor as Ebot had appeared in with his robot escort, but there was no one else around. Had his kidnappers already discovered that he was not actually the great scientist Eric Bellis, however similar they might appear to a computer system or a bunch of robots? Did this mean that they had just stepped into a hostile situation? What awaited them on this strange invisible spaceship?

'We're floating!' Annie drifted towards the curved walls of the corridor and grabbed onto a piece of pipe. 'We're in space! But I can breathe OK – can't you?'

'Shush!' said George. 'We don't know if anyone is listening to us.'

'I can't see anyone.' Annie looked up and down the corridor. At one end there was a door; at the other end it curved away out of sight. 'Let's go this way.' She edged towards the door. 'We've only got three minutes before they know we're here.'

'Why that way?' asked George.

'Just a hunch . . .'

'Fair enough. I've got your back.' George turned a quick somersault in the air, just as he had seen the robot do through Ebot's eyes. He suddenly realized something. 'How will Cosmos know when to open the portal and let us back? We haven't got any communication devices with us.'

241

'And he can only see through Ebot's eyes!' said Annie, reality dawning on her too. 'So we *have* to find Ebot if we want to get home. Otherwise we're stuck here. And we've got very little time before the time cloak expires; once that happens, the robot army might know we're here.'

'I hope they have some space provisions,' sighed George, whose tummy was now feeling very empty. 'Do we have a plan?'

'Yes,' said Annie. 'Find whoever is doing all this stuff and tell them to stop.'

'Or we'll . . . what – exactly?' asked George.

'Er, don't know . . . We'll have to make that bit up as we go along.'

'Great,' muttered George. 'That's just great.'

This was the hardest mission they had ever embarked upon. Previously, they had faced huge challenges and unravelled strange and mysterious events on Earth and in space. But this time they had taken a huge leap into the unknown, with no real idea how to get home, what to do or what they might find. It was by far the most frightening and bizarre of their adventures; moreover they were peculiarly plan-less. George realized that they were on the edge, cut off from civilization and human knowledge, completely on their own. It was a very odd feeling.

'Better than hanging around on Earth feeling useless,' Annie said firmly, using the pipes along the wall to

propel herself towards the door at the end. She floated down and grabbed the handle to steady herself. The door opened immediately, sending her flying backwards as something that must have been leaning against the other side of it lurched towards her.

Annie just managed to stop herself from shrieking, while George threw himself forward to protect her from whatever it was. It fell through the doorway in slow motion and floated horizontally for a moment.

'It's one of those robots!' said Annie. 'Nooooo! What are we going to do?' She grabbed hold of George and they hovered there together, unable to decide whether to stay and face their fate or try and make a quick getaway.

George looked around for an escape route. 'Maybe it

hasn't clocked us!' he whispered. 'C'mon – let's try and get away.'

But even as he spoke, the robot floated back upwards; for the first time they could see its face clearly. Unlike the ones they had met before, its expression was happy.

'Hello,' it said to them. Its voice was gentle – not what they had expected at all.

'Er, hello,' they both said nervously. Was this I AM? Could I AM in fact be a robot?

George had started to prepare a stern speech about the awful situation on Earth in his head; he intended to deliver it when he finally met I AM, using lots of long words, to impress upon whoever it was that this was very serious and that he, George, was not going to leave the spaceship until he was satisfied that the appropriate actions had been taken. But meeting a friendly, smiling robot with a sugary voice was so surprising that his speech was instantly forgotten.

'What's your name?' asked the robot.

'I'm Annie. And this is George,' said Annie.

'Would you like to be my friends?'

'Wow,' said George. This really *was* unexpected. He wouldn't have flinched if the robot had threatened him and Annie – or tried to arrest or even attack them. But befriending them? That was the weirdest of all.

'Er . . . yes, that would be lovely.' Annie sounded as baffled as George felt.

'What's *your* name?' George felt like a little kid trying to make friends on his first day at school. But he didn't know what else to do.

The robot was now floating straight in front of them so they could see his grinning face. 'My name,' he cooed, 'is Boltzmann Brian. I am a spontaneously

occurring sentient mind, able to replicate an infinite number of times.'

'I thought that was a Boltzmann *Brain*,' Annie muttered to George.

'There was a spelling mistake when the patent was registered,' replied the robot serenely.

George realized that it must have supersonic hearing. He and Annie would have to be very careful how they communicated with each other. Even though the robot was clearly trying to form a connection with them, George was instinctively reluctant to trust it.

BOLTZMANN BRAINS

Particles, particles, everywhere . . .

Every material on Earth is made of tiny particles called *atoms*.
These atoms are constantly knocking each other about by
exchanging particles of electromagnetic radiation called *photons*,
some of which we feel as heat, others being seen as light,
and others we use for communication by deliberately pulsing
them out of radio antennas. Photons and subatomic particles
produced by the Sun – and coming from more distant parts
of the Universe – are also constantly flying in from space. So
the Earth, other planets, stars and even space are all swirling
soups of tiny particles. How can a scientist possibly understand
the behaviour of anything when they have to consider such an
incredibly large number of microscopic moving parts?

. . . and more than a drop to drink!

Just one litre of water on Earth contains around 30 million million
million million molecules! But a litre of water doesn't look much
like a pile of particles – it appears to be a continuous material
that can exist as a solid, a liquid or a gas, depending on the
temperature and pressure. Add enough heat and water will boil
and turn into steam; lower the temperature sufficiently and it will
turn into ice. This is normal behaviour for water; we can observe it
easily. But why should *all* of these 30 million million million million
molecules behave the same way? No rebel molecules?

A nineteenth-century Austrian physicist, Ludwig Boltzmann,
provided a mathematical explanation of how the enormous
number of particles involved actually makes a particular behaviour
pattern overwhelmingly the most probable. For although the
multitude of particles effectively moves entirely randomly – each
one doing its own thing – it is most likely to produce an *average
overall behaviour* in which individual molecules can be forgotten.
In a litre of water, a small fraction of the molecules may randomly
and briefly deviate from this average, but the probability that
this fraction would be large enough to produce a
noticeable change in what we think of as the
normal behaviour of water is very, very small.

If the water were to be left alone for ever, however, large random fluctuations would eventually take place – for example, all the molecules could find themselves moving for a short time in the same direction. Now this is a very very very low probability, so if you leave a litre of water in a jug, you wouldn't expect to see it suddenly leap out. But if you could leave it for an eternity, such fluctuations would eventually occur – and occur an infinite number of times.

What does this mean for the Universe?

The Universe began 13.8 billion years ago in a Big Bang, and it is expanding at an ever-increasing rate.

If we apply the same principles to our Universe as we just did to water, we can see that a Universe which carries on for ever would contain *every possible* random fluctuation, an infinite number of times. This means that a perfect copy of our Universe today – after all, it is a perfectly good arrangement of particles – would eventually appear randomly somewhere *else* in the particle soup.

A copy of our Universe would obviously include copies of all our human brains, with all their memories too! But as creating all of that randomly is much, much more difficult than forming just one working brain on its own, it would be more probable that these random fluctuations would create *single* brains, complete with their memories, much more frequently than whole people or copies of the entire Earth.

A large enough particle soup, with a non-zero temperature and left for eternity, could therefore randomly create all possible brains – Boltzmann Brains – with all possible memories, infinitely many times. So if our Universe should last for ever, floating in space would be infinitely many *Boltzmann Brains* – each with all the brain's memories, right up to the moment when you thought you read this!

Are you sure you aren't one of them?

'Unfortunately it was not possible to change it once the patent had gone through,' the robot continued.

'Aw, poor you!' said Annie, not knowing quite what else to say.

'I like your hair,' the robot told her.

'What?' Automatically, she flicked her fringe.

'And you look very intelligent,' said the robot, addressing George.

'Erm, thanks!' he said. Was the robot pre-programmed to give out compliments to random people it met while floating about the spaceship? he wondered. What was the point of creating such an odd machine?

'Time is running out,' Annie whispered right in George's ear. 'We've nearly reached our three minutes.'

George nodded very slightly so she knew he had heard her.

'Boltzmann . . .' he said politely. 'Brian? Did you just say you could replicate an infinite number of times? Is that actually true?'

'I have been specially created to be able to copy my body in a simple and user-friendly fashion,' said the robot rather proudly. 'I can send my specifics to a 3D-enabled printer on Earth and then print out a version of myself.'

'And can you print yourself out anywhere you want?' asked George.

'Anywhere on the planet,' replied Boltzmann.

George felt a prickle of horror as the full implications

of this dawned on him. At the touch of a button, he realized, this robot could be re-created by 3D printers all over Earth, which meant that anyone who wanted to form a robot army there didn't need to manufacture them or import them. Just give the right command, and however many 3D printers there were on Earth – and George suspected there might be far more than people realized – would produce a robot which was presumably loyal to its creator. George imagined it must be the quickest way to take over the Earth ever, especially if the place was in a state of chaos and no one even noticed what was going on or tried to stop it until it was too late.

What if all the governments and armies and police forces and security services were distracted by collapsed transport networks, free giveaways from the banks, failing food supplies, grounded aircraft, bursting dams, exploding power stations and any number of the other recent catastrophes – and didn't notice a robot army seizing control? Even if it was a nice robot army, hell-bent on complimenting people . . .

George suddenly noticed that while they'd been talking, the robot had slowly, almost imperceptibly, been pushing them backwards along the corridor.

'So how many of you are there right now?' asked Annie.

'Just the one,' said Boltzmann Brian. 'There is only one true Boltzmann Brian.'

'But there are more robots than you on this space-ship?' said George.

'Correct.' Boltzmann continued to usher them back-wards. 'There are many copies of my robot body on this ship – an entire ensemble. But none of them have a brain. They're very unlikely to get one, you see, even if you cook the head for a long time . . . I'll let you into a secret.' The robot gave a self-satisfied grin. 'I'm much nicer than the others.'

'Are there more robots on Earth?' asked George.

'Correct once more!' Boltzmann replied happily. 'More units have recently been replicated via 3D printers in selected locations on Earth.'

'Do you mean the nasty ones?' asked Annie. 'The angry robots that keep chasing us around?'

'I have been specially educated to be extremely user friendly,' said Boltzmann Brian with a glassy smile. 'But the others . . .'

Annie and George didn't need to hear the end of the sentence to understand what it meant.

As it spoke, an alarm blared out and two of the other robots – the ones with the mean faces and vicious pincer grips – appeared behind Annie and George, grabbing them tightly.

'Ow!' cried Annie as a robot latched onto her arm and dragged her towards the end of the corridor.

Held in a vice-like grip by another of the menacing robots, George could do nothing to help her. Like

Annie, he was swept along the corridor by his robot escort.

Boltzmann Brian followed closely behind, bleating, 'But I'm a nice robot!'

For a moment George wished they'd been able to stay with just Brian – while that particular brand of nice had been a little creepy, it was a lot better than the threatening faces that surrounded them now. Where were they going? Would they find Ebot once they got there? he wondered.

He and Annie couldn't see their destination, given that they were travelling backwards, until the robots suddenly let go of them and they floated into the most extraordinary room that either of them had ever seen.

3D PRINTING

What is 3D printing, how is it different to *2D printing*, and why is it so exciting?

What does '3D' mean?

The 'D' stands for 'dimensional', so something which is 3D, three-dimensional, is something that has the following dimensions:

- a length (one)
- a width (two)
- a height (three)

So, while a picture on a piece of paper is a two-dimensional image (flat on the paper), physical objects that you interact with every day (like your bike, your dinner, and your nose) are all '3-dimensional'.

Slicing a sausage!

2D printing (two-dimensional) is what we usually think of when we say 'printing' – for example, using a printer connected to a computer at home or in your school or library.

A 2D printer usually:

- uses special inks to make the 2D images on paper.
- takes an *electronic file* that describes a whole 2D image - like a photograph from a digital camera or a document from a word processor – and then electronically 'slices' it up into lots of very thin strips. This process is sometimes called

salami-slicing because it's a bit like a chef chopping a salami-sausage into slices!

- takes each electronic slice in turn and carefully squirts coloured inks onto a matching section of paper to produce a precise image of that slice.
- then moves down and does the same for the next slice, and then the next, until finally the entire image has been built up on the paper one slice at a time.
- Artists and film makers can make 2D objects *appear* 3D by using tricks: like *perspective* in pictures and *3D Special Effects* in movies. But these are *optical illusions* and the images themselves are 2D as they only have a width (one) and a height (two).

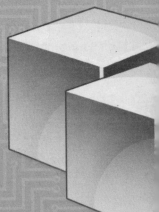

When my son was younger, he would watch with fascination as our printer whirred away producing photographs and letters. He'd also watch carefully if we bought something (like a toy) on the internet – he would wait expectantly by the printer for whatever we'd just bought to plop out of it! I guess that would make complete sense to a four-year-old. The funny thing is, for some types of toys, this is now close to reality.

Making a real 3D object

In 3D printing, what is made is not just a 2D image but a real 3D object. The machines that do this are called 3D Printers or Additive Manufacturing Machines.

- it begins, like 2D printing, with an electronic file. However this is now a special type of electronic file called a CAD Model (CAD stands for Computer Aided Design) which describes every single detail about the object to be 3D-printed.

If you look at the CAD model of an object on a computer screen, you can see an image of what the object looks like from the outside, but you can also 'fly through' to see what the object looks like from any point inside it.

- the 3D printer salami-slices the CAD model into electronic slices, one on top of another, where each slice might be about 20 microns thick.
- although all of the slices are 3D because they have thickness (or length) as well as width and height, the 3D printer treats each slice as a 2-dimensional cross section showing precisely what the object would look like if it were carefully cut through.

- the 3D printer prints out each slice – starting with the lowest – just like a printer would a 2D image. But instead of squirting ink onto paper, it produces all the details in each slice as a 20-microns-thick layer of 'stuff'.

- the material for one slice dries and hardens, then the 3D printer indexes (moves up) and produces the next slice as another 20-microns-thick layer on top of the previous one.

- this process is repeated over and over until all the slices of the CAD model have been printed one on top of another to produce a real 3D object!

> 20 microns – or 1/50th of a millimeter – is approximately 25% of the thickness of one of the hairs on your head! A CAD model of an object which is 10cm high would therefore be salami-sliced into about 5,000 electronic slices!

3D PRINTING

Facts about 3D printers

- The most common material used is plastic as it can be easily squirted out in very small amounts as a liquid and will quickly harden into a solid. It is also ideal for making prototypes (models of new things like buildings or cars). As modern machines can use several different kinds of plastic at the same time and can print in colour, prototypes can be very realistic. This is still the biggest application for 3D printers.
- There are two common types of 3D printers used today:

Extrusion Machines: the material is forced through a nozzle, rather like using a piping bag to ice a cake. These machines are especially good when using more than one type of colour of material, since more nozzles can easily be added.

Bed Machines: these are most commonly used with powdered metals. Enough powder is poured out to completely fill one slice, then a power laser fuses (melts and joins) the powdered metal into a solid shape at precisely the right places in the slice. Once the model is complete, the excess powered metal is brushed away.

- Over the next few years scientists expect that machines using plastic will become more common in peoples' homes, allowing you to download patterns and 3D-print things like made-to-measure bike helmets or fun personalized toys. Imagine printing yourself as a Star Trek™ or Harry Potter figure!

- 3D printers in factories use materials like metals and ceramics eg: to print out parts for jet aeroplanes that are lighter and stronger, thereby making the aeroplanes safer and more fuel-efficient.

- Medical devices like implants for new hips and teeth, and cranial plates (used to repair holes in heads) can also be 3D-printed, because this process allows them to be made specifically for the person they will be fitted into.

Robots of the future?

Today's 3D printers are still quite slow and can only make things out of a few different materials at the same time – it would not yet be possible to print a complete robot since you would need complicated inter-locking parts made of many materials: metal parts, gears and motors, magnets, wires, plastics, oil, grease, silicon, gold – even weird things like Yttrium and Tungsten!

But 3D printers could easily make parts for robots within a fully automated factory. The parts could then be unloaded from the 3D-printers by unloading robots, polished by polishing robots, and then assembled by assembly robots . . .

Robots using 3D printers (with other technology too) to make robots? Is this something you will see in the future?

Tim

It was as if they were in a spherical, clear glass bubble, floating through space. At regular points around the perimeter, openings led into more corridors: these tubes curved away from the central room to an outer circle, like the spokes of a bicycle wheel.

Apart from these, the room was completely transparent. When they looked down, they saw that even the floor (or was it the ceiling? It was hard to know in space) was made of the same glass-like material.

It was the most amazing thing George had ever seen; for a second it took his breath away. He had dreamed of diving through space; now, he realized, he was probably as close to this as he could ever get – suspended in a glass bauble with an awesome view of the Universe on all sides.

But when George gazed out, it wasn't just the emptiness of space or the dark sky peppered with stars that grabbed his attention. It was something far more beautiful: a jewel-like blue-green planet, clothed in a thin wispy veil of atmosphere. It was their home.

'It's the Earth!' breathed George as he and Annie drifted around the room. A lump came into his throat. He reflected that it would be difficult to explain this feeling to someone who had never flown in space. When you left the Earth and then looked back and saw it – fragile, ancient, mysterious and enchanting, suspended against the blackness of space – it made your heart burst with protective, homesick feelings.

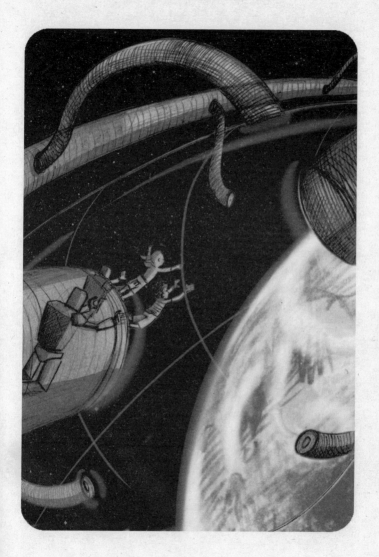

You wanted to stay in space for ever, but you also wanted to rush home and look after your beautiful planet, hanging there so courageously in the vast emptiness.

But George didn't have long to gaze in wonder. The angry robots had ushered them into the middle of the room and then taken up posts around the edges, where they lurked, silent and impassive.

Then, from another round opening, a figure emerged. 'Ebot!' cried Annie.

The android was no longer in Eric's spacesuit – he was now just wearing Eric's trademark tweed jacket, trousers and brightly coloured shirt.

George felt a rush of relief to see Ebot again in this strange place – he'd become oddly attached to the robot. More importantly, he was their route out of the alien spaceship.

'Ebot!' Annie shouted to him. 'We found you!'

But Ebot seemed to be asleep; he just floated into the room; and, they saw, he was not alone. The kids hadn't noticed his companion at first – but when they did, their mouths fell open in amazement.

Dressed in a onesie that was striped like the planet Jupiter, a peculiar figure rolled around the spherical room, flicking the tail of his suit and chuckling to himself. He orbited Annie and George and their robot, looking a little like a small planet. Holding onto each other for support, the friends gazed at him in astonishment.

'Hello!' the man – for it was indeed a man – cried, throwing out his hands in a gesture of welcome as he came to a stop in front of them. 'And welcome! I am so pleased you could join me. This has made my day! No – wait . . . not just my *day*! My week, my month, my *year*! I'm so happy you are here,' he continued, smiling broadly.

George felt himself relax a little. At least they seemed to be guests rather than prisoners now, and he knew which he preferred. Was this strange man I AM? Was this the voice they had heard on the radio? It certainly sounded rather familiar.

'George and Annie, right?' he continued, beaming away. 'From twenty-three and twenty-four Little St Mary's Lane, Foxbridge. George is 106 days older than Annie, who has the blood group AB positive, is working on a project to identify the elements of life and was recently diagnosed dyslexic by a child psychologist. She was sent to see a psychologist because her marks have plummeted and she has slipped down the class, losing out to her main rival, Karla Pinchnose. This has given her a complex, and she is determined to prove her intelligence and her ability to overcome her educational issues.'

One piece of information stood out for George. 'You're dyslexic?' He turned to Annie in surprise. 'You're doing badly at school? You told me you only went to the psychologist to have your IQ measured and they said you were probably a genius!'

Suddenly he realized why she had been trying so hard with her half-term project. She was attempting to reclaim her position at the top of the class – which George didn't even know she had lost. Now it all made sense: why she had started so many weird experiments, and why she had been unable to give up on the quest for life until circumstances had forced them to take another tack.

'The IQ test was part of the dyslexia assessment,' she said with great dignity. 'I didn't realize I had to tell you everything.'

'George,' continued their host, 'is harder to pin down in terms of information, which makes me think he is a less prolific user of technology than Annie. I know that he is a fan of computers and doesn't like humans nearly as much as machines. But given what I have also gathered of his parents – infamous eco-warriors with a marked dislike of the electromagnetic spectrum in domestic situations – he probably only gets to use the computer at school, and frankly I can't be bothered to wade through every single inane statement typed into a school computer.'

'You've been reading our private messages!' gasped Annie.

'Well, no,' chuckled the mystery onesie wearer. 'I think that's a bit too much to ask, don't you? I know about you because you tap away on Cosmos, and Cosmos is a computer that greatly interests me. I only investigated George because he is a registered user of Cosmos.'

'But how could you get into his system?' asked Annie, frowning. 'It's not possible!'

Their new friend chuckled. 'You're right,' he confided. 'There is no computer on Earth that could break into Cosmos.'

'Then you can't have done it!'

'Look around, dear clever girl, with your very high IQ and the partial disability which you are so keen to keep hidden from your friends and peers,' he murmured. 'Can you see what the answer is? Can you spell a seven-letter word?'

The colour rose in Annie's cheeks.

'Don't be horrible!' said George angrily. He hated seeing Annie being taunted like this.

'Me? Horrible?' said the man, swishing the tail of his onesie and simpering. 'I wouldn't know how! I'm full of love and kindness and joy. Just trying to help your little friend here work out the solution. She won't get it – I always said girls were no good at science.'

'Space,' said Annie defiantly. Inside, George cheered. 'You've got a space computer,' she continued doggedly. George gave her a double thumbs-up. 'No computer on Earth can break into Cosmos, so it must be a computer in space.

'And' – she thrust out her chin belligerently – 'I'm going to take a guess. It's *quantum*. Which is seven letters when space is five. That's the answer.'

'Can you spell that?' said the man sweetly. 'Or shall I do it for you?' He waved his tail and, in a loopy script, the word *Quantum* appeared on the clear surface of the bubble in red, blue and green lights.

'Now, children,' he purred. 'For a special prize . . . Who can tell me – where is the quantum computer?'

Chapter Seventeen

Georg looked around. Apart from the people, Ebot and the robots, the room held nothing at all apart from amazing views. He looked at the word *Quantum* spreading out across the transparent sphere, and a light went on in his brain.

'This is it, isn't it?' he said. '*This* is the quantum computer . . . We're inside it! I don't know how it works, but I just know that this is it.'

'Oh, so clever!' said their host. 'As you've made what some people would erroneously describe as a quantum leap, I shall fill in the rest for you. Embedded in the crystalline structure of this chamber are the billions of quantum dots that make up the quantum computer. The whole spaceship has them throughout, but in other locations they are ordinary non-quantum computer particles. This room is special because in here we have my quantum computer.'

'But what powers it?' For a moment George was lost in wonder at the technological brilliance of this achievement.

'Solar power, of course. The millions of dots inside the infrastructure of the spaceship scavenge power from the Sun.'

'Well, we know what you're using it for,' said Annie, sounding very unimpressed. The sharp tone of her voice woke George up and reminded him that they were not here to marvel at the technology and the view.

'Do you?' The man floated over to position himself right in front of them. They could just see the blue, yellow, green and white of their home planet, outlined against a dark sky, the view only slightly spoiled by the madman in a Jupiter-striped onesie.

He twitched his tail again and the glass sphere

around them lit up with tiny pinpricks of light. George and Annie felt as though they were suspended in the middle of a crowd of fireflies. 'It really has been the most extraordinary week so far,' the man told them. 'I can't remember when I last had such a good time. Who would have thought the dear old Earth would react so quickly to my little modifications? They were just supposed to be tiny tweaks to make it a better place. But – oops – I wonder if I overshot the mark, just a teensie little bit . . .'

The two kids looked astonished. George felt his jaw drop.

'Make the Earth a better place?' echoed Annie, having recovered the power of speech first. 'That's soooo not true! Who are you, anyway?'

'Take a guess!' said the onesie wearer. 'You did so well last time.'

'You're I AM,' said George.

'*I AM coming to save you* . . .' Annie realized now just what the voice had meant by this sentence.

'Oh, so many delightful possibilities!' said I Am. 'You see now how clever *I am*.'

'Yes, we do,' said George, hoping to get some more information by playing along. 'But you see, we're not so clever – at least, not as clever as you. We'd like to *learn* to be, if only you could teach us . . . To start with, could we know your name?'

'My name,' I Am replied, clearly pleased by George's

compliment, 'is Alioth Merak. I, Alioth Merak—'

'Hang on,' said Annie. 'That's not a real name. That's two of the stars of the Big Dipper!'

'Exactly!' crowed Alioth Merak. 'I don't really exist. That's the exciting part. That's why I'm so hard to find. You could search and search for me – and you won't find me anywhere. Not a single mention . . . It's the true luxury of our age – complete anonymity. Almost impossible in this era of information. But yet I have managed it.' He preened for a second, stroking his arm with his tail and looking extremely pleased with himself.

'Easy,' said George, 'with an invisible spaceship and a quantum computer.'

'*Easier*,' corrected Merak. 'Not easy – after all, I had to make the spaceship and the computer first.'

'Are you very rich?' asked Annie bluntly.

'Excessively so,' said Merak casually. 'That's what makes it all such fun!' He turned a few somersaults in mid-air to express his joy and happiness at being him.

George and Annie exchanged glances. It seemed very unlikely, thought George; he was talking to an adult, but he felt like the grown-up compared to the juvenile Alioth Merak.

'If you're so rich,' persisted Annie, 'why don't you

get a better onesie? That one is really uncool.'

Merak turned on her, furious, all the smiling good humour wiped off his face in an instant.

'How dare you, you horrible little girl!' he spat. 'How dare you – you insignificant, ridiculous vile little worm – make a comment about me, the amazing, the magnificent *I Am*! Don't you know, I am saving the world!'

'How are you doing that?' George intervened, anxious to screen his friend from further attacks by this cranky and probably very dangerous man.

'The Earth,' Alioth Merak began, sounding serious now, 'our beautiful planet, is beset with terrible evils: inequality, unhappiness, hoarding of resources; great wealth, great poverty. The rich have to police their land, their countries, their possessions with weapons, armies and guards, while the poor starve. No one is happy. No one is having fun.'

'So your plan was to make people have more fun?' Annie wrinkled her nose. 'That's the solution? Are you for real?'

'No,' said Merak, throwing her a scathing look. 'I would have thought it was perfectly clear that there is nothing "real" about me, idiotic small girl with intel-lectual pretensions.'

He turned to George and smiled. Clearly Merak had decided that he liked one of them and hated the other. 'My plan was, simply and brilliantly, to make the world a better place . . . What's that you say . . . ?' Suddenly he appeared to address some invisible person. 'Can you repeat? . . . Copy. I read you . . . What do you mean, the penguins have been exterminated?'

'What!' shouted Annie. 'You can't exterminate penguins!'

'Too late, I'm afraid,' said Merak. 'It seems they're already dead.'

'Who were you just talking to?' said George, horrified. It seemed to him that this man was becoming more deranged by the second.

'My head is a mobile phone,' Merak told him. 'I had an implant robotically inserted, deep into my brain, which means that I have no need of a handset to communicate with my mechanical troops.'

'Where *are* your troops?' said Annie, thinking of her mum and George's family in the basement and suddenly feeling very afraid. 'And do you just have robots or do you have people too?'

'People!' snorted Merak. 'Are you kidding? Why would I need people when I've got my own robot army? I think you've seen one or two of them already. A couple of them are in Foxbridge. For now, they are few and strategically placed, but soon they will be far more numerous. I just have to give the command to my network of 3D printers on Earth, and they will appear, as if by magic, ready to take control and make the world a better place!'

'I get it now,' murmured George to Annie. 'I see the link.'

'What's that, boy?' cried Merak. 'Speak up so everyone can hear you!'

'I get it!' said George loudly. 'The banks and the free money – the supermarkets and the free food, opening the dams, stopping the military aircraft, cutting off networks which might hurt people. You think all these things are *nice* things to do!'

'Clever boy! They were random acts of kindness,' replied Merak, thrilled to see that George had finally worked it out. 'They were poor, so I gave them money. They were hungry, so I gave them food. They were thirsty, so I made water in the desert. They were scared, so I made the bombs stop.'

'Whoa,' whispered Annie. 'He thinks he's a sort of God.'

'In a onesie,' added George.

'But why?' said Annie out loud. 'I don't understand why you have to do these things . . . Why can't you just live on your space station and leave Earth behind, if you think it's all such a disaster?'

'Because he wants power over everyone else,' chipped in George. 'He's not being nice. He's messing up the world so he can step in and save it afterwards. His robots take over, and no one will be able to stand against them – and then he will rule from the space station because he has control of all the computers on Earth!'

'I'm so misunderstood!' said Merak, pulling a sad face. 'I thought you "got" me, George – not like your illiterate little friend over there. We had to offer some goodies to the people of the world; then, once they've gorged themselves on an overdose of everything they thought they wanted, they'll be ready for a kind and compassionate but firm leader. Perhaps you're just not mature enough to appreciate the finesse of my plan.'

'And this "great leader" . . . that's you, is it?' asked George.

'You weren't very compassionate to the penguins!' said Annie hotly.

'Well, that was an accident . . .' Merak coughed. 'I didn't mean for that to happen.'

'Hang on . . .' said George slowly. 'I AM is not the only set of letters we've come across. There's QED as well. That's what your robot was trying to say when it came after us on the Moon. What does QED mean, and why did your robot want to kidnap Eric?'

'I know!' Annie declared. 'I know now what it stands for.'

'Do you?' sneered Merak. 'Is it Definitely Quell Excitement?'

'No!' she shouted. 'It stands for Quantum Error Detection!'

'It does!' said George, realizing his friend was right. 'Quantum error detection! That's what Eric does on the quantum computer – which is why you wanted him.'

'You can't work it, can you?' said Annie in sudden delight. 'It's just like Dad said – you can make a quantum computer but you can't control it. Dad is the only person on Earth who could help you, so you tried to capture him so that he would control the quantum computer for you!'

Merak looked mutinous. He folded his arms.

Annie stepped closer to George and whispered, 'If he twitches his tail, run!'

George nodded. They needed to get away, but where would they run to? Suddenly he realized something even more important . . . Annie must think that the control for the quantum computer was located in the tail of Merak's onesie – that's why he'd been twitching it. Aha! he thought. *So that's what we need to get hold of.*

'Maybe,' said Merak defiantly. 'Maybe you have a point. So what? What are you going to do about it? Whose spaceship is this anyway?'

'It's not just the quantum computer that's out of control,' muttered Annie.

Her words were suddenly written in huge glowing dots on the curved inner surface of the globe. *Out of*

271

control flashed up in red, green and blue.

'Well, tell me what you really think, why don't you?' said Merak unpleasantly, his words scrawled in loopy script against the dark backdrop of space.

'Did you mean it to do that?' asked George innocently as his words scrolled out in a pattern around him, like writing with a sparkler, only permanent.

'No!' said Merak. 'I did not. I did not order this to happen. Turn it off!' he shouted. 'Turn it off!' He grabbed his tail and twitched it several times. But it made no difference. His words kept appearing in great graceful curving arcs. 'The audio receptors have switched themselves on somehow!'

'Here's what I really think . . .' said Annie, ignoring him. As she spoke, her words flashed up in crazy squiggles, whirling around the globe. 'You don't want to help people at all. You're just pretending you do because in your fried little brain it means that you can justify taking over the world. If you tell yourself enough times that

272

you're doing the right thing, you start to believe it. But that still doesn't make it OK. Because we know the truth – we know that what you really want is to be the only person who gets to say what happens. You used the quantum computer to break every code on Earth so that you could get into all the different systems, read all the messages, change all the commands – a sort of massive cyber-terrorism attack. You did this so that you and only you would know everything. But we're not going to let you get away with it. I know you think I'm stupid and George is just a geek, but we're going to stop you,' she finished. If she hadn't been floating, she would have stamped her foot for emphasis.

By the time she stopped speaking, the whole sphere was alive with words, shining in an infinite maze of patterns and swirls. George watched with respect – Annie's speech was way better than the one he'd been getting ready for I AM. And she'd delivered her version with complete clarity and force. She was, he realized, pretty unique.

George wasn't the only one who was impressed by Annie's speech. While she was talking, the fierce-looking robots looked around, fascinated by the kaleidoscopic effect of the glowing words. Instead of standing guard, monitoring the chamber, alert to any threat to their leader, they had relaxed their rigid stances and simply gazed at the illuminated surface.

There was a loud crash, and George realized that

two of the robots had been so entranced by the word trail of Annie's speech that they had crashed into each other. The expressions on the faces of the others seemed to have softened in the multicoloured glow from the spherical screen.

'The robots have been hypnotized!' squeaked Annie to George. 'Look! They've gone into a trance!'

Brian floated in from the corridor, dancing around the spherical room like a robot fairy.

'When I say *now*,' George hissed to Annie (he was no longer worried about his words showing up on the screen – there were so many crisscrossing each other, it was impossible to make out an individual phrase), 'grab his tail and pull as hard as you can. You're right – it's got the control for the quantum computer in it: we need to rip it off his onesie.'

George snapped his fingers in his right haptic glove and was pleased to see Ebot come to life again. The android looked around, understandably surprised to find himself suspended in mid-air in a glowing glass globe floating in space.

Alioth Merak noticed the movement and, just as George hoped he would, headed quickly over towards Ebot to see how he had managed to wake up without his say-so.

While Merak peered at the android, George drew back his hand and punched the air very, very hard. Just a nano-second afterwards, Ebot, receiving the command

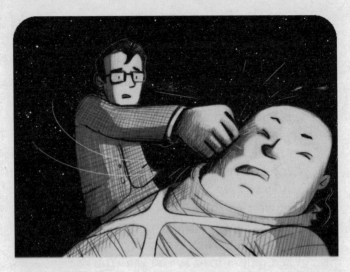

from the remote-access glove, mirrored his movement and punched Alioth Merak right on the nose.

Merak reeled backwards, unconscious, and as he did so, Annie grabbed his tail and tugged until it came away from the thin fabric of his onesie.

George and Annie looked at each other. They were longing to go home, but they knew they couldn't leave until they had, at least temporarily, closed down the quantum computer. But they had no idea how!

Annie grabbed Ebot's face and gazed into his eyes, wanting to attract the attention of Old Cosmos back on Earth.

'Cosmos!' she whispered, hoping her message would reach him. 'Help us! We need you! Come in, Cosmos!'

Chapter Eighteen

GeORGE and Annie waited anxiously for the antique computer back in Foxbridge to respond. Around them, the brainless robots tumbled and danced, entranced by the lights playing across the crystal sphere.

'How long have we got?' George muttered to Annie.

'Not long,' she said. 'Look – the pattern that hypnotized them is fading!'

For reasons known only to itself, the quantum computer was getting bored of its game. The coloured words it had been displaying across its crystal surface were gradually growing dimmer, and as they did so, the robots started to emerge from their trance.

'They're waking up,' said Annie urgently. This time her words didn't appear on the screen.

'But he's still out cold.' George watched Alioth Merak floating horizontally between them and their view of the Earth. 'He's the real problem.'

'He's not dead, is he?' said Annie fearfully. She didn't like him, but she didn't want him to be dead.

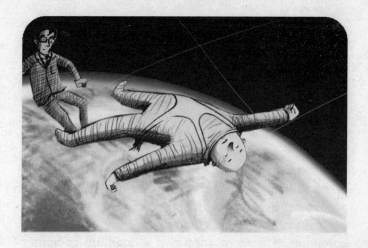

'No, just knocked out by Ebot's punch,' George replied. 'He'll come round in a minute, though. He may not be able to control the quantum computer without the switch, but I bet he can still give orders to those robots. And he's got that mobile phone in his head – there's no knowing how much damage he could still do.'

'Should we kidnap him and take him home with us?' Annie had taken Alioth Merak's stripy tail out of her pocket and was pressing the switch hidden in the end to see if she could work the quantum computer. But nothing seemed to be happening.

'No way!' said George. 'I don't want him back on Earth!'

'C'mon, Cosmos . . .' Annie gazed into Ebot's eyes

as she pressed the switch in the tail time and time again. 'Get us out of here!'

'Oh, no! Look at the Earth!' George saw that the space station's orbit was taking it over an area where night had fallen. There were only a very few pinpricks of light shining out. 'Most of the world must be without electricity! It's never normally that dark.' He turned to Annie. 'How are you getting on with that control?'

'I'm trying!' Annie was now performing all sorts of movements with the decapitated tail – swinging it around her head and stretching it between two hands to see if she could get it to communicate with the quantum computer. 'I have no idea how a quantum computer works,' she cried.

'Can we get in touch with your dad somehow?' George wondered. 'After all, Cosmos might not know . . . He might be too old. Can we call Eric?'

'How would we do that?' asked Annie. 'It looks like the only phone round here is installed inside I Am's brain!'

'Let's try Boltzmann,' said George. 'After all, it's supposed to be very user friendly. Maybe it will help us.'

'Oh, Boltzmann' – Annie acted on George's suggestion at once – 'can you help me?'

Boltzmann perked up. 'I would love to! I was created for the exact purpose of helping people! What may I do for you?'

'We need to call Annie's father,' explained George. 'We need his help. Can you make a call for us – like, an ordinary telephone call?'

'I most certainly can!' said Boltzmann proudly. 'Do you know his number?'

Annie reeled off a string of digits.

Boltzmann dialled the number on a keypad located in the palm of its robotic hand. They heard a phone ring, followed by a click as Eric answered.

'Hello?'

'Dad!' squeaked Annie joyously. Helpfully, Boltzmann held out a hand so that she could speak into it.

At the sound of Eric's voice George felt a lump come to his throat. Around them, the coloured lights in the

281

quantum dome sparkled and then resolved themselves into an image of Eric, picked out in red, blue and green.

'Dad!' said Annie again. 'We can see you!'

'Annie!' cried Eric. 'Where are you?'

'We don't really know,' she admitted. 'We're somewhere in orbit around the Earth, although I'm not quite sure which bit we've reached.'

'What do you mean *you're in orbit*?' Eric's face, displayed across the quantum computer, which was now functioning as a giant circular screen, looked worried.

'We're on a spaceship,' George chipped in, finding his voice. 'We found the quantum computer! The one that's broken all the codes on Earth.'

'You found a quantum computer? In space?'

'It's on a space station,' George confirmed. 'Belonging to a person called Alioth Merak – although we know that isn't his real name.'

'Alioth Merak . . .' Eric repeated, and he seemed to be looking over his shoulder, as though talking to other people in the same room. 'Get checking, guys.'

He turned back to the kids. 'How did we not know there was a rogue space station in orbit around the Earth?' he asked in confusion.

'He's cloaked it – made it invisible,' said George. 'We saw it, just briefly, when I was trying to take a photo of Saturn and snapped the ship instead.

282

We showed it to you – do you remember?'

'Oh yes . . . Oh, I wish I'd taken it more seriously!' Eric said. 'You guys' – again he turned to the unseen people behind him – 'Use this transmission to trace the location of the space station! Annie, George, we need to get you off that ship!'

'Dad, first you've got to tell us how to shut down the quantum computer,' said Annie urgently. 'We can't leave without stopping it – even Alioth Merak, who made it, can't control it. He's been trying to get your help all along. It might do something terrible – like cause nuclear missiles to blow up.'

'I just want you kids out of there.' Eric was ignoring her. 'Don't try and shut down the computer. I want you to leave the space station now. How did you get there in the first place?'

'We came through Old Cosmos,' said George. 'We used Ebot as our router to get us here.'

'Then you must come back the same way,' said Eric. 'Summon the portal – *immediately*. I think your transmission is allowing us to get a lock on your position and then we can target the space station.'

'Target?' asked Annie.

'Yes. That's why I need you to leave straight away. We have some computer systems restored now . . . they've got a missile lock on your location while we've been speaking. You must leave. They want to fire at the space station, so you must get off it, right now!'

'Cosmos!' George grabbed Ebot's head and stared into his eyes. 'We need the portal! And we need it *now*.'

As he spoke, Eric's face started to dissolve in the quantum dots on the screen. 'I'm losing you!' He sounded fainter now.

'Dad!' cried Annie, throwing herself towards the part of the globe where her father's image had been. 'Don't go!'

'Leave the ship!' Eric's voice echoed around the chamber.

Boltzmann snapped the phone closed. 'The connection has been interrupted.'

'Doesn't matter,' Annie muttered to George. 'We just need to leave. Dad's found the spaceship now, so he can deal with it. We need to get out of here.'

But before they could go anywhere, the unconscious figure in the onesie woke up. He stretched like a cat, opened his eyes and tossed back his head with an evil smirk. Alioth Merak had come back to life again. And not just Merak . . . his robot army also seemed fully functional; they were looking menacing again as they surrounded the two friends and their android. They closed ranks so that there were no gaps for the kids to squeeze through and escape.

Boltzmann, the one helpful robot that Alioth Merak had created, still floated outside the circle, bleating, 'Does anyone need my help?'

'I think you've done quite enough already,' said

Merak. 'Boltzmann – later, I will destroy you. You are a useless piece of malfunctioning machinery.'

'No I'm not!' cried Boltzmann. 'I'm a useful robot! I'm a friendly robot! I'm going to help humanity!'

'Humanity!' spat Merak. 'It doesn't deserve to be helped. Not yet, anyway. Not until they admit the error of their ways and beg me to make things better.'

'Not so kind now,' Annie taunted, 'are you?'

'TBH,' said Merak. 'Or BHT, as you would probably have it, my little dyslexic friend. I don't care what you think. You will give me back the controls for my computer. And then you will be ejected from the space station by my robots, where you will instantly explode!'

'What about me?' said George, hoping he could deflect some of Merak's attention – or at least keep him talking long enough for Cosmos and Ebot to create the portal, which was now their only hope of escape.

'Oh, I'm keeping *you*!' said Merak. 'I'm fond of you.' George shivered. 'After all, you want to live in a world without people, a world of robots. You're just like me.'

The full horror of what Merak had just said hit George like a steamroller. Why did Merak think he was like him? There was no conceivable connection between the two of them.

'How do I know that about you?' Merak gave a little smile. 'You made that comment when you were close to Cosmos, after I had penetrated the supercomputer. Your words resonated with me . . . You and me – we're the same. Clever. Good at technology. Able to work out complex problems. We don't like people. With my help and tuition, you could become my heir. Every great leader needs someone to pass the torch to . . . You will be mine. My second in command. You and I will rule the world.'

'Noooooooooo!' screamed George. 'I'm *not* like you!'

'Are you so sure of that?' asked Merak slyly. 'If I were you, I'd agree with me anyway. Because if you don't, I'll eject you from this spaceship with your little friend and you'll meet the same fate as her.'

'Then I'll do you a deal,' said George, hoping desperately that the portal was about to materialize. 'Either you keep us both – or you throw us both out. Whatever it is, we do it together.'

'Impressive!' Merak raised an eyebrow. 'And unexpected, I must admit. I thought you loved technology to such a degree that you wanted nothing more than to surround yourself with it, cutting out all human interaction.'

'I *never* said that,' George replied defiantly. He thought about his mum and his dad – they might be annoying and embarrassing sometimes, but he wouldn't be without them for a second. And his sisters – so they tried to follow him everywhere he went . . . It was irritating, but they only did it because they adored him. If it came to a straight choice between machines and his family, he would choose his family and friends over any piece of technology, no matter how amazing it might be.

'Oh, really?'

'Well, I might have said it,' George conceded, 'but I didn't mean it. Not like this. I didn't mean I wanted to live on a space station with just robots for company!'

'So here's the thing,' said Merak. 'You're trying to do a deal with me on a BOGOF with your friend. I keep you . . . I get the spelling-bee-challenged chum. But you don't seem to understand that you're not in a strong position. You don't get to set the rules – this is my spaceship, my robot army, my quantum computer; and when it comes down to it, it's pretty much my planet down there as well. Given that I am in control, here's how it works – either you stay and help me, or I throw both of you out into space, where you face certain death. Deal? Or no deal?'

As Merak was speaking, George noticed Ebot moving round so that instead of floating upright like Annie, George and the robots, he was now upside down.

'No deal,' he said firmly.

'No deal?' Merak sounded astonished. 'Why? Why would you do this? Why wouldn't you want to stay with me and break every code on Earth? Why don't you want to be the winner?'

'Because there's one code you'll never break. Or understand,' said George fiercely. No portal had emerged. He figured that, in a matter of minutes, either a missile from Earth would blow up the whole ship, or he and Annie would get hurled out into space. Either way, his final moments had come. A great calm stole over him.

'It's the code of friendship,' said George. 'Between people; real people who like each other, stand up for each other and care what happens to each other. You'll never crack that code. You can't decrypt it because it would make no sense to you. I don't know anything about you, but I *do* know that happy people don't behave like you behave. They don't go round bribing and bullying people into obeying them by intercepting their secret messages and then lording it over them and hurting them. You'll never be able to decrypt friendship. It's the code you can't break. Friends.'

'Yeah!' said Annie. 'Friends! That's what we are – George, you're brilliant.' She floated over to give him a hug. 'If this is our last minute, at least we're together.'

As George hugged her back, he spotted something. 'Look down – I think Ebot's finally come to the rescue,' he whispered.

He realized that upside-down Ebot's eyes had brightened. Two beams of light shot out of them as he started to outline the doorway, unnoticed by Merak and his robot army, who were still focusing on the kids.

'Oh, look!' said Annie loudly. 'Over there . . .' She hurled the tiger tail as far as she could. As she did so, all the robots and Alioth Merak leaped after it, away from Ebot and the doorway.

While their attention was elsewhere, Annie and George dived for the space portal. As they jumped through, Annie reached back, grabbed Ebot, and dragged him with her and George: instantly they were transported away from the doomed space station – towards Cosmos, Earth and home once more.

Chapter Nineteen

Travelling from micro gravity into normal gravity isn't a pleasant feeling, but Annie and George didn't care. They landed, the three of them, in a heap, on the floor of Old Cosmos's basement.

'Gerroff me!' Annie pushed George and Ebot off her and rolled over. 'Phew!' she said. 'That was horrible.'

George lay on his back beside her. Both of them still had their eyes closed as they listened to Old Cosmos's teletype, which had resumed its mechanical chatter, producing page after page of slowly unfurling paper.

When George finally opened his eyes, he saw that on the paper, spooling by him on the floor were dense blocks of text lines of complicated maths, presented like newspaper headlines (peppered with funny little numbers offset a little above and below), and also several diagrams drawn entirely out of characters – including one that looked like the space station from which they had so narrowly escaped.

The printer made a different sound as it produced these pictures, skimming quickly over large blank areas, then stopping to hammer a tiny part of the image, then shooting off to do the same thing a bit further on, and finally flying back to start the next line.

But when George looked up, past the reams of emerging paper, a horrible sight greeted him. Standing upright, holding his tail, as well as some fresh printouts from the supercomputer, was none other than Alioth Merak. He was smirking horribly.

George's heart sank. He squeezed Annie's hand and she opened her eyes in shock.

They thought they'd managed to escape from terrible danger, and at the same time saved the Earth from a power-hungry man in a onesie – only to find that they had brought their deadly foe back with them. The disappointment was shattering. To see Merak here when they thought they had vanquished him . . . it was even more frightening than their first encounter with him. They had guided him to the home of Old Cosmos, and who knew what damage he might be able to do if he got control of the supercomputer? It looked as though their happy ending had gone terribly wrong.

Merak himself looked immune to fear or anxiety. He seemed perfectly relaxed. '*Nanorobotic single qubit element*,' he mused, reading aloud from the pages. '*Operating temperature range 140 to 250 Kelvin. Accounts for space location – need to guarantee consistently low temperature range* . . . Oh, so that's why I built it in space, is it?' said Merak. 'Well, that's good to

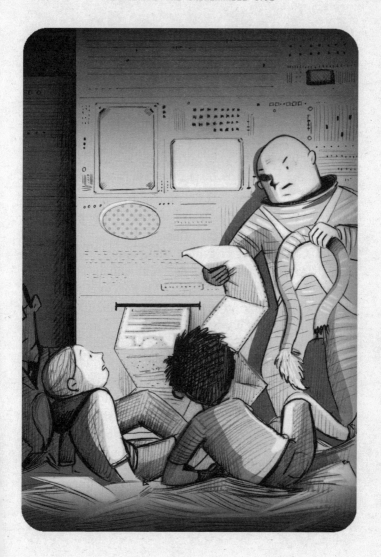

know! So glad two kids and a technological dinosaur turned up to tell me. Did you know' – he addressed the two children, who were still lying on the floor – 'that 250 Kelvin is actually 23 degrees below zero in centi-grade?'

He carried on reading while the kids lay there, petri-fied. 'Oh, and apparently I built a nanorobotic solar array to prevent my quantum computer from over-heating. Well, aren't I the clever one! Look at this – so sweet! Your ancient and outmoded friend has printed the code of an entire program written in the program-ming language "C". What's this . . . ?'

Old Cosmos began typing once more. Merak read out: '*Current time: 04:31:18. No malicious activity detected for 153 seconds.* Oh dear! Is he trying to tell me that my space station has been destroyed? Obviously that's a pain, but it's hardly the end for me. Being a positive sort, I choose to see it as a beginning.'

'How did you get here?' George got to his feet and pulled Annie up with him. He wasn't going to let this nasty piece of work stand over them any longer.

'I followed you through the portal,' said Merak. 'I just had time to dive after you – you were so keen to escape that you forgot to look behind you! A schoolboy error, one might say . . . so appropriate.'

'It's the end for you, if you don't have a quantum computer any more.' Annie wasn't going to let him get the better of them. She and George had come through so many challenges together – they weren't going to let this madman bring them down.

'I can rebuild it,' said Merak casually, dusting down his onesie. 'Wow – that portal thing is old school. I didn't think they made them like that any more! So slow to shut down as well – that's how I was able to jump through after you. Hey, Grandpa!' He kicked Old Cosmos. 'How does it feel to be entirely irrelevant in the modern age?'

'Don't kick Cosmos!' said Annie angrily.

Merak smiled at her and kicked him again.

Annie threw herself at him, pummelling her fists against his onesie. 'I hate you!' she burst out. 'You're evil and rude and nasty, and you want everyone to do

295

as you say rather than let them choose what they actually want.'

Merak pushed her away and she fell at George's feet.

'There's nothing more you can do,' George said bravely, stepping in front of his friend. 'Eric knows we are here.' He hoped this was true. 'He's sending people to meet us. You won't get away with it! You've got nothing left to bully us with!'

'So sad,' tutted Merak. 'I wish you wouldn't keep harping on about bullying! It's just a show of superior strength, which you silly little kids find demoralizing and overwhelming.'

'I thought you said George was your heir!' protested Annie, getting up again.

'I was wrong . . . Not something you will often hear me say.' He smiled. 'I have now given the command to my global network of 3D printers to start replicating my robot army. A few of them are already on the planet, as you know. I have now summoned them here. They weren't far away.'

'Are you replicating the Boltzmann?' asked Annie.

'I have decided to discontinue that model,' Merak told her. 'They are incredibly hard to pull off and not at all reliable when you succeed. I hoped I could be nice when I came to save the Earth, but your negative reception has made me change my plans. I have now decided to implement a regime of punishment instead. You will have to watch while I rip the world as you know it to pieces, and know that it is entirely your fault. Fun, huh?' He swished the tail around like rope charm. 'Well, for me, anyway.'

A great pounding noise resonated from outside the basement room. The two friends gulped. As they watched helplessly, the door was relentlessly pummelled until it gave way. For a moment George hoped they'd see Eric and his fellow scientists, but it wasn't to be. Two of Merak's identical robots forced their way into the basement.

George turned to look at Ebot: the android had survived the kidnap, the space station and the portal, returning to Earth with his hair only slightly ruffled, seemed to have lost power and was now uselessly slumped in the corner.

The magnificent ancient machine, Old Cosmos, offered no obvious protection, either. In any case, George realized, to reach their old friend they would have been forced to go round Merak. Had they really survived all their adventures only to end up the prisoners of an evil robot army with a madman in a planetary onesie who sought world domination? Was this really the end of everything for them?

Once more, George reached out for Annie's hand, and the pair clung onto each other, determined to face the threat together, united.

But just as they'd given up even a tiny glimmer of hope, they realized that the robots hadn't actually seized them. Instead, they were grabbing hold of Alioth Merak, who was struggling in their pincer grips.

'Let go of me, I command you!' he snapped. 'You've misunderstood my orders . . . It's not me, you pathetic piles of metallic junk! It's *them*!' He tried to free his hands to point, but they were pinned tightly behind his back.

As the robots held their former leader, Annie and George heard Cosmos tapping away once more.

George ran over to the computer and ripped off the sheet.

'*He's not the only person who knows how to break a code,*' he read out loud, '*or intercept a message and*

change the contents. ROFL!'

He burst out laughing. 'Annie!' he said gleefully. 'Cosmos has taken control of the robot army. Isn't that right, old fella?'

Cosmos twinkled. *Yes it is*, he replied. *I shall direct them all to be extremely helpful, wherever they are. Except for these two, which I will use to keep this man in custody until Eric arrives.*

'Wowzers, Cosmos!' exclaimed Annie, who ran over as if to give him a hug, but then stopped, realizing that this was kind of impossible. 'You saved the day!'

Next time, said Cosmos, *remember that there is wisdom in age as well as innovation in novelty.*

'OK!' said George. 'We'll do that, you marvellous machine! You' – he turned to Merak, who was still vainly struggling to get free – 'can stay here until Eric arrives! I expect he'll have some Quantum Error Detection to do with you!'

'Where are you going?' Alioth Merak asked sulkily. 'You can't just leave me here in this basement, with these robots! That's not fair. I've got nothing to eat, nothing to drink, nothing to do. This is against the International Convention of Robotic Activity. I'll get my lawyers on to you! You'll pay for this!'

'Typical,' said Annie as she and George turned to leave the room. 'Now that he's lost, it's unfair. When he was winning, he didn't care what rules he broke.'

WHAT CAN'T A COMPUTER DO?

All known computer designs (including quantum computer designs) can compute no more than a Turing Machine could compute if given enough time and memory. However Turing was able to prove that some problems in mathematics are uncomputable, that is to say, they cannot be solved by a Turing Machine – and hence not by any known computer today! He demonstrated this with a problem concerning Turing Machines themselves, known as the Halting Problem.

The Halting Problem

When will a Turing Machine halt? If it only has one state (state 0), then only two rules are needed - what to do if the machine reads 0, or 1. There are varied ways these rules could lead to different results, depending on how the 1 rule is formulated:

- the 0 rule says leave 0 and march right, continuing until it finds the input of a number 1, then halt. The machine halts and outputs the answer.

- But a Turing Machine could find itself in an endless loop: choosing 'if 1 is read, write 1 and move left' would make the machine move back to the previous 0, then move back to the 1 at the next tick of the clock (following the 0 rule), and then repeat these two moves for ever.

- It is also easy to make a Turing Machine that will not ever halt. Changing the 1 rule to 'if 1 is read, write 0 and move left' will cause the machine to move back to the previous 0, then return, but this time it sees 0 and continues past until the next 1. The machine will turn all the 1s into 0s and then disappear off to the right for ever.

Machine 'H'

Alan Turing himself posed the question: is there an algorithm that, when fed with the program of any Turing Machine and some extra input, will output the answer 0 if that machine with that input doesn't ever halt and output an answer?

Suppose for the moment that such an algorithm existed – then there would be a Turing Machine to perform it. Furthermore, there would be a machine that could test whether any Turing Machine would not halt when the input was its own program. Let's call this machine H and input data such that H halts if, and only if, its input is the program of a Turing Machine which doesn't halt when input with its own program.

So what happens if we feed H with its own program?

If it does halt, then it is an example of a Turing Machine which does halt when input with its own program – but then H was designed not to halt when fed with the program of such a machine!

If it doesn't halt, then H is a machine which doesn't halt when input with its own program, but that means that H fed with the H program should halt, because it was designed specifically to detect such machines.

Either way, this is a contradiction! A nonsensical situation like this tells a mathematician that what they were assuming is true was wrong. Constructing the imaginary Turing Machine H – which cannot exist – was therefore very clever. It proved there cannot be a Turing Machine able to compute whether any Turing Machine with any input doesn't halt. And if this question cannot be settled by a Turing Machine, therefore it is uncomputable on any computer we can currently imagine building.

Put simply, a computer can't solve this problem!

302

Infinite numbers

The number of possible programs and Turing Machines is infinite, but because every computer program can be turned into one big binary number a mathematician would describe the set of all programs or machines as countably infinite, because we can list them in order of size.

But there are much bigger infinities, for example the infinity of decimals with infinite decimal places – these are called the 'real numbers'. There are real numbers whose digits cannot be generated by a computer.

For example, the real number pi (which you use in working out the circumference of a circle, for instance, and probably know as standing for 3.142) can be written out to any number of decimal places by a computer. The first few are 3.1415926535 and a computer has done this to trillions of decimal places. Most real numbers, though, cannot be generated like this: they are fundamentally uncomputable – a computer can't do it!

The future?

Some theorists speculate that new types of computer, relying on as yet unknown physics, will be discovered in the future that can compute more than a Turing Machine can compute, and that the human brain (the original 'computer') may even turn out to be one of these.

There is no general agreement on whether the human brain could be described by a sufficiently complicated Turing Machine.

'Let's go home, Annie . . .' George picked up his skateboard and headed towards the stairs. 'I don't know about you, but I'm hungry!'

'Wait!' said Annie. 'We have to say goodbye to Old Cosmos!'

'Thank you.' George looked at the massive computer and smiled. 'Thank you, Cosmos. You've saved not just us but the whole world.'

It was my pleasure, Cosmos said, and his lights seemed to glow. *It is nice to be useful. Please make sure you tell Eric all about it, just in case he was thinking of decommissioning me.*

'We won't let that happen,' Annie promised. 'You're our friend for ever now!'

Outside on the street, a silvery dawn was just breaking over the quiet streets of the beautiful university town; the stone facades of the ancient building reflected the newly minted sunlight. In doorways and under arches, people slumbered as the two friends trundled past on their skateboards, discussing what they most wanted to eat for breakfast.

'Pancakes,' said George, his mouth watering at the thought. 'A huge tower of them with maple syrup.'

'Bacon!' said Annie. 'Hot crispy bacon!'

'Bacon?' George was thinking of his old pig, Freddy.

'*You* don't have to eat it,' Annie told him. 'Anyway,

it's not like we've actually got any food at home.'

George thought of the empty kitchens in their two houses. 'Wow, it's going to be hard to put everything back together,' he said as they rolled along.

'I wonder what will happen now . . . I mean, how will Dad and the others explain this to the world?' Annie wondered as they approached Little St Mary's Lane.

'What do you mean?'

'They can't just say, "Oh, by the way, people of Earth, we were attacked by a madman in a onesie who pretended he wanted you all to have free money and food but in fact wanted to rule the world."'

'I don't know,' said George thoughtfully. 'Perhaps

305

LUCY & STEPHEN HAWKING

it would be best just to tell everyone the truth?'

'Maybe,' Annie replied.

They drew up to George's front door, which still lay on the ground, ripped off its hinges by the furious mob. But the street itself was quiet and empty: no cars, no aeroplanes overhead, no phones ringing, no televisions blaring; none of the usual hustle and bustle of a small city waking up to greet another day.

'Wow, this is so strange!' remarked Annie. 'Do you think this is what life was like before computers were invented?'

'Suppose so,' said George. 'But it won't stay like this for long – not if your dad and all the other scientists are working to get everything started up again. In a few hours it could all be back to normal.'

They went into George's house. 'Talking of peace and quiet . . .' he said as they stood in his kitchen looking down at the trapdoor. They could hear the twins singing away merrily and someone saying groggily, 'Girls! It's really early!'

Annie laughed and shot back the bolts that were keeping the trapdoor closed. She and George lifted one flap each, opening the basement below to the light of the beautiful Foxbridge morning. As they did so, Hera and Juno scrambled quickly towards the ladder, eager to leave their underground shelter.

'Let there be life!' said Annie as they burst into the kitchen once more.

306

LIFE IN THE UNIVERSE

In this chapter, I would like to talk to you about the development of life in the Universe, and in particular, the development of intelligent life. I shall take this to include the human race, even though much of its behaviour throughout history has been pretty stupid!

We all know that things get more disordered and chaotic with time. This observation even has its own law, the so-called *Second Law of Thermodynamics*. This law says that the total amount of disorder, or entropy, in the Universe, always increases with time. However, the Law refers only to the total amount of disorder. The order in one body can increase, provided that the amount of *disorder* in its surroundings increases by a greater amount.

This is what happens in a living being. We can define life to be an ordered system that can keep itself going against the tendency to disorder, and can reproduce itself. That is, it can make similar, but independent, ordered systems. To do these things, the system must convert energy in some ordered form - like food, sunlight, or electric power - into disordered energy, in the form of heat. In this way, the system can satisfy the requirement that the total amount of disorder increases while, at the same time, increasing the order in itself and its offspring. This sounds like parents living in a house which get messier and messier each time they have a new baby!

A living being like you or me usually has two elements: a set of instructions that tell the system how to keep going and how to reproduce itself, and a mechanism to carry out the instructions. In biology, these two parts are called *genes* and *metabolism*.

What we normally think of as 'life' is based on chains of carbon atoms, with a few other atoms such as nitrogen or phosphorous. There was no carbon when the Universe began in the Big Bang, about 13.8 billion years ago. It was so hot that all the matter would have been in the form of particles, called protons and neutrons. There would initially have been equal numbers of protons and neutrons. However, as the Universe expanded, it cooled. About a minute after the Big Bang, the temperature would have fallen to about a billion degrees, about a hundred times the temperature in the Sun. At this temperature, neutrons start to decay into more protons.

308

If this had been all that had happened, all the matter in the Universe would have ended up as the simplest element, *hydrogen*, whose nucleus consists of a single proton. However, some of the neutrons collided with protons and stuck together to form the next simplest element, *helium*, whose nucleus consists of two protons and two neutrons. But no heavier elements, like *carbon* or *oxygen*, would have been formed in the early Universe. It is difficult to imagine that one could build a living system out of just hydrogen and helium - and anyway the early Universe was still far too hot for atoms to combine into molecules.

The Universe continued to expand, and cool. But some regions had slightly higher densities than others and the gravitational attraction of the extra matter in those regions slowed down their expansion, and eventually stopped it. Instead, they collapsed to form galaxies and stars, starting from about two billion years after the Big Bang. Some of the early stars would have been more massive than our Sun; they would have been hotter than the Sun and would have burnt the original hydrogen and helium into heavier elements, such as carbon, oxygen, and iron. This could have taken only a few hundred million years. After that, some of the stars exploded as supernovas, and scattered the heavy elements back into space, to form the raw material for later generations of stars.

Our own solar system was formed about four and a half billion years ago, or about ten billion years after the Big Bang, from gas contaminated with the remains of earlier stars. The Earth was formed largely out of the heavier elements, including carbon and oxygen. Somehow, some of these atoms came to be arranged in the form of molecules of DNA. This has the famous double helix form, discovered in the 1950s by Crick and Watson in a hut on the New Museum site in Cambridge. Linking the two chains in the helix are pairs of nucleic acids. There are four types of nucleic acids - *adenine, cytosine, guanine*, and *thiamine*.

We do not know how DNA molecules first appeared. As the chances against a DNA molecule arising by random fluctuations are very small, some people have suggested that life came to Earth from elsewhere – for instance, brought here on rocks breaking off from Mars while the planets were still unstable - and that there are seeds of life floating round in the galaxy. However, it seems unlikely that DNA could survive for long in the radiation in space. There is fossil evidence that there was some form of life on Earth about three and a half billion years ago. This may have been only 500 million years after the Earth became stable and cool enough for life to develop. The early appearance of life on Earth suggests that there

LIFE IN THE UNIVERSE

is a good chance of the spontaneous generation of life in suitable conditions. Maybe there was some simpler form of organization which built up DNA. Once DNA appeared, it would have been so successful that it might have completely replaced the earlier forms. We don't know what these earlier forms would have been, but one possibility is RNA.

RNA is like DNA, but rather simpler, and without the double helix structure. Short lengths of RNA could reproduce themselves like DNA, and might eventually build up to DNA. We cannot make nucleic acids in the laboratory from non-living material, let alone RNA. But given 500 million years, and oceans covering most of the Earth, there might be a reasonable probability of RNA being made by chance.

As DNA reproduced itself, there would have been random errors, many of which would have been harmful and would have died out. Some would have been neutral - they would not have affected the function of the gene. And a few errors would have been favourable to the survival of the species - these would have been chosen by Darwinian natural selection.

The process of biological evolution was very slow at first. It took two and a half billion years to evolve from the earliest cells to multi-cell animals, and another billion years to evolve through fish and reptiles to mammals. But then evolution seemed to have speeded up. It only took about a hundred million years to develop from the early mammals to us. The reason is that fish contain most of the important human organs and mammals – essentially, all of them. All that was required to evolve from early mammals, like lemurs, to humans, was a bit of fine-tuning.

But with the human race, evolution reached a critical stage, comparable in importance with the development of DNA. This was the development of *language*, and particularly written language. It meant that information can be passed on from generation to generation, other than genetically through DNA. There has been some detectable change in human DNA, brought about by biological evolution, in the ten thousand years of recorded history, but the amount of knowledge handed on from generation to generation has grown enormously. I have written books to tell you something of what I have learned about the universe in my long career as a scientist, and in doing so I am

transferring knowledge from my brain to the page so you can read it.

The DNA in human beings contains about three billion nucleic acids. However, much of the information coded in this sequence is redundant, or is inactive. So the total amount of useful information in our genes is probably something like *a hundred million bits*. One bit of information is the answer to a yes/no question. By contrast, a paperback novel might contain two million bits of information. So a human is equivalent to about 50 Harry Potter books, and a major national library can contain about five million books - or about *ten trillion bits*. So the amount of information handed down in books or via the internet is a hundred thousand times as much as in DNA!

This has means that we have entered a new phase of evolution. At first, evolution proceeded by natural selection - from random mutations. This Darwinian phase lasted about three and a half billion years and produced us, beings who developed language to exchange information. But in the last ten thousand years or so, we have been in what might be called an *external transmission phase*. In this, the *internal* record of information, handed down to succeeding generations in DNA, has changed somewhat. But the *external* record - in books, and other long lasting forms of storage - has grown enormously.

Some people would use the term 'evolution' only for the internally transmitted genetic material, and would object to it being applied to information handed down externally. But I think that is too narrow a view. We are more than just our genes. We may be no stronger, or inherently more intelligent than our caveman ancestors. But what distinguishes us from them is the knowledge that we have accumulated over the last ten thousand years, and particularly over the last three hundred. I think it is legitimate to take a broader view, and include externally transmitted information, as well as DNA, in the evolution of the human race.

But we still have the instincts, and in particular, the aggressive impulses, that we had in caveman days. Aggression, in the form of subjugating or killing others and taking their food, has had definite survival advantage, up to the present time. But now it could destroy the entire human race, and much of the rest of life on Earth. A nuclear war is still the most immediate danger, but there are others, such as the release of a genetically engineered virus. Or the greenhouse effect becoming unstable.

There is no time to wait for Darwinian evolution to make us more intelligent, and better-natured! But we are now entering a new phase of what might be called self-designed evolution, in which we will be able to change and improve our DNA. We have now mapped DNA which means we have read 'the book of life'. So we can start writing in corrections. At first, these changes will be confined to the repair of genetic defects - like cystic fibrosis, and muscular dystrophy, which are controlled by single genes, and so are fairly easy to identify and correct. Other qualities, such as intelligence, are probably controlled by a large number of genes, and it will be much more difficult to find them and work out the relations between them. Nevertheless, I am sure that during the next century, people will discover how to modify both intelligence, and instincts like aggression.

If the human race manages to redesign itself, to reduce or eliminate the risk of self-destruction, it will probably spread out, and colonize other planets and stars. However, long-distance space travel will be difficult for chemically based life forms — like us - based on DNA. The natural lifetime for such beings is short, compared to the travel time. According to the theory of relativity, nothing can travel faster than light, so a round trip to the nearest star would take at least eight years, and to the centre of the galaxy about a hundred thousand years. In science fiction, they overcome this difficulty by space warps, or travel through extra dimensions. But I don't think these will ever be possible, no matter how intelligent life becomes. In the theory of relativity, if one can travel faster than light, one can also travel back in time, and this would lead to problems with people going back and changing the past. One would also expect to have already seen large numbers of tourists from the future, curious to look at our quaint, old-fashioned ways!

It might be possible to use genetic engineering, to make DNA-based life survive indefinitely, or at least for a hundred thousand years. But an easier way, which is almost within our capabilities already, would be to send machines. These could be designed to last long enough for interstellar travel. When they arrived at a new star, they could land on a suitable planet and mine material to produce more machines, which could be sent on to yet more stars. These machines would be a new form of life, based on mechanical and electronic components, rather than macromolecules. They

could eventually replace DNA-based life, just as DNA may have replaced an earlier form of life.

What are the chances that we will encounter some alien form of life, as we explore the galaxy? If the argument about the timescale for the appearance of life on Earth is correct, there ought to be many other stars whose planets have life on them. Some of these stellar systems could have formed five billion years before the Earth - so why is the galaxy not crawling with self-designing mechanical or biological life forms? Why hasn't the Earth been visited, and even colonized? By the way, I discount suggestions that UFOs contain beings from outer space, as I think that any visits by aliens would be much more obvious - and probably also, much more unpleasant.

So why haven't we been visited? Maybe the probability of life spontaneously appearing is so low that Earth is the only planet in the galaxy - or in the observable Universe - on which it happened. Another possibility is that there was a reasonable probability of forming self-reproducing systems, like cells, but that most of these forms of life did not evolve intelligence. We are used to thinking of intelligent life as an inevitable consequence of evolution, but what if it isn't? Is it more likely that evolution is a random process, with intelligence as only one of a large number of possible outcomes?

It is not even clear that intelligence has any long-term survival value. Bacteria, and other single-cell organisms, may live on if all other life on Earth is wiped out by our actions. Perhaps intelligence was an unlikely development for life on Earth, from the chronology of evolution, as it took a very long time - two and a half billion years - to go from single cells to multi-cell beings, which are a necessary precursor to intelligence. This is a good fraction of the total time available before the Sun blows up. So it would be consistent with the hypothesis that the probability for life to develop intelligence is low. In this case, we might expect to find many other life forms in the galaxy, but we are unlikely to find *intelligent* life.

Another way in which life could fail to develop to an intelligent stage would be if an asteroid or comet were to collide with the planet. It is difficult to say how often such collisions occur, but a reasonable guess might be every twenty million years, on average. If this figure is correct, it would mean that intelligent life on Earth has developed only because of the lucky chance that there have been no major collisions in the last 67 million years. Other planets in the galaxy, on which life has

LIFE IN THE UNIVERSE

developed, may not have had a long enough collision-free period to evolve intelligent beings.

A third possibility is that there is a reasonable probability for life to form – and to evolve to intelligent beings but the system becomes unstable, and the intelligent life destroys itself. This would be a very pessimistic conclusion and I very much hope it isn't true.

I prefer a fourth possibility: that there are other forms of intelligent life out there, but that we have been overlooked. There used to be a project called SETI – the Search for Extra-Terrestrial Intelligence - which involved scanning the radio frequencies to see if we could pick up signals from alien civilizations. But we need to be wary of answering back until we have developed a bit further! Meeting a more advanced civilization, at our present stage, might be a bit like the original inhabitants of America meeting Columbus – and I don't think they thought they were better off for it!

Stephen

Acknowledgements

Like the other books in the series, George and the Unbreakable Code is made possible by the willingness and great enthusiasm of scientists and technology experts to explain their research. I'd like to thank our distinguished contributors for their brilliant and entertaining work, taking the abstract, the cutting edge or the simply baffling and making it accessible to readers young – and not so young. They are: Professor Michael Reiss, Professor Peter McOwan, Dr Raymond Laflamme, Dr Tim Prestidge, Dr Stuart Rankin, Dr Toby Blench and, of course, Professor Stephen Hawking.

In particular, I would like to thank Dr Stuart Rankin for his long-term assistance and input into the George series, which includes writing the fantastically informative text boxes on computing, as well as his advice and his numerous contributions to the book as a whole. I would also like to thank Dr Toby Blench for introducing a chemical element to the series and for his authorship of Annie's half-term chemistry project, more of which can be read online. Alastair Leith of the Online Astronomy Society provided very helpful advice on the astronomical elements of the book and IT expert Dawn Mancer wrote the advice on how to keep safe online.

I'd like to thank our young readers who read and helpfully commented on an early draft of George and the Unbreakable Code. They are: Marina McCready, Jamie Ross, Francesca Bern and Lola and Amelie Mayer.

Garry Parsons has given the characters and the storyline a visual life with charm and verve. I'm so grateful to Garry for taking on the challenge of drawing a quantum computer in space and doing such a fabulous job!

The team at Random House Children's Publishers have gone on a cosmic journey with George and his adventures – and produced a really beautiful book. Working with Ruth Knowles and Sue Cook as editors has been a joy, and Annie Eaton and the rest of her team have given us the chance to explore the universe in style.

I'd like to thank my agents at Janklow and Nesbit, Claire Paterson and Rebecca Carter for their unstinting hard work on the series, and Kirsty Gordon for managing such a complex project so very well.

Most of all, I would like to thank all our readers for their interest and excitement at the prospect of a new George story! Originally, there were only going to be three – and now there are more. Thank you for travelling with us – the universe is a big place and there is still so much more to discover. In the words of my awesome co-author and father, Stephen – Be Curious!

Lucy

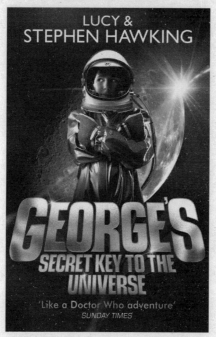